LOVER
BIRDS

LEANNE EGAN

LOVER BIRDS

h
HARPER FIRE

First published in the United Kingdom by
Harper Fire, an imprint of HarperCollins *Children's Books*, in 2024
HarperCollins *Children's Books* is a division of HarperCollins*Publishers* Ltd
1 London Bridge Street
London SE1 9GF

www.harpercollins.co.uk

HarperCollins*Publishers*
Macken House, 39/40 Mayor Street Upper
Dublin 1, D01 C9W8, Ireland

1

ISBN 978-0-00-862657-0

Leanne Egan asserts the moral right to be identified as the author of the work.
A CIP catalogue record for this title is available from the British Library.

Typeset in Adobe Caslon Pro by Palimpsest Book Production Limited,
Falkirk, Stirlingshire
Printed and bound in the UK using 100% renewable electricity
at CPI Group (UK) Ltd

This book contains FSC™ certified paper and other controlled sources
to ensure responsible forest management.

For more information visit: www.harpercollins.co.uk/green

To the messy queer kids.
Thank you for being unapologetically yourselves.

CHAPTER ONE

We're talking about celebrity crushes when I see her for the first time. The tall girl in the fancy suit with the long red hair that falls, shiny and straight, down to the small of her back. She's standing a few metres from us, looking down at her phone, leaning against the sixth-form building that we're making our way towards.

'I'm just saying,' Katie insists, blonde ponytail swinging as she whirls round to stop us in our tracks, like this is the most important conversation we'll ever have. 'Every girl's got a list of female celebrities they think are fit. That doesn't make me a lesbian – it just makes me a person with eyes.'

She's looking at each of us in turn, like she's waiting for one of us to back her up, but I can't take my eyes off the fancy-suit girl. I've never seen her before, which is weird. It might be our first day as sixth-formers, but we've been going to this school for half a decade now and we know everyone in our year. And she's got to be in our year because she's wearing sixth-form clothes. Even if she does seem to have taken the 'black and white officewear' instruction a bit more

1

seriously than the rest of us, in our multipack Primark white shirts and black jeans.

'That would make you a bit of a lesbian, Katie.' Lily's voice draws my attention back to the conversation briefly. 'Like, one woman, *maybe*, but having a whole list is fairly high up there on the gayness scale, you know?'

Maybe she's in the year above? But we know most of the people in upper sixth too. I've definitely never seen her before.

'It's called the Kinsey Scale, actually,' Mel interjects, and everyone rolls their eyes except Jas, who I don't reckon is even capable of rolling her eyes. I think all the muscles required to do it just didn't form in her, and went instead to whichever muscles you need to smile warmly at somebody.

My eyes flick back to the suit girl. She puts her phone into her pocket and seems to shrink into herself as soon as she no longer has something to occupy her, reaching up to tuck her hair behind her ears, eyes darting across the school grounds too quickly to land on anything.

'You're telling me –' Katie is in full flow – 'that if some dead fit celebrity walked up to you right now and was like, *come to my mansion in Hollywood, and we'll adopt a dog together*, you'd all be picky about gender?'

'The question would be whether or not you're *actually* attracted to them,' Jas says, as if this is genuinely a burning question that Katie needs help with instead of just some sidenote about having celebrity girl crushes that we somehow stumbled upon. 'Acknowledging that a celebrity is classically gorgeous isn't necessarily gay, but if you could see yourself, like, actually *fancying* them, then you might want to give your identity some thought.'

I watch as the girl practically melts with relief as Mrs Anderson, the head of sixth form, approaches her. The girl reaches out to extend a hand, all formal and delicate, and Mrs Anderson shakes it, a little taken aback. They're saying something to each other now, but we're still too far away to hear them.

'Well, yeah, I'm *attracted* to them –' Katie rolls her eyes – 'but not in, like, a gay way.'

I snort, and she zeroes in on me.

'Was wondering how long it'd take for you to have an opinion, Lou.'

'Yeah, you're not spouting your usual fountain of shit,' Lily teases. 'You feeling okay?' Jas gives her a gentle swat about the head for that.

I shrug and start walking again. 'Depends on the celebrity.'

'Well, that's not even the point.' Katie sounds exasperated as she hurries to keep up with me. 'The point is that there are some women who are so fit they transcend gender.' I snort again, but she ignores it. 'Women are better looking than men; that's just a universal truth.'

'Nah. First of all, I've seen some of the weirdos on your celebrity crush list, so you might want to re-evaluate your concept of *universal truth*,' I point out, finally tearing my eyes away from the tall girl in the suit. 'And second, your concept of celebrity is, like, alt-girl indie singers. If we're doing absolute fantasy scenarios, I'm defo going for, like, an Oscar-winning actress or something.'

'Calling it a fantasy *definitely* makes you a bit of a lesbian,' Lily says, wrinkling her nose.

When I look back, the girl in the suit is gone.

Katie groans. 'But see, that just proves my point.' She looks far more disgruntled than the conversation really warrants, to be honest. 'Even Lou gets it, and she's the straightest person I know. Just ask Jay Henderson,' she says, walking backwards to open the door to the sixth-form building. 'And Tom Bryson. And Ollie Wyatt. And—'

'All right!' Jas laughs, giving Katie a gentle shove through the door. 'She gets the point.'

'Yeah,' I scoff, following the others into the common room, 'the point being that I'm a massive heterosexual and a bit of a slag, apparentl— Oh, hiya, Mrs Anderson.'

The others have all stopped, too, giving little waves and awkward smiles to Mrs Anderson, who's standing right in front of us, the suit girl in tow.

'Hello, girls,' Mrs Anderson says, trepidation in her voice that suggests she definitely heard the end of that conversation. Good start to sixth form, really.

'I was hoping to find you all,' she presses on. 'We've got a new student this year, Isabel Williams here. She's just moved to Liverpool from *London*, and I was thinking you girls would be perfect to welcome her to the school.'

The way she says London is like it's some magical land, and we should all be wildly impressed.

'Eloise.' Mrs Anderson turns to me, and I try not to wince at the use of my full name. 'You two have English literature together with Ms Price this year, so I thought you in particular could be helpful to Isabel.'

'Er, yeah, sure,' I say as if sixth form isn't already going to be A Lot. As if there isn't already so much pressure to do well this year.

'Great. So, Isabel, this is Eloise Byrne, Jasmine Olowe, Melanie Powell, Lily Hyun and Katie Fletcher. These girls are inseparable, but I'm sure they'll be lovely and welcoming.'

The girl – Isabel – offers a tense smile as Mrs Anderson leaves her standing awkwardly with us, clutching a pile of papers: timetables and maps and term calendars by the looks of things.

'Nice to meet you,' says Jas, beaming. Isabel just grimaces back. Jas, social butterfly that she is, barely misses a beat. 'Mrs Anderson insists on calling everyone by their full names, but you can call me Jas, and Mel can't stand being called Melanie, and Lou thinks Eloise makes her sound like the heroine in a period drama.'

'Yeah, and not in the sexy *Bridgerton* kind of way, either,' I explain, 'but in, like, a *never see another person naked until you marry your cousin, have sex once, have a child, then grow old alone on the secluded moors* kind of way.'

She winces while I'm speaking. Like actually winces. I know I have a bad habit of not knowing when to shut up, but isn't it polite to at least *pretend* not to have second-hand embarrassment about it?

'We've actually got English lit first lesson,' I say to her, rocking back on my heels after the silence has stretched out a bit too long. 'I can show you around before if you want?'

She looks at me like I've just threatened to murder her entire family or something. Her eyes go wide and her lips form such a tight line they basically disappear. But she nods, albeit tersely, and I wave her onwards before turning back to my friends.

'Anyone got a free third lesson?'

'Me,' Lily and Mel say in unison.

'Fab, see youse in here then? And, everyone else – caff at lunch?'

They all nod, and I shepherd the new girl further into the sixth-form building.

'I like your hair,' she blurts out suddenly as we turn a corner away from everyone else. And for a second I barely even register the compliment, I'm so distracted by her accent.

I remember when Lily started going out with this lad from Southport. Massive posho, went to that all-boys' grammar school and lived in one of those big white-bricked houses that he was always throwing parties in. We mocked him – and her, by association – mercilessly for months, for being a wool. Every time he opened his mouth, he'd say something that sounded so unbearably posh, and we'd just lose it. But this girl is on a different level entirely. I kind of didn't really think people actually spoke like that in real life.

'Oh, thanks,' is all I say, tugging at the ends of my hair. 'It defo wasn't supposed to look like this,' I add with a nervous laugh because, well, when have I ever known when to stop talking? 'I dyed it blue at the end of last year because the teachers were too busy trying to make sure we all got our GCSEs to actually crack down on the no-crazy-hair-colours rule, and I forgot to keep up with it this summer so the roots grew out, and then I got it cut short, and it kinda worked.'

I run my hands through the hair in question, like I might be able to feel the place where the natural dark brown melds into turquoise round the tips of my ears, the ends, splintered from the copious amounts of bleach I used, just brushing my jawline.

'This is the sixth-form building, by the way. Not much to show. We've basically just walked round the whole thing. This is the study area; that bit we were just in is like a common-room-lounge type of situation. Just don't go upstairs – that's where the nuns live.'

She looks at me like she's not sure if she should laugh.

'Not a joke,' I say, smiling a little at her expression. 'That's actually where they live. There's only, like, three left, and they're all retired from teaching. But y'know –' I shrug – 'can't exactly kick 'em out.'

She does laugh then, just a bit, a surprised little hiccup that makes her press her fingertips to her mouth like she might be able to hide that it had happened in the first place. I suppress a grin of my own while I check the time on my phone.

'Lessons are all in the main school building, though. I'll show you the way to English now, and then we can figure out the rest after?'

She just nods, and we head back outside, cutting over the grass to the main building, and I start to feel antsy and nervous again in the silence that settles.

'*Sooo*, London?' I ask as we weave through the hallways.

She just nods, which – fair enough. It's not like it was an intelligent question or anything.

'Whereabouts?' I ask as if I know anywhere in London apart from the Monopoly squares. 'These are the big loos, by the way. There's a few more single ones around, but there's never a queue for these.'

'Hampstead,' she says, her voice tight.

'Oh, nice.' I have no idea if it's nice. But, based on her suit and her accent and her general *everything*, it's probably safe to assume it is.

'Yeah, it was.'

Squeaking of shoes against the wooden floors. Distant footsteps of a few early birds down the hall. Tumbleweed somewhere probably.

'That's the office through there, but you've probably already been there for enrolment stuff. You don't seem thrilled about leaving. Why'd you move?'

'My mum's office is setting up a new headquarters in Liverpool. My brother goes to university up here, so Mum volunteered to relocate. I didn't really get a say in the matter.'

I hadn't thought it possible, but her voice gets even tighter then, dripping with resentment, like I personally forced her to move here.

'Oh. Cool that you get to stay near your brother, though. You two close?'

'Yes, very.'

'Neat.' I actually say that. *Neat.* 'Er, this is us. Ms Price's classroom. We're a bit early, but we can go in now, since it's the first lesson of the day.'

She just nods and takes a seat in the back corner of the classroom, next to the window. I park myself in the desk beside her, drumming my fingers on the surface, the sound feeling deafening in the silence.

All right, cool. So we're done, I guess. Because she's staring intently out of the window, turned so far away from me that it almost looks uncomfortable for her to be sitting like that. Which I'm obviously not going to take to heart or anything. It's fine. It's not like I'm *incapable* of sitting in silence or anything.

CHAPTER TWO

Thankfully, other people start to file in just around the time that the silence stretches so taut it's becoming unbearable.

A few people flash Isabel strange looks, though most don't even notice her, huddled in the back corner of the room, head turned to the window.

"S'appenin', Byrnie?"

I hear his voice only half a second before Jay Henderson plants himself on the desk in front of me.

'Get fucked, Henno.'

'I'd say it's good to see you out of uniform,' he says with a smirk, 'but we all know I've seen you out of your uniform before.'

I can't believe I went out with this dickhead, really I can't. In my defence, it was two years ago, and he wasn't as much of a dickhead then. Or, no, that's too generous. More like he did a better job of hiding the fact before. Lads do that pretty well when they're trying to get with you, I think.

When I don't give him anything more than an eye-roll, he presses on.

'Who's the new girl?' He only half whispers, nodding at Isabel.

Her head is still turned towards the window, her face obscured by her hair, but out of the corner of my eye I see her stiffen.

'Which new girl?' I ask, just to be annoying.

I've been told I'm insufferable. Multiple times, actually, by multiple different people. In fact, I've been told it for so long that the first time someone said it to me, I had to go home and google it on my mum's laptop because I wasn't old enough to know what it was or even have a smartphone of my own to google it on.

Sometimes it's kind of a badge of honour, I think. Especially when I'm being insufferable to a dickhead lad who told the whole school I was a lesbian because I swerved him after two weeks of him groping me in the back of the big Maccies in town.

It's his turn to roll his eyes. 'The ginger bird, obviously.'

He doesn't bother to keep his voice low any more, and she definitely tenses up. There are a few people still milling around the classroom now, but most have taken their seats, so Jay is drawing more attention than I'd like.

'Oh yeah,' I say with a shrug. 'That's the new girl.'

God, I enjoy being insufferable sometimes.

'Think you can do me a favour?' he asks with another smirk. 'Can you ask her if the carpet matches the drapes?'

Except, as he says it, Ms Price walks in, and the background chatter of the classroom falls to a hush just in time for his words to ring out loud and clear. Isabel does turn round at this, her face all tight and a furious red.

'Oh, hon,' I sigh, fighting to keep my voice cool and level in

11

the newly fallen quiet, 'if you don't know what a vagina looks like, you don't need to go asking strangers. There's websites for that.'

He doesn't like that answer very much. He especially doesn't like how a couple of his mates, a few desks down, let out whoops of laughter at his expense.

'Devo'd, lad,' one of them says with a chuckle.

'Devastated indeed,' Ms Price adds, a cool, neutral expression on her face that looks like hard work and makes me think she's at least a bit happy someone put Henno in his place. 'Is there a reason you aren't in your seat, James?'

He slinks off to an empty desk as Ms Price makes her way to the front of the classroom. I chance a look at Isabel, and she seems to have frozen in place, except the scowl that she'd aimed at Henno now seems to be fixed on me instead.

I tilt my hands up at her, the universal hand gesture for *what do you want from me?* But she just whips her head back round to stare out of the window, face hidden again by that shiny sheet of red hair.

'All right,' Ms Price calls out. 'I'm sure you all had lovely summers, but this is where the real work starts. Mock exams are serious. Just because your A levels aren't for another year doesn't mean lower sixth isn't vital. The work you do now will dictate your futures.'

Yikes, just diving in the deep end, I guess.

I feel my leg start to twitch under the desk already, even though I told myself I'd do better this year – even though I *have* to do better this year. I place a hand on my knee to stop it, but it doesn't do much, just knocks my knuckles into the underside of the desk, making a bit of a racket.

Ms Price shoots me a Look. One of her signature Looks. It's a Look that I think she reserves just for me that says, *you know, if you were anybody else, I'd bollock you for that.*

She actually said that to me once. About forgetting to bring my homework or my books in or something. She likes me, I think, even if she gets fed up with me. She knows I'm trying, but she also knows I'm not succeeding very often. It was her who first suggested I should consider making an appointment for an ADHD assessment. I need to speak to her about that, actually, after class. Tell her thank you or whatever.

Problem is, now having a name for the way I am doesn't really change much. The medication might, if my mum gets her way. But she won't get her way. Not if I can pull my shit together and do well enough in the mocks this year.

I remove my hand from my knee slowly, with a small – and I'm hoping at least slightly angelic – smile at Ms Price, who continues her little speech about how important this first year is. It doesn't take long for her words to kind of just slide over me again, and I turn to look out of the window, but Isabel's obscuring my view. And it's weird, but I'm pretty sure she's just been *staring* at me. Her head whips back round to face the front almost as soon as I look, but she's just half a second too late for me not to have seen it.

Fucked-up vibes from this one, seriously. First thing she says

13

to me is some blurted-out compliment, but then the second I try actually talking to her she gets all stoic and sulky, like I've done or said something specifically to piss her off. And now, apparently, she's staring at me.

The best thing to do, I decide, is just not to bother with her. She clearly wants nothing to do with me. Mrs Anderson asked me to welcome her to the school, and I've done what I could: I've shown her around a bit, walked her to class. My duties end there, if that's all she wants from me. I wash my hands of the girl.

Thankfully, the class isn't a particularly important one. I don't take much in. Papers are handed out, booklets and sheets of module outlines and exam guidelines, reading lists, that kind of thing. When the bell rings, I've got sociology, but it's only next door, so I hover to talk to Ms Price before I leave. Isabel sees me waiting, takes one look at me and just pelts it out, like the idea that maybe I'm waiting for her is the worst thing imaginable. Whatever. *Crank.*

'Lou,' Ms Price says when she sees me lurking. 'First day and you're already zoning out.'

'I know, sorry. But the doctor gave me some tricks and stuff. Just got to put in the practice, I guess. I'm gonna do better this year.'

'So you got an assessment?'

'Yeah, you're talking to the proud owner of a freshly minted ADHD diagnosis.' I shoot her a peace sign, and she rolls her eyes, but fondly, I think. I hope.

14

'Has the medication been helping at all?'

I shake my head. 'Not on it. Don't want to. Mum agreed that if I get my shit together this year, before the A levels, I don't have to.'

'Eloise—'

'Anyway, I've got to get to sociology, miss. Just wanted to say thanks, for the suggestion, for having my back, or whatever.' I give her a small wave and dart out of there before she can give me the same speech I've been getting from my mum all summer.

CHAPTER THREE

'Hemel Hempstead?'

'No, that's not it. Look at it on the map – it's barely in London.'

'Hampstead! No, I see it. Yeah, it's mostly just a big field.'

Lily gasps, and Mel and I both turn to look at her. She grasps my arm, still staring at her phone with wide eyes.

'What?' I prompt after a second.

'*Harry Styles* lives there,' she breathes.

I snort, rolling my eyes, but Mel jumps in, too, staring at her own phone.

'And Helena Bonham Carter. And Ricky Gervais.'

'Christ.' Of course this is where Isabel lived. She's not just from London, she's from *rich people* London.

I kick back, planting my feet on the empty chair opposite me while Mel and Lily keep scrolling, Lily listing off names of more famous people from Hampstead, Mel calling out 'fun facts' about its history. We've pretty much got the sixth-form common room to ourselves. For the most part, the second years are too cool or too stressed to be spending their frees on-site or out of

16

the library. And I don't think people in our year have got used to this area being available to them yet. I've been sneaking in here on rainy days for years.

I've filled them both in on the morning, thoroughly. Lily's firmly on my side. She always is when one of us says we have a reason to hate someone. No questions asked, ride-or-die, she'll hate whoever we need her to. She trusts us. Mel's a bit slower to jump in than Lily is, more insistent on getting the facts first, but whatever she's currently reading about Hampstead on her phone seems to be doing the job.

'Jesus, Lou, you should see the price of the houses in this place.'

'Well, we knew Isabel was posh,' I say with a shrug. 'Just didn't know she was, like, crack out the guillotine, first one on the menu when we eat the rich level of posh.'

'No wonder she's so stuck-up.' Lily rolls her eyes.

There's a small squeak from the far end of the room. This tiny, strangled noise that makes us all look up just in time to see a flash of red hair disappear out of the door of the sixth-form building.

'Fuck,' I breathe. 'How much of that do you think she heard?'

'Oh, none of it, for sure. She just turned round and legged it because she heard nothing.'

'Thanks, Mel,' I say, hauling myself from my seat and picking up my bag. 'You're delightful as always.'

She sends a lazy and unbothered middle finger my way as I start to chase after Isabel to do some damage control.

I think I've lost her at first, stepping into the pale early-September sun and squinting for a moment, eyes roving round the paths and grassy patches, trying to see if she's still outside. I'm about to head for the main building and look for her there when I hear her voice from behind the massive gnarled oak tree nearby. I can only see her feet poking out.

'Yeah, I know,' she murmurs, and I freeze. 'I just wish she'd waited, like, two years, you know? I hate it here. I hate that I had to leave.' Her voice breaks on that last part, and she falls silent for a moment, listening, I assume, to the person on the other end of the phone.

I'm torn for a moment between pity and prickliness. It is shitty that she had to leave her home, but is she really not going to give my city, my school more than half a day before she decides she hates it?

'Not really,' she says then. 'One girl, I suppose. A teacher asked her to show me round, so I talked to her a little before first lesson, but I *highly doubt* we're going to be friends.'

More silence, and I shrink back towards the door to the sixth form, making sure I'm hidden from view.

'Yeah, we've got English together. She was very, uh, chatty.' Isabel says this like it's an insult. As if I wasn't having to single-handedly carry the entire conversation. If you'd asked me a couple of hours ago, I'd have said that Isabel could do with a bit more *chattiness* in her life, though she seems to be plenty *chatty* when it comes to slagging me off over the phone.

'Well, yes,' she continues after a moment, 'but it's like

18

somebody forgot to tell her that sometimes it's okay to just *not* speak. It's – it's allowed. You can actually stop talking and that's fine. And that's not even taking into consideration the fact that I could *barely* understand her. It surely can't be that hard to tone down your accent just a tiny bit, make it a little less . . . difficult.'

Okay, now *that's* an insult. I'm not even sure which part of that to be more offended by.

'God, no, of course I don't *like* her. She's . . . tolerable.'

I can't make out any words on the other end of the phone, but the tinny sound rings out loud enough for me to hear, and she laughs, a kind of derisive scoff.

'Scouse girls are not all you made them out to be, Benji. You're too sweet. Plus, I think you're dating the only nice one in the city.'

CHAPTER FOUR

I'm out of there. Fast. As much as my mum likes to complain about my impulsivity, even *I* know that if I stick around and listen to the rest of that phone call, I'm going to say something I'll regret.

I mean, it'd feel bloody fantastic while I said it. Just *dreaming* about saying it feels pretty fantastic. But yeah, I guess, I *suppose*, it probably wouldn't work out well for me in the long run.

See? The new and improved Lou Byrne. The mature Lou Byrne. The one who's getting her shit together in time for A levels, and who considers how things will work out in the 'long run' before delivering a tirade of insults to the new girl that I haven't quite come up with yet, but I'm sure would have been incredibly witty and creative.

Except now I'm in the main school building, all twitchy and flustered and on edge, and all I can think to do is wrench open my locker and start pulling out my trainers and my kit. It might be a stupid idea, but it was, technically, doctor's orders. Well, actually, no – that's a stretch. His actual orders were that I start taking a terrifying medicine with the word *meth* in it that took three tries for me to pronounce. And, when I gave him a hard no, he suggested exercise. Running helps with focus. It always has. It leaves me awake and alert and just lets my brain sit still for a minute.

Thank God for the newly found freedom of being a sixth-former. A quick change in the loos then I'm pelting it before I even leave the gates, trainers pounding against the gravel, music blasting in my headphones. I think I might pass Isabel on the way out, but I barely see her. I'm supposed to be training for the London Marathon next year, but I've never exactly been great at *slow and steady*. I push until my legs are screaming, my lungs burning, and then I turn round and push some more, the warmth of the last leg of summer clinging to my skin along with my workout clothes.

I don't know how long I've been running for, but when I get back to school, sweaty, breathless, hair sticking to the nape of my neck where it's too short to fit into a ponytail, the exercise hasn't done much to drum out the fury I'm feeling. The only thing that does is the sudden swooping realisation that I've got bigger problems than some swot who thinks I'm too *chatty*.

I don't think I've ever seen a shower at this school.

I'm standing at the gates, catching my breath, drops of sweat falling with little *plod*s on to the gravel while I consider my options.

Option 1: the sinks in the girls' loos. I could just grab some paper towels and make do, hope nobody walks in.

Option 2: the boys' PE changing rooms. I have a feeling they've got at least one shower in there. But there's multiple flaws with this plan. I'd have to be in the boys' changing room for one, and you couldn't pay me enough to even walk past the open door without pinching my nose. It's also communal, meaning I'd have to get all publicly naked, which might be a bit frowned upon if someone found me in there.

Option 3: slightly rogue but not *completely* ruled out, I run all the way home, fuelled by adrenaline and shame, and skive off the second half of the first day of sixth form. Which isn't a great look, but it *could* look better than stinking out every classroom between now and the end of the day.

But then I think about Ms Price, and how disappointed she'll be in me. I swear I'm not some kind of teacher's pet, okay? I wouldn't care this much if any other teacher was disappointed in me – and they usually are, in my experience – it's just that Ms Price actually cares, you know? And when she gives me The Look, it's the same as when my mum gives me The Look. It's like they both hope for *my* sake that I can do better.

Taking Option 3 right now would definitely get me The Look from both of them.

Okay, so Option 1 then. Girls' loos. Even if it is the middle of lunch and seemingly *everyone* is milling about right now. Maybe if I stride in there with enough confidence, it won't be so mortifying. Shoulders back, sweaty hair pushed out of my face, chest held high. If anyone gives me any shit, I can just shrug. *How many miles did you run today, huh? Yeah, that's right. Tell it to my thighs of steel, bitch.*

As it turns out, I don't actually get to use the line. Nobody says anything to my face as I stride up to the main building. Only a handful of Year Nines have a little giggle at me as I rush in to grab my clothes, but the Year Nines are class-A wankers this year so I don't really care what they think.

'Eloise?'

I'm clutching my clothes in a little bundle, trying to decide which loos to head for, when she appears behind me. Because of *course* she's here right now. Of *course* she is.

I fix an obviously fake smile on my face before I spin round and straighten up a little to look her in the eye. 'Yeah, Iz?'

That seems to stump her, actually. Don't know what she expected when she called out *my* name. Her eyes are just darting around as if she doesn't know *where* to look, like the sight of me, red-faced and dishevelled, sweating in my shorts and sports bra, is simply too much for her delicate sensibilities. She's exactly like one of those dogs who's just been caught raiding the fridge and can't look anybody in the eye from the guilt of it all.

'I just wanted to— I just— Are you okay?'

Obviously not.

'Do I look okay?'

She does manage to meet my eye then. The guilty-puppy act

23

drops just long enough for her to take me in fully, and wrinkle her nose a little in disgust.

Is she serious?

'Are you serious?'

Whoops, didn't mean to say that part out loud. She at least has the decency to seem embarrassed about it. She turns away, starts rummaging through her bag.

'Here.' She thrusts a handful of stuff in my direction.

I stare at them for a second. 'Deodorant and wet wipes?'

She just nods, waving them at me again. Great, so now she's being generous?

'I don't—' I try to swat her away.

'Trust me, you need them more than I do.'

Oh, okay, so not generosity then. Just repulsion.

Neither of us say anything as I take the deodorant and wipes from her, and the silence starts to feel awkward, so I just turn round. I take a step towards the toilets before I hesitate.

'Not to sound ungrateful for the barely concealed insult or anything, Isabel,' I say, 'but why are you helping me?'

She's gone. Of course she has. Because it's all *women supporting women* until she has to stick around and listen to me being *chatty*, I guess.

She avoids me the rest of the day. Which I'd thought was for the best, but I'm hanging around at the school gates for her as a sea of tiny Year Sevens in brand-new blazers and neat little ties pour out of one of the classrooms as the last bell rings, and if I thought the last couple of hours after my run would have helped me cool down, I was hilariously wrong.

Instead, I've had an afternoon to agonise over it all. How the resentment had clung thick to her voice when she called me 'chatty', the way I could hear the sneer in her words as she told this *Benji* guy that I was '*tolerable*'. The way she wrinkled her nose at me.

When I finally see her, head down, hurrying out of the gates alone, I'm so worked up that it gives me a frankly unhinged amount of satisfaction to hear the little yelp of surprise she lets out when I step into her path and thrust her deodorant and wet wipes at her.

After she recovers from the shock, she reaches out and wordlessly takes them, her face set in a grim, stony expression.

'You're welcome,' I say.

She closes her eyes and takes a long breath, like she's trying to be patient. It's infuriating.

'You're returning *my* things,' she says then, slowly. 'If either of us should be saying thank you . . .'

'Oh, I would have, back by the lockers, except you left. I was probs just being too *chatty* for you.'

I watch her frown turn briefly to confusion, see her brows turn up in the middle just slightly before furrowing back downwards as she realises what I'm talking about. Well, I'm in it now. In for a penny, or whatever.

'Shame, really. I must not have been that *tolerable*, after all.'

For a moment, she doesn't respond, just blinks a couple of

25

times, then takes a sharp intake of breath, like she's about to start shouting. But instead her voice turns to a hiss as she takes a furtive step towards me as if she's embarrassed to even be having this conversation.

'You don't get to be angry about that,' she whispers. 'It's not like you were exactly saying wonderful things about me behind my back.'

I laugh. 'Oh, which part didn't you like? The part about you being rich, or the part about you being stuck-up? Because you've made it perfectly clear you're not ashamed of either of them.'

She twitches. 'I don't need to be rich to be better than you, Eloise.'

'Oh, we're just saying the quiet part out loud now, are we?'

'Well, *I* would never greet a new student by firing ceaseless questions at her, then using that information to gossip behind her back.'

'No, you wouldn't say anything at all, would you? You'd just stay silent and stoic and rude because better that than being cringe like *me*, right?'

She seems to shut down for a second. I watch the rage just fall out of her expression to be replaced by this perfect blank mask.

'Got it on the first try. Good for you,' she says simply, before hefting her bag over her shoulder and barrelling past me.

Right. Okay. Well, that's her stance settled then.

CHAPTER FIVE

'**S**o what then do we think that says about Jane's relationship with Rochester?'

Couldn't tell you, Ms Price. Honestly, gun to my head, not a clue. Too busy pretending not to notice Isabel staring daggers at me to know what you're going on about. When nobody answers, Ms Price pauses for a moment. The rest of the class all either looks away or shrugs.

She groans. 'I *know* some of you know this! Rochester's been keeping his supposedly mad wife in the attic. Jane's just expected to trust him. But what does that tell us, as readers, about their dynamic?'

Of *course* Isabel's raising her hand right now. As if it isn't her fault I've spent the first few weeks of term so distracted. Because here I was, totally content to go our separate ways after our fight and just spend the next two years ignoring each other. It might have worked, too, if we hadn't been stuck in the desks that we chose on the first day, close enough to feel her fuming, the disdain bubbling over from her every time I so much as shift in my seat.

Apparently, though, Little Miss Better-Than-Me is fully capable of splitting her attention span evenly between simmering at me and listening to the teacher, and, now that her hand is raised, the teacher in question is looking at Isabel with an almost painful amount of relief. Well, nice try, Iz, but I'll always be Ms Price's fave.

'Yes, Isabel?'

'I think Brontë's showing us that nobody's exempt from the patriarchy.'

'That's interesting – can you expand a bit, explain why?'

Isabel's looking very much like she'd rather not expand right now. If anything, she seems to very much want to shrink, preferably into non-existence. I won't lie: it's a little bit satisfying to watch her struggle. At least until she opens her mouth.

'Jane is portrayed as this perfect woman.' Her voice is quiet but measured. 'Educated, plain, humble. And Bertha's supposed to be her opposite – she's described as animalistic, insane, passionate, *literally* fiery. But they're both at the mercy of Mr Rochester, or the other men in their lives. It doesn't matter how ideal a woman you are, the only way Jane and Rochester are able to be equal at the end is because of her inheritance and Rochester's blindness, because he has to be dependent on her for them to be anything close to equal.'

Pfft. I could have told you that. But now Ms Price is looking at Isabel like she's just shown up on her doorstep with a bunch of flowers and a winning lottery ticket.

'That's an excellent point, and I think we should touch on

28

that for a moment: the concept of the *madwoman in the attic* as Jane's supposed opposite—'

She goes on a bit more, but I'm busy wondering how the hell Isabel gets away with that whole *oh no, I'm so shy, I couldn't possibly expand* act, and then immediately comes out with the most eloquent literary analysis Ms Price has apparently ever heard in her classroom.

It's as if Isabel hears me think it. She just snaps her head over in my direction, glaring at me, and I jump a little in my seat, knocking my pen into the desk with a sharp clatter that – just my luck – draws Ms Price's eyes.

Great, so now I've got to spend the rest of the lesson looking like I'm paying attention to avoid getting called over for another concerned chat when the bell goes. I think I'm doing an all right job of it, too, for the most part, but as soon as the lesson's over, just as I'm standing to stuff my books back in my bag—

'Eloise?'

Yep, there it is.

'And, Isabel, could you both wait behind for a second?'

Wait, what?

I risk a quick glance over at Isabel, who seems to be having roughly the same train of thought. We both approach Ms Price tentatively, from opposite sides of her desk.

'Isabel.' Ms Price shoots her a smile. Still not sure where this is going, but I already know I'm not gonna like it. 'You were part of a mentor/mentee programme at your old school, weren't you?'

Oh *Christ, no.* I definitely do not like where this is going.

Isabel just gives a stiff nod.

'That'll look great on your uni applications. Better still if you continue it this year.'

Isabel stammers for a second. 'I-I'm not sure – with me being a new student, I just don't think it makes sense.'

'Why not? It's an opportunity to show how you adapt to change, that you're willing to hit the ground running in a new environment. And, Eloise, it's an opportunity for you, too. You need a lot of help this year.'

Oh, we're just going straight for the jugular today I see, okay.

'You're capable of good grades. I know that – you know that. But you need help focusing. And Isabel here –' she smiles, waving a hand over at Isabel who is most definitely not smiling back – 'has as much to gain as you do.'

Isabel's face pales in almost comical symmetry with mine.

'I don't think that's a good—' I begin, at the same time as Isabel says, 'Thank you for thinking of me, but—'

Ms Price waves both of our protestations away, looking, well, a bit smug if you ask me. She really thinks she's on to something here, doesn't she?

'Isabel. If you're willing to tutor Eloise, I'd be happy to write you a glowing reference to add to your personal statement. You've told me you want to apply to King's College, and, if you're serious about getting in, you'll need something to make you stand out. And, Lou, if you'd like to get through sixth-form without a repeat of my near-weekly calls to your mum last year . . .'

'You *know* my mum works shifts, miss.'

It was the source of so many arguments last year. Mum refused to ignore any of my teachers' phone calls, kept telling me that my education was the most important thing to her, but how many times did she answer those calls at the expense of a few hours' sleep between shifts?

'Well, if you benefit from this mentorship programme, I'll have nothing to call her about, will I?'

Here's the problem with Ms Price. She's *so* like my mum. She's frustrating in a way that's sincerely supportive, but when it's my mum making me do things I hate *for my own benefit* I can argue back to my heart's content. When it's Ms Price, I have to remind myself that it's not socially acceptable to groan at a teacher about what is and isn't fair. So I restrain myself, just barely. Isabel seems to have done the same, her facial expression shutting down into the kind of neutral look that *has* to be carefully constructed.

'We could try some tutoring sessions after school,' Isabel eventually concedes, her voice flat. And I've got no choice but to agree, have I?

'I can't stay late this week,' I tell her. Mum's on nights, which means early evenings after school are the only time I get to spend with her. 'I can do after tea tomorrow maybe, but it'd have to be at mine. I can't get a lift.'

'I could . . . probably ask my mum or dad to drive me.'

Ms Price is beaming, like she's just facilitated something ground-breaking.

'Excellent.' She smiles at both of us, clapping her hands together to emphasise just how excellent she thinks this is. 'That's a start!'

It's a start, yeah. Not sure it's the start of anything good, though.

CHAPTER SIX

'Okay, but isn't the main point of this to learn?' Mum pauses, a chunk of hash brown speared precariously on the end of her fork while she makes what I'm sure she thinks is a very astute observation. 'You won't have to get all chummy – you don't even have to talk about anything other than school. Just treat it like you would a normal tutor – that is, if you'd ever let me get you a tutor. It's a professional relationship. I don't like most of the consultants at the hospital, but we still do our jobs. Or I do, at least.'

I try to ignore the little jab there about hiring a tutor. She knows why I didn't let her: she can't afford it. I don't think she likes it when I say that out loud, though, but it's obvious, isn't it? She works enough overtime as it is to keep the two of us comfortable. I'm not about to throw however much a tutor costs into the mix.

'That's the point, though, isn't it? It's not like we just don't want to be friends. If we were just, I dunno, *normal* about each other, then it'd be fine, but she *hates* me. She thinks she's better than me – she said so herself. And did you forget that she's already got her opinion on *Scouse girls* as a whole? Because I didn't.'

'Well then, prove her wrong.'

I almost spit out my eggs with indignation, which my mum seems to find really funny for some reason.

'I shouldn't have to – it's not like I can change her mind anyw— I mean, that's not even the point!'

'You literally just told me *that's the point.*'

I don't like her tone.

'Okay, well, the new point is that there isn't even anything she can teach me. I'm not stupid. It's not like Isabel is *smarter* than me or has, like, I dunno, Secret Literature Knowledge that I don't have. It's literally just that I can't focus. How's Isabel telling me stuff I already know going to fix that?'

'I see,' Mum says, standing up to take her plate to the sink. She sounds very sage, and it's making me nervous. 'I think I've figured out what this is about.'

I'm pushing the last bits of sausage round my plate. I don't want to waste it. Mum goes out of her way to make both our meals veggie, even though she hates the veggie sausages I like, but I have a feeling that whatever she's about to say is going to make me less sympathetic to her plight anyway.

'And what is it you think you've figured out?'

'Your feelings are hurt.'

'That's what I've been telling you. Isabel was a dick.'

'No, not by Isabel, by Ms Price. You're hurt because she asked Isabel to tutor you. It implies that she thinks Isabel knows more than you.'

'Obviously, she doesn't think that because I'm well smarter

than Isabel,' I grumble into my plate. I hear Mum finish up at the sink, the clattering of her plate in the dish rack, then suddenly she's standing next to me, leaning down to place a small kiss on my head, hugging me from behind.

'You're right. And I'm sorry, it must feel awful to think your favourite teacher is doubting you.' I stop pushing my food round on my plate, lift my arms to clutch hers where they're wrapped round me, feeling my lip wobble a little as I do. 'We both know you're intelligent, love. So, like I said, prove it to her.'

Okay, that ruins the moment a bit, I will admit. What's the age where it stops being socially acceptable to just groan and cry *but Muuuuummm*? Because I'm tempted to give it a shot. Just as I'm considering it, though, the doorbell rings.

Fuck. Of course she's early.

Mum grabs my plate as I jump up and hurry to the door, wrenching it open to reveal Isabel, looking up only briefly before she returns her gaze to her shoes.

'Hi. Sorry I'm early. Mum insisted – she hates being late.'

'You're fine. Just means it'll be over with faster, right?'

She just cringes, holding what looks like an actual, literal briefcase with both hands in front of her like it'll shield her from my presence.

'Oh, hiya. The famous Isabel, is it?' Mum's somehow finished washing the dishes at record speed just to come and be as embarrassing as possible. 'Are you just going to leave her standing outside, Lou?'

I resist the urge to groan, stepping aside to let her in.

35

'Mum, Isabel, Isabel, Mum,' I mumble, gesturing between the two of them.

Isabel reaches out a hand to shake, and Mum takes it with a little bemused smile.

'Nice to meet you,' Isabel says.

'You too, love. Don't worry about me, though. I'm off to work in just a second.'

I watch Isabel look my mum up and down. She's not subtle about it, either. When someone habitually keeps her eyes fixed on the ground, it's pretty clear when she's using them to judge a person.

For a second, I see my mum through her eyes. Hair a bit on the greasy side, thrown messily into a bun. Heading off to work in a rumpled T-shirt, pyjama bottoms and Crocs. Isabel doesn't have the context I have. She doesn't know that Mum's hair is greasy because this is the last of a long string of night shifts before her day off, or that she's dressed like that because she prefers to change into scrubs at the hospital, or that the Crocs – well, I have no excuse for them. They're hideous, but apparently all the other nurses wear them, too. Isabel can only go off what she sees.

'Uh, Isabel?' I point her over to the kitchen, the table just visible through the open door. 'Mind setting up over there? I'll be two seconds.'

She nods, hurrying off, and I interrupt my mum in the process of grabbing her coat and keys with an emphatic hug.

'Kill me, please.'

She laughs. 'Can't. I don't have time to hide the body before work. Just be nice, okay? I'll see you tomorrow – love you.'

'Yeah, love you, too, Judas.'

She laughs on her way out of the door.

Isabel, while this is all happening, has apparently managed to spread out the entire A-level syllabus on the kitchen table, and, by the time I'm pulling out the seat across from her, she's sitting with her hands between her knees, looking round at my kitchen like she's taking mental notes on everything she sees. Probably planning on calling whoever that Benji guy was and telling him all about the bubbles in the lino and the bit of ketchup on the worktop.

'All right, let's do this,' I say, sighing. She gives a grim nod in response.

'I thought since it's our first session we could just run through the syllabus and the exam specs. That kind of thing.'

'Sure. I have all of that already – Ms Price handed it out on the first day – but why not?'

Her eyes narrow. 'What do you want from me, Eloise? You agreed to this, too.'

'Only to get Ms Price off my back.'

'Well, same here. And the best way to do that is to just suck it up and do some work.'

'I didn't object.'

'Fine, okay, so you already know the syllabus? Tell me about it then.'

I can't get my mum's voice out of my head. Prove it to her.

'Love Through the Ages,' I tell her. 'We'll study one Shakespeare text – Ms Price chose *Taming of the Shrew* – *Jane Eyre*, and one modern novel, which. Er. I don't remember what that one is, actually. Maybe she hasn't mentioned it yet. And, uh, some poems.'

'Almost,' Isabel says. And the way she says it is *smug*. She's so pleased at having caught me out, I feel the tips of my ears burning and my leg start to bounce under the table. 'It's actually one Shakespeare, one book and one poetry anthology. Of the last two, one of them has to be pre-1900s. So that's *Jane Eyre*. There'll be a question that is just going to ask us to analyse the Shakespeare play, a question that will ask us to compare two . . . Are you listening to me, Eloise?'

That's the bit that sends me into a fury if I'm being honest. Because I'm actually, genuinely, paying attention. I'm looking up at the ceiling, yes. Tapping away at the table with my fingers, sure. But I'm doing those things because I'm *concentrating*. Fat lot of good it does me, though, when she comes out with that patronising tone.

'Maybe it's just difficult. Because of your accent. Maybe you could try and, I don't know, tone it down a bit. I'm getting most of it, though. You're doing well – keep going,' I add with a smile that matches the level of condescension she offered me.

I watch the contours of her cheekbones grow a blotchy, angry pink. I watch as the muscles beneath the redness tense and twitch as she clenches her jaw. She looks me right in the eye when she speaks.

'You think you're so above this, Eloise, don't you? But Ms Price wouldn't have asked me to do this if she didn't think you needed it. So either you deal with it and let me help you, or you go and tell her yourself that you don't plan on passing your exams next year.'

She's really picked out the sorest spot she could find and gone to town on it, hasn't she? I'm starting to think that she only agreed to this because she thought it'd be fun to humiliate me. I take in her expression carefully, painstakingly, and though she does match my gaze with an almost impressive steeliness to her glare, I can see those blotches of colour that sprouted on her cheekbones starting to spread. Her whole face, even her neck and ears, turns a warm, flushed pink as she continues to meet my eye. I let her struggle for another long moment.

'So what, exactly, do you think you can do to help me?'

She visibly relaxes when she looks away, needlessly rearranging the papers on the table for a second too long.

'I think we can work together to organise the syllabus in a way that helps us out,' she says finally. 'If we get a jump on the kinds of questions they ask, we can spend the year tying everything we learn back to the exam. I was thinking that tonight we could analyse the phrasing of past-paper questions, making a list of everything we need to know, the kinds of points they want us to make, so, as the year goes on, we can keep coming back to those notes and compose perfect answers.'

Christ, this is going to be the longest year of my life.

CHAPTER SEVEN

'I think you're overreacting.' Jas's voice is soft, but everything else about her tone indicates a clear and decisive point being made. We're sitting in the common room again, along with Mel and Katie, each with a cup of tea or coffee while we try to wake up a bit before our first lesson. Caffeine is a bit touch and go with me. Sometimes it wakes me up, sometimes it calms me down, but it seems to be the former today, because what started out as a harmless griping session about Isabel is rapidly turning into a full-blown rant. And I don't see myself running out of ranting material any time soon.

Let's see, we've already covered the exasperated way she explained the plot of *Taming of the Shrew* as if I was dumb for not already knowing, despite us not having even *started* on it in class yet. And the part where she gave an 'example' analysis of a poem that isn't even *on* the syllabus just to show off how clever and well-spoken she is. What next? Oh, I know. There's always the part where she set me actual homework: reading her personal copy of *Jane Eyre* because she thinks her oh-so-insightful annotations could really help me 'grapple with the more complex themes of the book'. That one's my favourite, personally.

'I am *not* overreacting.'

'Oo-er!' Lily, late again, sinks down into the empty seat at the table with her eyebrows raised. 'What's boiled her piss?'

'Isabel,' Mel and Jas both sigh in unison. Katie, though, who had been a thousand miles away for most of the conversation, looks up at Lily's entrance.

'Where were you last night?' she hisses. 'Your mum called me to check you were at mine. I had to cover for you again.'

'A lady never tells,' said Lily with a smirk, which is hilarious because she *always* tells, but this time she just turns to me instead. 'What's the posh fuck done this time?'

I can see Katie deflate at the evasion, but I can't resist filling her in. Lily's the only one who's still on my side in this thing.

'We had that tutoring session last night. And she just shows up at my house, immediately pulls a face at my mum, then spends the next two hours finding every opportunity to humiliate me.'

'Absolute crank.'

'I don't think that's actually how it went down,' Mel says.

'Why would I lie?' My voice is thick with frustration.

'No one's saying you're lying,' says Jas, 'but maybe you misinterpreted *how* she said it.'

'You do have a bit of trouble with tone sometimes,' Katie points out, her voice small. Great, welcome back to the conversation, Katie, just in time to stab me in the back.

41

'*Et tu, Brute?*'

'It's true, though,' she says, but she looks apologetic. 'Not in a bad way. Just sometimes you tend to assume people are being worse than they are.'

Jas sighs. 'Just give her a chance, Lou. You might not actually hate her.'

I groan, but I think it's pretty big of me to not keep arguing, so I count that as a win for this year's new, more mature Lou Byrne. The thing is, I still haven't told them about our argument on the first day of school. It's important context. Sure, her acting a bit stuck-up during a tutoring session seems harmless on its own. But not when she's already made how she feels about me perfectly clear.

I'm not sure why I'm keeping it from them exactly. Except that I think if I told them, they'd want to know why I got so worked up over it. And honestly? I can't even figure that one out myself. Like, okay, she insulted me. We argued. But it was a few cheap jabs in angry whispers with a girl I'd known less than a day. I've had screaming matches with my mum – hell, Lily and I have raised our voices to each other a few times – shouting much crueller things than Isabel and I did. But I've never felt the blood rush to my ears like that, never felt my heart pounding so hard mid-fight that I'm breaking a sweat. Not until Isabel.

Maybe it's because I know Isabel means it. She believes in her superiority so strongly that, for all her blushing and hiding behind her hair, she can still look me dead in the eye and tell me so to my face.

Jas, though, isn't willing to take my sullen silence as an answer.

'You might want to make a bit of an effort,' she says eventually. 'Because she's got *no* mates, and I'm not about to let her keep eating lunch on her own.'

'No chance in hell,' I tell her. But then it's Jas, and she's looking at me all disappointed and maybe a little hurt, and I deflate just a bit. 'I just think she's probably happier with no mates than she would be stuck with us,' I huff, to save myself.

Mel, infuriatingly perceptive as always, leans forward.

'Lou, did something happen to make you think that?'

'No,' I say, too fast. Mel just raises an eyebrow.

I think about telling them for a second. I think about having to explain that I got my precious little feelings hurt by some perfect snob who said a couple of mean things a week ago and is now trying to make me feel stupid by helping me pass my exams. I really do consider it. But then Katie's voice comes out of nowhere, sharp and tense.

'Who are you texting?'

We all follow her gaze to Lily, who looks up from her phone, a smile still on her face. When nobody says anything, she just shrugs.

'Wouldn't you like to know. Did the bell go already?'

It hasn't, but she doesn't wait for anyone to answer, just stands up and gives us all a wave before heading to her next lesson.

'Okay, not to pry,' Jas begins cautiously, 'but that was weird, right?'

Katie just frowns, sinking deeper into her chair.

43

'Yeah,' she says after a moment. 'It's not like Lil to stay quiet about it if she's seeing a new lad.'

'If anything, she usually tells us too much,' I add with a shudder, remembering the graphic details from the last guy she went out with.

'Lou.' Mel gives me a little prod in the ankle with her foot. 'You were saying?'

Nope. No way. Moment's passed.

'Just that Isabel's too much of a snob to want to be seen with the likes of us,' I tell her with a dismissive wave.

Thankfully, the bell does ring then, and whether Mel believes me or not becomes a Mel problem.

CHAPTER EIGHT

Jas makes good on her threat. The next day, when I join the others in the caff for lunch, Isabel's sitting with them at our table. I hesitate in the dinner queue, trying to figure out if it's too late to skip lunch and go for a run instead. I'm weighing up how hungry I am versus how willing I am to deal with an hour of cold, awkward silences, when I realise what seems off about the picture.

I can't hear what they're saying from here, but I don't need to. Isabel's being . . . nice? Or at least friendly. She's chatting in between bites of her meal, putting her knife and fork down on her plate to gesticulate. The girl *gesticulates*. Also, apparently nobody warned her that it's – for reasons unknown to literally everybody – deeply uncool to use an actual plate at lunch here. You've got to get your dinner in one of those Styrofoam pasta pots, and if it's a Roast-Dinner-Wednesday, good luck to you. I don't plan on breaking that news to her. Call that my little victory if I'm being forced to spend my lunchtimes with her.

When I sidle up with my food, the atmosphere shifts. Isabel doesn't even look up at me, but stiffens as soon as I approach;

what looked like easy laughter from across the caff shifting into a mouth clamped shut into a solid line of discomfort.

Well, good to know it's just me she hates, I guess.

'*Eeeeverythiiing okay?*' I ask. My first mistake is using that kind of lilting *awkward* voice that has never in the history of spoken language served to do anything but make a situation *more* awkward.

Isabel doesn't say a word.

'All good.' Jas smiles as I sit down. 'We were just talking about Isabel's last school.'

'I see. Loads better than here, I assume?' Isabel does not miss the sarcasm in my voice. Good. She narrows her eyes.

'She was actually just saying how much she prefers our uniforms to her old ones,' Jas says, still wearing her best peacekeeping smile.

'They had to wear little hats,' Lily adds, and even I feel a little bit guilty about the conspiratorial smirk she sends my way. I'm hoping Isabel didn't catch it, actually. I'll happily say any number of cruel things to her face, but there's a special place in hell for girls who don't try to hide that they've been saying bitchy things behind another girl's back. Tell Satan to put me on the list, I guess.

'Uh,' I say, trying to brush past that moment of conscience. She did say she was better than me, after all. It's not like she doesn't deserve it. 'What else? I assume the kind of school that makes you wear little hats is nothing like this one, so what *was* it like?'

She frowns at me, like I'm trying to catch her out. I am a bit, but it's not *my* fault if her old school was fancy enough to embarrass her.

'What about clubs?' Jas asks. 'You mentioned you were in a few. We don't really have any except, like, hockey and football. There's rugby, too, but girls aren't allowed, I think.' Jas wrinkles her nose in distaste, before returning her expression to a warm smile, and Isabel echoes it. Now that it's Jas asking the questions, Isabel's face lights up again.

'There were a few. Some I don't miss. I was never any good at choir. But we used to do a book club every month. I miss that a lot.'

'Ooooh, what kinds of books did you do?'

'A bit of everything.' Isabel sounds almost excited to be talking about this, and it's *weird*. 'We'd alternate – we'd do something contemporary one month, then a classic the next. It was mostly just a ruse to get us to read more widely, like they thought we'd be tricked into reading Dickens if they gave us a teen romcom the month before, but I really enjoyed the classics, actually.'

She dips her head a bit then, like she's embarrassed herself.

'Let me guess, you found the romcoms too unsophisticated.'

I can't stop myself. I really can't. It was the embarrassed little dip of the head that got me, I think. Like, *oh, look at me, I'm Isabel, I read Dickens and it doesn't make me want to gouge my eyes out, how quirky of me.*

But her head snaps up when I speak, and suddenly she's glaring at me. 'I didn't say that.'

'You didn't need to.'

Out of the corner of my eye, I see Jas and Mel glancing between the two of us like they're watching a tennis match, concern laced through both their expressions, but Lily and Katie seem otherwise occupied with hissing furiously at each other from the end of the table about something.

'Well, what about you, Eloise? What kind of books do you read?'

The question catches me off-guard for a second, not least because the last thing I'd expected was for Isabel to take an interest in anything I'd have to say. Though maybe an *interest* might be too strong a word for it. Maybe she's just looking for something new she can giggle about on the phone, tell her mates something else about the chatty, uncultured girl at school that she can't seem to shake.

'Eloise?'

'Oh, I heard you. Just figuring out what you want me to say.'

I lean forward a little, and she keeps her eyes fixed on me. 'Because I'm pretty sure you want me to list off a few of my favourites so you can judge my taste. But see, I'm actually deeply annoying, so just for the fun of it I think I'll go ahead and say no, I don't like books at all, actually. You go ahead and judge me for that if you like.'

Mel and Jas share a look of vague alarm next to us, but Isabel is still looking at me. Still narrowing her eyes. And seriously, if looks could kill, I'd at least be severely maimed right now.

'I wouldn't dare.'

48

But then she does the strangest thing. She kind of, I dunno, gives this little – there's no other way to describe it – *smirk*. Like she's seriously enjoying this little enmity we've cultivated.

I don't have much time to process that because, at that moment, Lily and Katie's odd little whisper-fight at the end of the table boils over into what looks to be a real fight.

'Give your head an absolute wobble,' Lil is saying, face furious. 'I don't owe you shit.'

'It's not about what you *owe* me, Lil, it's about being a fucking friend for once.'

Lily laughs. 'Sorry I have a life, Katie. You should try it sometime.'

And Lily's off, flying out of the caff, Katie following shortly after, face red and furious as she jogs to catch up with her.

A long, tense silence stretches out across the four of us left at the table.

'Well, that's something,' Mel says, slapping her knees in an unintentionally hilarious gesture. 'You might not get a book club at your new school, Isabel, but you do get to watch a real-time murder mystery play out between those two. Except the mystery is just guessing which one will murder the other first.'

It breaks the tension so thoroughly that we all let out a little nervous laugh, marking a definitive end to mine and Isabel's stare-down.

CHAPTER NINE

'So, what, they just hugged and made up?'

I shrug, but Jas seems to want more.

'Dunno, guess so. They seem all right to me.'

Jas shifts forward in her seat. 'Were they as tight-lipped with you as they were with me? Did they give you *anything* about what the fight was about?'

'Nope, I tried. With Lil *and* Katie, and both of them just kept insisting that it's fine, saying it doesn't matter anyway because they're okay now.'

She lets out a long breath and slumps back in her seat again, staring into the empty common room.

'But, if they won't tell us, how can we know they've worked through it *properly*?' She sounds exasperated.

'Jas, my angel, light of my life. Please don't take this as an insult—'

'Because that sentence always ends well when you say it.'

'—But I do think they're capable of working out their problems without you sometimes.'

She pouts. This silly, overdramatic pout that has me giggling.

'But it helps, right?'

I laugh. 'Of course it does.' I take my feet off the empty chair between us so that I can reach over and pull her in for a hug. 'A sprinkling of Jas helps any situation.'

She hugs me back for a second, with a contented little *mmm*. The long stretch of silence as we pull apart is my first red flag. The second is the face Jas pulls after a moment. Jas's thinking face.

'So, when you say *any* situation . . .' she begins. This isn't going to end well for me, is it? 'Could a sprinkling of Jas maybe help the Lou and Isabel situation?'

Of course. All red flags point to Isabel Williams.

I put my feet back up on the chair between us, groaning.

'Not unless you can fashion her a whole new less pompous personality.'

'What about if I fashion you a less judgy one?'

She says it jokingly, I think, but I splutter for a moment, too indignant to form words.

'Me, judgy? *She's* judgy, Jas. *She's* judgy.'

Not exactly an argument that's about to win me any national debate awards, but I think it gets my point across.

'You're both judgy in your own way,' she says eventually, which I'll count as at least a partial victory for me. 'She's, okay, yes, maybe a little . . . let's say a little sheltered.' Jas ignores my scoff at that. 'But you, Lou, are trying so hard to see the worst in her.'

'Well, it's not my fault I'm the only one who gets shown the worst parts of her.'

51

'What actually happened between you two? Don't try to deny it. That show at lunch the other day was not about *nothing*.'

'Yeah, that thing at lunch was *weird*, right?'

I see her clock my evasion of the question, but the new intrigue seems to win out. She lowers her voice slightly, leaning in. 'It kind of was, wasn't it?'

'Did you see her smirk?'

'No?'

'She smirked! Like she was having fun with it or something.'

'Are you sure she wasn't just smiling? Trying to bury the hatchet?'

'No way. Only place she was planning on burying any hatchet was in my face, Jas.'

'I don't know – maybe she realised it was all a bit too intense and tried to lighten the mood?'

'With a smirk?'

'With a smile!'

In the moment's hush after Jas's exclamation, the common-room door creaks open, and we both turn to look at whoever just came in.

Isabel – because, of course, where *isn't* this girl? – freezes when she sees us, like maybe she's wishing as much as I am that she could just turn round and run away. Jas, though, is on a completely different wavelength.

'Isabel!' She beams, waving her over, before giving my legs a couple of not-so-subtle nudges until I begrudgingly remove them from the empty seat. 'All right?' she asks as Isabel sits, stiff and slow, and Isabel just nods.

There's a beat of awkward silence, in which I pick at a scab on my neck, the tension eating at me and making my whole body feel like it's about to start vibrating. Jas, though, is the definition of casual as she examines the ends of her braids and sighs.

'Are the braids working?' she asks cheerfully into the uncomfortable silence, and I see Isabel visibly relax, the tense, upright stiffness in her shoulders easing as the silence is broken. 'Mum doesn't like them.'

'Your mum also doesn't like you wearing your natural hair,' I point out. 'So are we really going to trust her opinion?'

'They're very cute,' Isabel says after a moment.

She speaks! Good to know it's just me that she refuses to converse like a person with.

'You think? They're new. I wanted locs, but Mum wouldn't let me get those, either.'

'You could always do what I plan to,' says Isabel. 'Just save all your major hair decisions until you turn eighteen. I plan on getting an undercut the second I move back to London for uni. My mum can find out through Instagram like the rest of the world.'

Jas laughs, but I think I might be glitching or something. The thought of Isabel – perfect, uptight, *better than you* Isabel – getting an undercut just floors me for a second. I can't explain it. It's like I've been hurled a few centimetres out of my own body at the thought of it. It just doesn't compute with the tiny scraps of personality she's given us to work with. Maybe I've been glitching too long because Isabel leans forward a little in her seat, frowning at me, but Jas, thankfully, has apparently been forming coherent thoughts in the time it's taken me to rotate the image of undercut-Isabel around in my head a few times.

'So what you're saying,' Jas says slowly, fixing her face into an expression of concern, 'is that you've come all the way to Liverpool, *objectively* the best night out in the UK, and you're planning on running back to London as soon as you turn eighteen? For what, five-pound pints and posh wankers grinding on you in a club?'

This, at least, is solid ground. This I can contribute to.

'In her defence,' I chime in (not words I thought I'd be saying today, but here we are), 'you get wankers grinding on you in a club anywhere you go. They're just less likely to be posh here.'

Isabel flashes me a smile that *almost* seems genuine. 'Plus, I don't even like beer. So the cost of a pint is kind of irrelevant.'

Jas gives a kind of satisfied nod. 'Fair do's, you got me there.'

'Weren't you saying you wanted to go to uni in London, too?' Isabel asks, her voice small and tentative again.

Jas looks a bit embarrassed at that. 'I think about it sometimes, but then I remember how expensive it is and—'

'What Jas is much too nice to say,' I cut in, 'is that she only ever mentioned wanting to go to uni in London to be polite, and sociable, because she's Jas and she's a polite and sociable

54

gal.' I don't say it to be cutting or whatever, just matter-of-fact, and though Jas winces a little at my words, she does so with that angelic kind of guilty smile that dissipates any tension that my words might have caused otherwise.

Isabel gives her a small smile in return, but when she glances back over at me the smile drops just a bit. Her eye contact is just a little too intense.

'You can't fault her for it,' I say, scrambling for something new to say under Isabel's stare, choosing instead to throw an arm round Jas, who leans into me, closing her eyes for just a second, smiling. 'She has no faults at all. She's an angel.'

'I'm *not* an angel,' Jas says, an embarrassed, airy laugh escaping her. 'I *have* faults.'

'Technically, false humility is a fault,' Isabel says quietly. 'So, a bit of a catch twenty-two there, I suppose.'

Jas laughs. 'Oh well, in that case I'm fucked either way.'

But, even though Jas laughs it off, it irks me. Who is she to criticise Jas?

'And what about you, Isabel? Any faults of your own? Or are you *practically perfect in every way*?' I'm doing a Mary Poppins accent, but I see a steely glint in her eye at the words, and I realise that it kind of just sounds like I'm mocking her accent instead. Well, she did say she wanted me to adjust my accent, make it less *difficult*. That one's on her, I'm afraid.

'I have faults,' she says, and the words are in that same cold tone that I'm used to hearing from her when Jas isn't around.

'Oh yeah, like what?'

From the corner of my vision, I see Jas's eyes flicker between me and Isabel, but our eyes are fixed on each other, a challenge in them, the air suddenly tense and weird.

'Like, for example, if somebody does something to offend me, or hurts someone I care about, I never forgive them.'

I actually laugh out loud at that, thinking about me trying to make an effort with Isabel for Jas's sake, despite what I overheard of her phone call last week. At least I've got the one-up on her in something.

Her brow creases just slightly at my one bark of mirthless laughter.

'Sorry,' I say, pulling my face back into a neutral expression. 'It's just that I can respect that. Really, I can. Can't fault you on it. I think it's perfectly fair to not want to forgive someone who's insulted you. Sensible even. So, guess you are flawless, after all.'

There's a slight flush creeping up her neck, climbing above the collar of today's probably stupid-expensive silk blouse. But her gaze stays fixed on me. I meet it, a challenge I won't back down from, and there's a flutter at the corner of her lips, this twitch. It reminds me of that smirk, back at lunch the other day. It makes my stomach squirm.

'I'm not flawless. Nobody is. Everybody has some major fault.'

'And yours is to dislike pretty much everyone?'

The twitch becomes a definite smile then. It's small, like she can't help herself. The little smirk pulls at the corner of her lips, and her eyes, still fixed on mine, narrow just a bit.

'And yours is to wilfully misunderstand them.'

What in the fuck does that mean?

Jas looks between the two of us, biting her lip like she might just gnaw a hole through it from the tension. The way she slaps her knees, pitching forward in her seat suddenly, makes both me and Isabel jump a little.

'Well, I need a wee,' Jas says chirpily as she jumps up. 'Back in a mo,' she sing-songs. 'You two just chat among yourselves.'

Oh fab. Nice one, Jas. That was super smooth and not at all an obvious ruse to get your two friends who hate each other to break the ice.

I lean forward, too, like a panic instinct. Everyone keeps insisting that it would be 'uncouth' or 'completely insane' to actually *fight* Isabel, so I guess the next best thing is flight. Except I can hardly plead with Jas not to leave me alone with her when Isabel's sitting right next to me, so I just freeze, leaning forward in my seat, and Jas gives me a little wink on her way out. *Traitor.*

By the time Jas is out the door, Isabel's dropped her gaze, the smirk gone.

I want it back. I want proof that I'm not going crazy, that she seems to actually be *enjoying* this.

I don't even take a second to gather my thoughts. I'll figure it out as I go along – I usually do.

'Soooo, *Iz*—'

She's standing bolt upright before I can even finish.

'I just remembered I left my lunch at home,' she says, her voice tight and her tone cold. 'Sorry.'

She's out of there faster than I can process.

'What . . . the hell just happened?' Jas's head peeks out from the doorway – where I can only assume she's been lurking since she left.

CHAPTER TEN

'It was . . . a bit weird, Lou,' Jas is saying over lunch once she's filled the others in on the bizarre interaction between me and Isabel.

'Sounds like sexual tension to me,' Lily teases with a snort, and Katie gives her a gentle swat round the head for it.

'Hah,' I deadpan. 'Sure.'

I don't have much of a comeback. My head's not right at the minute. I can't stop thinking about the way Isabel looked at me, the steely glint in her eye and the slight smirk that she couldn't seem to stop. It *was* a bit like flirting if I'm honest. But not exactly. I mean, she's a girl for one thing, and also we both hate each other. So obviously not real flirting, but *like* flirting.

'I'm starting to wonder if maybe she does have it in for you,' says Katie. 'Don't get me wrong, I still don't think she hates you as much as you think she does, but I talk to her a bit in psychology and she's *never* been like that around anyone else. Normally, she's just embarrassed by everything that comes out of her own mouth.'

'You mean that stick up her arse isn't a permanent feature?'

Lily titters, and Mel rolls her eyes, but Jas fixes me with a look that's way more serious than I expected.

'She's shy, Lou. Like, painfully shy. Around everyone, but you especially.'

I scoff, but Jas puts a finger out to show that she's not finished.

'I'm serious. It might not, like, compute with you or whatever because you're incapable of not speaking every thought and acting on every impulse—'

'Wind your neck in.'

'I didn't say it was a bad thing. But shy people do exist. And people like you can be intimidating. We all love that you're loud and outspoken, and your brain moves at, like, triple speed, but she's just not like that. She's just a bit awkward, okay? Stop taking it personally.'

'Maybe she is shy, but what if she weren't? The only difference if she was a bit more extroverted would be that she'd be telling me to my *face* that she thinks I'm common as muck.'

I still don't mention that she already did tell me as much, back on the first day of the school year. Jas does seem to genuinely consider my point for a second, though, which I wasn't really expecting, and suddenly I'm on edge, waiting for her response.

'No,' she says slowly, 'I don't think so. I think she came out of her shell today. I think what we saw was what's underneath the shyness. And honestly? It was strange, for sure, but I don't think it was hatred.'

I can't argue the point any further without mentioning the phone call, and the fight. The fight that, okay, yes, I might have sort of instigated. Which is exactly what they'll all pick up on if I mention it. Not the fact that, regardless of who started it, Isabel showed me her true colours.

When I see her on my way out of the school gates at the end of the day, it's impossible to act like I've been normal about the whole thing. Katie's mum's offered me a lift home, so I'm just standing here by the side of the road, minding my own business while I wait. But I don't realise I'm staring until I see her notice me.

It throws me for a second, when she moves towards me. But she's not marching up to me; she's marching *past* me. I'm the weirdo who's staring at her, yes, but I'm apparently also in her way. So she's extracting herself from the situation as quickly and seamlessly as possible.

Or at least she's trying to.

But I mean, hey, I could have warned her. I might not have the most common sense in the world, but even I know that if you're going to leg it down a busy road, then you should probably be looking where you're going. Isabel is absolutely not looking where she's going. I want to say that's on me, but there are plenty of places to look that aren't *me* or *her shoes*. There's surely got to be a middle ground somewhere.

But no, she's looking at her shoes. And charging past me with so much gusto that when one of the gargantuan Year Eleven boys shoulder-barges her, she goes flying.

I'll be honest: my instincts are much kinder than my conscious mind is, because if I'd had a choice in the matter I'd probably

61

have just let her go. But my stupid traitor limbs act on stupid traitor instinct, and I reach out to grab her anyway.

She's halfway to the ground when I finally make contact, right on track to be face first in the cobblestones if not for my arm wrapped round her waist. Not that she's grateful for it or anything. She just lets out this little squeak, then straightens up to glare at me, the two of us standing oddly close.

In the stumble, her hair's fallen out of place, and there's a strand stuck to her lipgloss. It's honestly kind of satisfying to see Isabel a little mussed up for once. I'm still staring at it, that strand of hair clinging to her lower lip, when I realise my arm is still round her waist. I might have noticed it sooner if I'd seen her eyes getting wider, her cheeks turning redder, but instead what happens is that when I finally look away from that piece of hair on her lips, it's because she's taken a sharp step back from me, her face a shade of red I can only describe as *call an ambulance, please*, and is staring at me with wide, horrified eyes.

'Gee, you're welcome, Iz.'

'I didn't . . .' She takes another step back, touching the spot on her waist where I'd grabbed her. 'I didn't ask for your help.'

She finally notices the hair, swiping it away from her lip just in time to turn on her heel and march off again.

It's not until I'm alone that I notice how hard my heart has been pounding, feeling like it's taking up too much space in my chest.

Okay, Isabel, so you hate me? Then prove it. If I have to

prove myself to her, then I need her to prove herself to me, too. Really show me what she thinks of me. I reckon that might make me officially, entirely batshit insane. But I want steely glares and poorly suppressed smirks. I want fire and rage and whatever it is that's making my breathing shallow and my pulse race right now. I want *more* of that.

I'm done trying to avoid Isabel Williams. New goal: get a rise out of her. Get her to tell me how she feels about me to my face. It's time for me to do what I apparently do best and be goddamn *insufferable.*

CHAPTER ELEVEN

My first chance to test-drive the new fucked-up little dynamic comes the next day.

I shouldn't even have come to the caff this early, I'm supposed to be using my free to write my sociology essay. And I did try, swear down. I tried *really* bloody hard. Not that it'd have looked that way to anyone passing me in the library while I scrolled through TikTok.

It's hard to explain, that feeling of desperately *wanting* to do something but being totally, painfully, incapable of doing it. I know because I've attempted to explain it to multiple people, and it only ever results in a raised eyebrow or a scoff, like I've decided to go for the world record in worst-excuse-ever-made. Like, *sorry sir, I tried to do my homework, but I spent four hours ugly-crying and begging myself to do it, until I eventually had to give up and switch to begging myself to go to bed instead.* Doesn't really check out, as far as explanations go. It's maybe the most frustrating part of this whole ADHD thing. Like, on paper, it's really not that difficult. Put the phone down, look at the open book in front of you. A small action, a quick motion, you're set.

And the way I hear some people talk about it, it really *isn't* that difficult, which seems fake but okay. Like, apparently, there are people who don't have to spend hours pleading with their own body to just *do* the thing they want to do? I've thrown the phone across the room before in frustration, only to get up a few seconds later, nearly in tears, pick it up and keep scrolling.

Can't throw my phone across the room in the library. Well, I could, but I reckon it'd be frowned upon. So, I did the next best thing and gave up. I thought I'd grab our usual lunch table and wait until the others finished their lessons.

But here she is. Sitting there, reading, all casual like this isn't my friend group's sacred lunch table. And honestly? It's kind of a relief, after fighting with my own body for the better part of an hour, to be able to pick a fight with someone who isn't me.

Her eyes widen as I approach. She's definitely not expecting me to sit down in the seat opposite her. Good. I'm already winning.

I don't say anything as I stretch out on the chair, pulling out my previously abandoned sociology books and pen – just for something to do with my hands – but I feel her eyes on me the whole time. Perfect, just as planned.

'Something on my face?' I ask, not looking up, not giving her a chance to look away first.

She's silent for a moment, until I do look up, and her eyes meet mine, that hardness in them again, that smile playing across her lips. She holds my gaze for a long moment, then I watch as her eyes rove pointedly across my face.

65

'No, you're good.' She turns back to whatever book she was reading, though the smirk lingers.

I pause for a moment, allowing myself to appreciate the full weight of what I'm letting myself in for.

'So, Iz. How about another tutoring session?'

It's honestly hilarious. The way she snaps her head up at me in total shock. I've officially won this round. She's too taken aback to even speak for a moment. Then I watch her eyes flitter across my face – trying to work out if I'm joking maybe – and she composes herself.

'Are you sure you're up for that?'

'Only if *you're* sure you're willing to put up with the effort of helping to educate the poor little simpleton.'

She scoffs. 'I've always loved a challenge.'

There it is. This is what I wanted. I can't even put my finger on what's shifted exactly, but the dynamic's definitely different. She's insulting me, yes. She's saying exactly what I've always known she's thought of me, but there's a playful glint in her eye, the ghost of a dimple that reveals the smile she's fighting.

'Well then. Consider yourself challenged. You're free now, I'm guessing?'

She turns the corner of her page, setting the book aside slowly.

'Yes, but I don't have all my tutoring notes with me. Though I was thinking about what Ms Price was saying in that last lesson . . .'

'About how men and women feel love differently in the book?'

Her eyes light up, seemingly in spite of herself.

'Yes! There was a question in one of the past papers about it—'

'I remember.'

'We could spend some time separately making notes now, of examples and arguments, then compare. And maybe read something else ahead of our next session and write up a mock answer using that as a comparison.'

'Works for me. At least that way we don't have to talk for a while.'

She just gives me this sarcastic little *hmm*, then starts pulling her notebook and pen out of her bag.

Yeah, I definitely like whatever this is more than whatever we had going on before. Even if it feels strangely risky, even if my pulse is racing in a way that doesn't seem to match the conversation. I'd rather have this strange, giddy anxiety pooling in my stomach than the little ball of hurt that fed into rage every time I felt her eyes on me. If we're going to hate each other, at least let it be fun.

We stay like that for a while, silently writing, only the sound of the occasional flipping through of pages to find passages and quotes to break the tension. Or at least those are the only sounds I notice. Isabel, however, seems to pick up on something I'm missing.

'What,' she asks eventually, her voice tight, 'has that pen ever done to hurt you?'

I glance down at the pen in question, the one I'm holding

in the middle and tapping either side against the desk while I think.

'Collateral damage.' I shoot her my best angelic grin, but it's wasted on her. She still hasn't looked up from her notes. 'I suppose it can only be grateful it hasn't done anything to hurt *you*. Otherwise you'd never forgive it.'

Her head snaps up, and she glowers at me. I imagine it'd be intimidating to anybody else, but we've spent weeks now silently resenting each other for no good reason, and seeing it now, seeing her anger kindle after I've intentionally lit the flame, it's kind of a thrill.

I wink at her, and that flush from yesterday creeps up her neck. I see her take a deep breath before she turns back to her book slowly, deliberately.

'I'd forgive it,' she says, her voice all faux-casual. 'Poor thing's been through enough, having to draw that same wonky tree over and over every English lesson.'

'Well, that's just below the belt. My tree doodling is perfectly symmetrical.'

She reaches over, barely looking up, and flips over my page of notes. On the side now facing up is my usual doodle of a tree, spindly branches splaying out from the trunk, except because it was doodled absent-mindedly in class, I hadn't planned ahead – half of it is smushed up against the few notes I actually made in the lesson, stopping short so as not to cover the words. She just smirks, like she's won this argument.

'Jesus, and *I'm* supposed to be the one with an attention

deficit? How much literary analysis do you actually learn while you're watching me doodle?'

'I can hardly be blamed for that,' she says. 'You make it incredibly difficult not to watch you, Eloise.'

It happens again. Something in me just kind of stutters when she says that. It's just so bizarrely unexpected, and there's this strange swooping sensation in my stomach that I can't place. I actually feel my palms get a little sweaty as I keep my eyes fixed on her. I honestly have no idea what she means, but there's no *way* it's anything good.

I watch her panic, like maybe she's just realised she's overstepped some line, too. And, when she finally drops my gaze, I see her let go of her pen to flex a slightly shaking hand. I frown at her. If it's made her this nervous, it definitely wasn't complimentary.

'Well, you don't seem to be making much of an effort there, do you, *Iz*?'

Her eyes narrow, just slightly, when I shorten her name again.

'I just . . . I only mean to say—' She stumbles over the words a little, and, when her hands fly up to tuck her hair behind her ears, it seems to only panic her further that her hair is already thoroughly tucked behind them. Her fingers hover there for a second before she lands on pulling all her hair back across one shoulder and smoothing it out anxiously. The movement leaves one side of her neck bare, and I can see little flyaway baby hairs at the base of her neck. She's wearing perfume, too. I hadn't noticed it before, but I get a wave of it now. A sharp sweetness with something a little warmer and woodsy in it.

She's still stammering, though.

'Not to say— It's just, I only mean, the human eye is drawn to movement. And you are *never not* moving. No wonder you don't get any work done in class. I barely get any work done myself with how much you fidget. Would it kill you to sit still for five minutes? It's infuriating.'

What starts off as nervous murmurs rolls into a steady rant, like she's been sitting on that for a while. And, well, I was right. It wasn't anything good. But I mean, did she have to go ahead and ruin the moment by poking at what she *surely* knows is a sore spot? And to make things worse I can still smell that perfume. Which is bothering me more than it should.

I don't even know what to say now. I just glare back at her for a moment, trying to come up with something, until a voice nearby forces me to shift my attention.

'It's almost October. There's no way.' Mel's voice carries as she and the others make their way over to the table with food. Isabel wrenches her eyes away from me, too, looking around with some alarm at the sound of Mel's voice.

'Check the app. It's supposed to be nice,' Katie insists, showing Mel her phone. As they sit, Mel takes it, frowning. 'See?' Katie adds.

'Okay, yeah, that's really nice, actually.'

'Trying to figure out if it's warm enough for the beach tomorrow,' Jas explains in response to my puzzled expression.

'Full sun all day, high of twenty-three degrees,' Katie tells us smugly, sitting back a little.

'Sick,' Lily adds, though she doesn't take her eyes off her phone. 'I'm in then. Last chance to crack out my cute shorts before they go in a box until, like, next June.'

At Lily's words, Katie practically lights up. It's kind of hard to watch, actually.

'I'm down,' I say. 'Mum's on nights all weekend anyway so I'd only be either home alone, trying to be as quiet as possible, or nagging one of youse to come into town with me.'

I look at Jas to see if she's in, but she's looking at Isabel, who's been silent beside me since everyone showed up.

'You're obviously invited, too, Isabel,' Jas adds with a smile.

'Oh,' she says, and then she frowns just slightly, perfect eyebrows furrowing. 'Is there a beach close by?'

I suppress a snort. I can basically see her mapping out the Northwest in her mind and coming up blank. Southerners.

Isabel shoots me one of her glares – what I'm realising now is actually kind of her signature glower – and glances of horror from some of the other girls suggest that maybe I didn't suppress that snort well enough. I try to cover it with a cough.

'Formby's the closest,' I tell her, hoping to brush over it. 'It's maybe forty-five minutes on the train. Southport is the nearest proper beach town but, like, who can be arsed?'

She nods slowly.

'You should defo come!' Katie jumps in, oblivious to the way I'm widening my eyes at her, trying to shake my head without Isabel seeing.

My only remaining shred of hope is that she'll say no. Of

course she will. She's clearly come to the same understanding as me that whatever we've got going on does not work when there are other sane people around. Normal people who don't get off on pissing each other off.

'Sure,' she says, her voice small, and my stomach plummets. Making the most of the time I'm forced to spend with her is one thing, but this whole rivalry dynamic feels like too much effort to waste a beach day with my friends on. 'That'd be really nice, yeah. How, uh, how do I get there?'

'Oh, we can meet you at Formby station and show you the way to the beach,' Jas says, beaming. 'You live around here somewhere, don't you? Best to get the train from the station by the school.'

'You'll have to change at Sandhills,' Mel chips in, and I see Isabel turn to a blank page in her *Jane Eyre* notes, writing out the words *Sand Hills*.

'No, she's not on the Kirkby line, so she doesn't have to change,' Lily says, looking up from her phone briefly.

'To get to Formby she does.' Mel rolls her eyes. 'We all do unless we're getting on at Bootle.'

I watch with faint amusement as Isabel scribbles down names of stations and crosses them out with every piece of conflicting information. She looks like she might start crying or something, and, God help me, I take pity on her.

'It's fine, Iz,' I tell her, and the only thing making me not instantly regret the words is the way she winces just slightly at the way I shorten her name again. Well, if I'm doing it now, I might as well have some fun with it. 'I'll show you the way,' I say with a sigh. 'We can meet the rest of youse at Formby station.' I gesture weakly to everyone else, who all seem oblivious to the massive self-sacrifice I've just made for this girl.

'You know this means you can't be late this time, right, Lou?' Mel says.

'I've never been late a day in my—'

'You are late literally every single time we go anywhere,' Lily interjects with a scoff.

'It's not a bad thing,' Jas says. 'It's good to be consistent.'

'Yeah, consistent enough that we can usually tell you to get there a solid twenty minutes earlier than we need you,' Katie points out, and I can't help but notice Isabel's switched pretty quickly from deer-in-the-headlights mode to trying her best to hide a laugh behind her hand. Which, y'know, at least she's trying.

'Katie, if you *tell* her we do that, it doesn't work,' Mel says in a stage-whisper.

'Oh. Right, sorry.'

Isabel's stopped trying very hard to pretend she's not laughing, but at least she doesn't look like she's about to flee the scene any more. This is what I get for being a nice person, I suppose.

CHAPTER TWELVE

Okay, fine, so maybe I'm running a *little* late on Saturday morning.

Which isn't exactly my fault. I have a piece of paper from a doctor diagnosing me with *chronically late disease*, but sure, let's all make fun of Lou for not getting out of bed until fifteen minutes before she needs to leave. Which, yeah, I guess makes it a little bit my fault. 'Time blindness' is a thing with ADHD apparently, but sometimes I'm hyper-aware of the time. Sometimes I'm lying there, watching the clock, knowing full well that I won't be able to drag myself out of bed until I absolutely *have* to. Because my brain's never met a deadline that it didn't consider a challenge. But I've also never been especially good at rising to the challenge. So, yeah, I'm about twenty minutes late by the time I'm actually on my bike and heading over to Isabel's, but it's nothing that a bit of reckless cycling can't fix (it's not *that* reckless, calm down. The address Isabel gave me is so close to school I could do it with my eyes closed. Whether or not I've actually done that, on the occasional bone-tired Monday morning, is neither here nor there).

I get off my bike when I reach the school so that I can check the map on my phone, and I turn off on to the canal, wheeling my bike alongside me, but I've reached the address before I've been walking for five minutes. Her house is one of the huge McMansions that line the canal, the kind with stone lions out the front and security cameras, the kind that I'd thought only drug dealers could afford. The successful drug dealers, too, the high-ups.

She'd said her mum's office was setting up headquarters here and that's why they'd moved. What does her mum even *do*? Something in banking, maybe? That would check out, looking at this place. Honestly, if you showed me this house and told me that her parents were part of the Mafia, I'd actually believe you.

I'm still trying to figure out if I should ring the bell when the door is flung open, and Isabel's standing there, normally so tall and imposing, but looking about half her normal stature in the doorway of this massive house. Or maybe it's not the house, but the fact that she looks like a halfway normal person now that she's not in her sixth-form clothes. She's just standing there, in this pretty white sundress, all light and floral and rippling a little round her knees in the wind.

'Hi,' she says, her voice small. 'Sorry, I saw you out the window. Thought maybe you weren't sure if you had the right address.'

'Oh. Er, yeah. Yeah, that's it.'

No, Isabel, I was just contemplating how many organs I'd have to sell on the black market to afford a house like this.

'Do you want to leave your bike inside?'

'Sound, yeah.'

She smiles, and there's a hint of that smirk – laughing, probably, at my use of *sound*.

I try to pick the bike up when I step inside, so as not to scuff the hardwood floors.

'You can just leave it there.'

I do so, as gently as possible, while she throws on a small cross-body handbag and picks up a set of keys.

'*Muuum!*' she bellows, to nowhere in particular, and I swear I think it's the loudest sound I've ever heard her make. 'I'm going!'

There's a muffled response from somewhere in the house, something that sounds like it's probably *bye, darling, have fun*, but Isabel doesn't stick around to translate, leading me out the front door as soon as my bike is propped up against the wall.

We walk for a minute or so in silence, the only sounds the gravelly canal path crunching beneath our feet and the sound of ducks somewhere in the distance. My mind is racing through conversation starters, but nothing sticks, like one of those anxiety dreams where you're a waiter and someone's listing a complicated order and halfway through you realise you've forgotten your notepad.

So, in the absence of something good, my brain hurls out anything it can. The rest of the walk to the station is just me trying desperately to keep my stupid mouth shut, but instead blabbering on about stuff like *so, have you done that assignment for Ms Price yet? And I really love walking down this canal, don't you? And oh, that bakery there does the nicest hot butties you'll ever eat for, like, a quid, you should try it sometime.*

'Feel free to jump in at any time,' I tell her as we arrive at the station, after a solid ten minutes of the Marvellous Lou Byrne one-woman show. (Gather round! Step right up! Watch as the blue-haired girl single-handedly carries a two-person conversation without once pausing for breath!) 'I'm not sure how it's done down south, but where I come from it's generally considered standard to contribute something when having a conversation.'

She glares at me for a moment as she pays for her ticket, then, pocketing it, turns to me slowly – the smirk is back. There we go. Solid ground again.

'Is it?' is all she says after a long moment.

I nod. 'I mean, that'll do, as responses go. But usually you want to be a bit more expansive than that.'

'Do you normally keep a running quota of each person's response in a conversation?'

I shrug. 'Not generally, but it doesn't hurt to say *something*. I'd rather be chatty than dead silent. Wouldn't you?' I don't mean to make it into such a challenge, but I lock eyes with her, and she doesn't look away. When she doesn't say anything, I shrug again, adding, 'Though I'm sure there's ways to make it so that we both have to say as little as possible without it being *completely* rude, right? Maybe that'd be best.'

'Would that be for your sake or mine?'

I'm still trying to decipher that when the train arrives, and we both turn away from each other. Something happens, though, when I sit beside her on the train. Me in my shorts, her in her dress, our knees bump together, and she jumps about a mile in her seat at the contact.

Something about it seems to break the spell, and all hope of wittily tormenting each other for fun seems to be dead. She's just staring steadfastly out of the window, like it's her only goal in life to look anywhere but at me.

God, why did I offer to do this?

'Lou, you're out of it again.' Mel squeezes my shoulder to bring me back, lagging behind the others to fall into step with me.

'Is rivalous a word?' I ask her, and to her credit she only looks slightly taken aback. I think she's used to it by now.

'Frivolous?'

'No,' I sigh. 'Like, okay, so you can be a friendly rival, right? But can you be a rivalous friend?'

She frowns. 'I don't think there's a word for that.'

'There should be.' I don't mean to, but I look up ahead when I say it. Everyone's kind of paired off since we met up at Formby station. Katie is linked arm in arm with Lily – a temporary respite, it seems, between their now increasingly regular arguments – and Jas seems to have taken Isabel under her wing for the walk to the beach, but at some point while I've been zoned out Isabel's fallen back just a bit. Close enough to hear what I've just said, apparently. When I look at her, she's glancing over her shoulder at me. And it's kind of hard to tell, squinting through the sunlight at her, but I *swear* she laughs quietly at me when I meet her eye.

'I see the squirrel woods!' Lily calls out then, picking up speed a bit, Katie still trying to cling on to her arm, laughing as she runs.

They're off too fast, and we're all too lazy to follow at their pace, but Mel and I at least manage to catch up with Jas and Isabel. The walk from Formby station to the beach is always the most boring part of any beach trip, and we're all a bit antsy to get to the sand.

'I . . . thought we were going to the beach?' Isabel asks hesitantly as she eyes the trees in front of us.

'We are. We've just got to go through the woods first.'

'Liverpool's so strange,' Isabel mutters, almost under her breath. I see Jas shoot me a nervous look, like I'm about to go off or something, but I just laugh.

'And proud of it. I'll have you know we have actual real-life red squirrels in these woods.'

She doesn't have a snarky comeback to that. She just widens her eyes. 'I thought they were basically extinct?'

'Liverpool's strange like that, I guess,' I shoot back with a smirk. 'Now be nice to me because *I* –' I pat my backpack – 'brought the monkey nuts.'

'Don't get your hopes up,' Jas teases, but she mostly just looks relieved that I didn't try to bite Isabel's head off. 'I haven't actually seen a red squirrel here since I was a kid.'

'That's because you never bring the monkey nuts!'

I shout out to Lily and Katie to wait for us, but they're too far ahead, so Mel texts them to say we're hanging back in the woods for a bit on a squirrel hunt. Lily just sends back a sun emoji, which I assume means they'll meet us on the beach.

It should feel like a waste of the sunlight, hovering in the woods, waiting for squirrels, but it doesn't. For one thing, we're all trying to keep quiet, to not scare any of them off, which means the silence no longer feels awkward because it's *intentional*. It does feel kind of something, though. Not awkward, but still thick somehow. Heavy. Jas and Mel are hovering a bit further away from me and Isabel, so it's like we're just standing here alone in the silence together.

When I hear a rustle in a nearby tree, Isabel doesn't notice, so I reach out and touch her shoulder with two fingers. She looks up at me startled, but I just point noiselessly to the squirrel, handing her the bag of monkey nuts. The squirrel perks up at the rustle, and she breaks out into a huge grin. I've never seen anything like it on her before; it changes everything about her face. Her smile is wide when it's real. That's when I realise my hand is still on her bare shoulder. I don't know why that's weird, but it is. I can feel her collarbone beneath my fingers, her skin slick with sunblock. I remove them as she crouches, slowly, extending a hand as the squirrel watches her.

I watch her, too. I'm still fixated on her shoulder for some reason. As she crouches, her hair falls over it, before parting to cascade down her front. There's a constellation of freckles spreading out from beneath the back of her sundress to the base of her neck, her shoulder blades, climbing right across to her collarbone. I've never seen that many freckles on a person before. I bet if I traced my finger over them, I could connect the dots, make a whole damn artwork from them. I curl my hand into a fist, just in case I do accidentally reach out and trace a finger over them. That'd be weird, for *sure*. Even weirder than me staring at her shoulders.

She doesn't notice, though, thankfully. She's holding her breath while the squirrel approaches. She throws a nut about half a metre away from her, and the squirrel grabs it and legs it back again. She's not deterred. She throws another, and it doesn't scramble off as quickly this time. Another, and it lingers. Not quite close enough to touch.

This time, she clutches the bag in one hand and, with the other, stretches out an arm as far as she can – which really is quite far; I knew she was tall, but Jesus, she is *long* – a nut poised lightly between her thumb and forefinger. I hear Jas gasp as we all watch the squirrel take it from her. Isabel's still holding her breath, I think.

Then, I swear, I almost missed it, it happened so fast. The squirrel darts towards her. She hasn't even taken out another nut for it yet. It just launches itself at her, and it isn't until I see it struggling to climb back up the tree that I realise it's taken the entire bag of monkey nuts. Isabel's no longer crouching. She's fallen on to her bum in the dirt with a yelp and an *oof.*

There's only a single beat of silence before I crack up, howling

81

with laughter, clutching my sides. Even Jas is doing her best to politely stifle a giggle behind her hand. Isabel stands, brushing the dirt off her dress with a lot of huffing and *hmph*-ing. She sends me a glower, this truly terrifying death stare that might have affected me five minutes ago, but I'm too far gone. I'm crying with laughter now.

'Come on,' Jas says, trying so hard to keep a straight face. 'Let's get to the beach.'

Just when I think I'm done laughing, the memory of Isabel's little yelp as she falls arse first into the dirt replays in my mind, and I'm off again. I swear I see her clench her fist by her side as Jas and Mel shepherd her away.

'Tell me one of you got a video!' I call out before jogging to keep up with them, the underbrush melding into sand beneath my feet bit by bit as we breach the edge of the treeline, looming sand dunes stretching out ahead of us.

CHAPTER THIRTEEN

Lily and Katie are already stretched out on towels on the sand when we find them, Lily on her back, eyes closed, smiling into the sun, Katie on her front, propped up on her elbows, talking to Lily.

I park myself cross-legged beside them, straight into the sand, watching Jas extract a towel from her bag and Mel perching on the end of Katie's towel, but Isabel is still hovering a bit uncomfortably, arms wrapped round herself. Judging by the little cross-body bag she's wearing, she didn't think to bring a towel. I pat the sand next to me, grinning up at her.

'You're on the beach – you can't seriously be afraid of a little sand?'

Jas looks over at us, and opens her mouth, but Isabel's already glaring at me, spinning round and smoothing her skirt over the back of her legs before sitting next to me, her jaw set.

'I was going to say you could share mine,' Jas says.

I beam back at her. 'Too late,' I say. 'Besides, what's a little bit of sand after falling into all that dirt?'

'Oh, of course you'd have that mentality,' Isabel throws back. 'When do you not have a stain on your shirt?'

'Why are you looking?'

Her frown grows steelier then, but it shuts her up, at least. We sit in silence for a while, soaking up the sun, until Isabel speaks again, her voice more tentative this time.

'This might be a stupid question—' she begins.

'From you? Never.'

She rolls her eyes at me. 'But where's the water?'

'See the horizon line?' Mel points out towards where the dark sand meets the sky, pausing for effect. 'Further,' she deadpans.

I laugh. I actually do not remember the last time I came here and got anywhere near the ocean. It's always so far out. For some reason, from here all the way up to Southport, tides mean nothing. The water is always unreachable, no matter what time of day it is.

'You can actually get to it,' I add. 'It's just ages away.'

Katie perks up. 'We could try, though. I haven't paddled in years. And we've got all day.'

'Ugh,' Lily groans, 'the sand is *vile* over there, though.'

'Nothing we can't handle,' I say, getting to my feet. 'Iz here's never seen the Irish Sea. We can't deprive her of that.' I offer a hand to help her up, along with my most evil smile. 'Call it trial by sludge.'

She takes it, letting me pull her upright, and when she's standing she's unsettlingly close to me.

'Just be careful,' she whispers, close enough for only me to hear. 'I might try to take revenge for you laughing at me. Falling into the sludge feels like a much worse fate than mine was.'

I don't know if it's the sudden proximity, or the fact that her friendly teasing really does just feel *friendly*, but I'm thrown for a second. My breath catches a little as she keeps her gaze fixed on me, her smirk just playful enough to not feel completely threatening.

This feels right. Like maybe what I'd been aiming for the whole time, with the fighting and the insults and the two of us trading jabs like the world's laziest swordfight. I think, maybe, what I wanted was just this.

'Oh yeah?' I breathe after I've recovered from the initial shock, raising an eyebrow as I try to play it cool. 'You might be *better* than me,' I tell her, 'but I'm faster.'

At first, I'm worried it might be too far, bringing up that fight. But she surprises me by laughing.

I can't help but smile, part in shock, part in relief, and she beams back, that wide smile that rearranges her whole face. This, I decide, is even better than the smirking.

I'm not sure how long I stare at her, but eventually her smile falters, head ducking slightly as she reaches up to tuck her hair behind her ear. Her eyes dart over to the others. Mel, Katie and Lily are all marching off towards the sea, but Jas hangs back, watching us with a small curious frown.

'Come on,' Isabel mutters, shaking her head as she jogs off to catch up with Jas.

I jog along with her. Whatever the hell just went on in her

head, it's making me feel a bit like maybe she'd rather I didn't fall in step with her, but when has feeling unwanted ever stopped me?

We slow when we reach Jas, which is for the best, since this is about the point where the sand turns more to dark sludge around our feet.

Isabel winces as her toes sink into it. I don't blame her. The sand around here, it's not just soggy, it's *slimy*. It's a uniquely grim experience.

A little way ahead, Lily retches, loudly and theatrically.

I think about turning back. Everyone else seems to be thinking about it, too. But I look at Isabel.

'You're a brand-new honorary Scouser,' I tell her, chin jutting out high and defiant. 'And every Scouser has to wade through the beach scum at least once. We're doing this.'

Her eyes light up at my words, and it makes me realise just how much I mean them. I *want* Isabel to fall in love with Liverpool. Not just to prove her wrong, but because today I've seen a glimpse of the person she can be when she's not being a complete snob. And *that* person might just deserve the beauty this city has to offer.

She nods once, firmly. 'We're doing this.'

There's that wide smile again.

It's not all grim as we walk. There is some respite from the sludge, the sand occasionally becoming dense and firm beneath our feet.

'Hey, Mel,' I call out. 'You know stuff. What causes these

86

little ridges?' I point with my toes at alternating lines of raised clumps and divots in the firm sand.

'Wind and water. Same concept as the dunes, but on a smaller scale, and with siltier sediment.'

'Right. Yep. Sure. Makes total sense, everything you just said.'

Isabel chuckles, and for the life of me I cannot tell if she's mocking me.

'Watch yourself,' I tell her, just in case she is. 'You want to make sure there's no squirrels about.'

That gets me the glare. I don't even have to see it to know. I look down at my feet as I walk to hide my grin.

It's not so bad, the walk, after a while. We all get kind of used to the texture – except Lily – and the sun is still strong, and we call out to each other from time to time, mostly just to laugh whenever Lily squirms.

Lily is the first to reach the water, wading in without a second thought, getting in as far as the hem of her booty shorts allows. Katie's next, beaming as she watches Lily throw her head back to the sun, the water lapping at her thighs. Jas follows shortly after, paddling in to about her knees, dampening the bottom of her long-line linen shorts, though she doesn't seem to mind much.

Isabel, beside me, hesitates. Her fingers bunch round fistfuls of her dress, lifting it just slightly, but she's looking at the water like it might leap up and bite her. Or maybe she's worried that the murky waves will stain her beautiful white dress. She's possibly right on both fronts, to be honest.

I roll my eyes pointedly at her when she doesn't move.

87

'Oh, come here, princess,' I sigh, enjoying her little yelp of indignation as I drop into a squat in front of her with as much grace as I can muster, and scoop up the hem of her dress. She lets go immediately, hands uncurling from the material and raised in the air, like maybe now *I'm* about to leap up and bite her. I don't. I just bunch as much material up as I can and tie it into a clunky knot at the side of her thigh. The result is a much tighter, much shorter skirt, and sure, it's got an ugly-as-hell ball of material sticking out of it, but it'll keep it clear of the water.

When I press my hands into my thighs, pushing myself back up, she's just staring at me.

'What now?' I ask as I focus on folding the hems of my own shorts up as high as they'll go. 'Worried about it creasing or something?'

I look up at her when I get no reaction, and her eyes are following the movement of my hands on my shorts. She blinks, moving to give an exaggerated eye-roll instead.

'Well, creases are better than dirty seawater, I suppose,' she said with a sigh, and I grin back at her.

She's still Isabel, but she trusted me enough to let me mess up her pretty dress, so there's got to be some hope for her. Some hope for us, maybe, to be friends. Not just friends by proximity, or friendly rivals. Real friends. Friends that get to laugh when the other falls down and know it won't hurt their feelings. Friends that get to tease and call each other out and know there isn't any real resentment bubbling behind the words. Friends who get to mess each other up a little and still receive big, beaming, heart-stopping smiles in response. It's almost embarrassing how much I want that to be true. How quickly I can turn from complete loathing to whatever this is.

But I'd rather drown myself in the sea sludge than actually say any of that out loud, so I settle for the next best thing.

'Exactly,' I tell her, offering my hand. To my surprise – and possibly even to her own – she takes it. And when I pull her out towards the water she follows.

'Well, we fucked the timing on that one,' Lily says, shivering a bit in her damp shorts.

Mel groans, squinting up at the sky. 'The weather app said full sun all day.'

Jas follows Mel's gaze. 'Maybe it's just, like, a rogue cloud?' she suggests. 'Maybe it'll pass in a minute.' But she doesn't sound so sure.

'That,' I say, pointing to the cloud currently covering the sun, 'is just a rogue cloud. But that –' I wave over to the sheet of angry dark grey leering over the horizon – 'is not.'

Isabel huffs a little as she wrings out her dress, which still managed to get soaked despite my handiwork, so now it's both damp *and* covered in deep creases. It didn't seem to matter much when the sun was shining. Nothing did. But now that we're cast in grey again, the mood's shifted.

'Come on,' Katie begs, tugging on Lily's arm. 'We can stay out a bit longer, can't we?'

'It's already going to take forever to walk to the station,' Mel says. 'If we're tired now, we should start heading back so we're not knackered by the time we leave.'

'Mel with the sensible suggestions as ever,' Jas says with a smile even as Katie groans.

CHAPTER FOURTEEN

A long walk, a disheartened, quiet train ride later, and it's just me and Isabel on our own again. I'm tired, cold, a bit grumpy – too tired to keep up any kind of verbal sparring with Isabel – but I stay on those extra few stops anyway, because of course I left my bike at her house.

Stupid move, in hindsight.

'Oh,' I whisper, the two of us standing under the awning of the station, a downpour of rain preventing us from making the walk to Isabel's. She just nods.

'No sign of it stopping,' I say after a moment, checking the weather app on my phone. I glance over at Isabel, who's staring out at the sheets of rain, wincing.

'Run for it?' she suggests after a moment, her voice quiet. I almost didn't hear her. It's the last thing I thought she'd say. I was expecting her to want to waste money on an Uber or something rather than dash through the downpour with me.

But she just smiles, extends a hand – just like I had to her on the beach – and pulls me out into the rain.

The run wakes me up. I'm faster than her, but even though

I *finally* have the upper hand in something, whenever I get too far ahead I keep jogging back to drag her along with me. Both of us are slick with rainwater, but we're also laughing. I'm not sure when it started, the laughing. It was gasping, at first, gasping with the shock and cold of the rain pounding down on us, gasping for breath as we ran without stopping, but then, slowly, laughing, breathless and dizzy, all the way to her house. She fumbles for her key, and we tumble inside, still laughing.

'Oh my God,' I breathe, swiping a hand over my soaking-wet hair, pushing it out of my face. Isabel just laughs harder. 'What?'

'I don't think that was the look you were going for,' she giggles, and then before I can stop her she pulls her phone out of her bag and snaps a picture to show me. My hair's sticking up everywhere. I run another hand through it frantically to fix it while Isabel regains some of her composure.

'You can*not* bike home in this,' she says after a beat of silence in which we can still hear the rain thudding against the door.

'Mum's on a night shift,' I say. 'I can't ask her for a lift.'

Her mood changes then, the remnants of laughter falling away to be replaced with a nervous grimace. 'I think my parents went out. But you could wait it out here? Stay the night or – or maybe just a few hours?'

Poor girl is so clearly hoping I'll say no. Nobody gets that nervous unless they're already regretting the question before they've even said it.

'No, really, it's fine.' I step towards where I left my bike, but she takes a panicked step to block my path.

'I could call Benji?' she squeaks. 'He could give you a lift?'

'Benji?'

I've heard her mention that name before. That's who she was talking to on the phone that first day.

'My brother,' she says.

Somehow I don't think I want to meet the guy she's been shit-talking about me to. Especially not after such a good day together.

'I can't ask your brother to come all the way out just to—'

'He was planning on coming round tonight anyway!' And she sounds really desperate to not let me bike back in the rain right now. 'He comes over most weekends.'

I stare at her for a moment longer.

'Really, he won't mind. He's, like, a literal puppy. He'll just be excited to see me and meet a new friend of mine.'

That makes me laugh. And honestly? I'm mostly just too surprised by her use of the word *friend* to argue back.

Not that I care or whatever.

She calls Benji, who sounds eager enough to come, and there's an awkward twenty minutes or so where Isabel goes into straight-up hostess mode. She offers towels and a hairdryer, then, once I've used both, she starts asking if I want any food or snacks.

Her house really is huge. The ground floor is all open-plan, and round the back of the house there's this kitchen-dining-room set-up that seems filled with light even in the heavy grey evening. She parks me at a huge marble kitchen island while she crosses over to the double-doored silver fridge on the other side of the room, calling out drink options.

The kitchen's so big that I hear the voice before she does.

'Hi there. You must be Eloise.'

I jump, spinning on the little stool next to the kitchen island. A boy – a young man, I guess – is leaning against the open archway that leads from the kitchen to the living room, car keys in hand. He's giving me this big, open, dimpled smile, dark blond curls falling messily into his eyes.

'I'd say you must be Benji,' I tell him, eyebrow raised. 'But there's no way Isabel's related to someone who smiles so much.'

He laughs, and for most people not laughing is their baseline, right? Neutral is a more natural state, and they laugh when they find something funny. But for Benji Williams it seems as if laughter *is* his natural state. Like, when he's not laughing, he's holding it back, just waiting for someone to say something funny so he can go back to what feels right.

Yeah, one of them's gotta be adopted, for sure.

'She's exactly like you said, Iz,' he calls over to her, still chuckling. And there's so much to process there. First of all, she's been talking about me? Second of all, what has she been saying? And third, fourth and fifth, *Iz*? She hates it when I call her that. But I don't really get to process it because Isabel's noticed he's there and is hurrying over, her expression horrified and her cheeks turning red.

'I didn't say anything,' she grumbles as she reluctantly allows herself to be pulled into a hug.

94

He gives a sarcastic little *mmhmm* and shoots me a wink over Isabel's head as he hugs her back. There really should be no way for a twenty-something guy to wink at a teenage girl that isn't creepy, but somehow Benji manages it.

'Ready to get home?' he asks, jangling the car keys when Isabel squirms free.

'Thank you,' I tell him, feeling a bit embarrassed. 'Sorry you had to come over just to drive me home. Mum's on night shift and—'

'Nonsense,' he says, waving my apologies off. 'Not a chance either me or Isabel were going to let you cycle home in the rain. I don't think the bike will fit in my car, though . . .'

'I can bring it to school on Monday?' Isabel suggests, not looking at me directly.

'That works,' I tell her. 'I can get the bus Monday morning.'

'Wonderful.' Benji beams at us, holding the front door open so we can dash to the car.

I scramble for the back seat, and Isabel hovers awkwardly in the rain for a second, seeming to agonise over where to sit. She settles on the passenger seat, and I watch this bizarre little interaction happen between her and Benji. He quirks an eyebrow at her, and she shakes her head slightly. He raises his hands a bit, palms up, like a kind of a *what the fuck?* gesture, and she gives him this glare. He just grins, and turns on the satnav. He glances at me in the rear-view mirror, and I realise I've just been caught watching their silent exchange. If he's pissed about it, he does a really good job of hiding it. Mostly he just looks amused.

'What's your address, Eloise?' he asks.

I tell him, then add, 'Just Lou is fine, by the way.'

'So, Lou,' he says as he pulls out of the driveway, 'you said your mum's on night shift? What does she do?'

'Oh, she's a nurse at Alder Hey.'

'Ooh, nice. Must be hard work over there – that place is huge.'

'She's tired, like, all the time,' I tell him with a small laugh.

'What's . . .' Isabel asks, her voice quiet and hesitant.

'Big children's hospital,' he tells her, not even needing her to finish the question. 'One of the best in the country. It's the reason I wanted to do medicine in Liverpool in the first place.'

Benji's a doctor-to-be. Of course he is. Because apparently everyone in this family is smart and attractive and put-together.

'What, er—' I feel suddenly awkward. I'm used to not being particularly sociable around Isabel, but Benji makes me feel like I should be a bit friendlier. 'What's your mum do? Isabel mentioned she moved up here for work, right?'

'Wow, you two really just have not shared anything about your lives at all, huh?' He chuckles. 'What do you even talk about?'

From my position, I see Isabel sink further into her seat, and I don't even need to see her face to know she's burning red. It's wild seeing her like this. Seeing her play the role of pissed-off little sister.

'She's head of a sales company,' she mutters, ignoring his last question. 'Something to do with selling machinery and stuff to factories. I . . . honestly couldn't tell you much more than that.' She looks to Benji then, like she's tapping him in. He just shrugs.

'Hell if I know. She's explained it a few times, but it all just goes over my head. All I know is she wears power suits, and says things like *if I don't have those invoices on my desk by Monday, Johnny, I swear to God.*'

Isabel laughs. Like actually laughs. Not a derisive snort, not a giggle that escapes involuntarily. A laugh that makes me believe, just for a second, that she and Benji could actually be related. The sound is like a revelation.

Benji catches me staring. I'm not sure how long I've been doing that since she laughed. Long enough for a silence to fall and for him to glance at me in the rear-view again. When I look up, and accidentally catch his eye, his whole face is pure joy. He presses his lips together as he looks away, giving his head a small shake.

When we reach my house, instead of just parking up on the kerb like a normal person, Benji, bless him, inches up the empty space in the driveway, keeping the car at a crawl for a second to get as close to the front door as possible. It's barely even drizzling now, but he turns round in his seat anyway, bracing his arm on Isabel's headrest and grinning back at me.

'Ready to make a break for it?'

And it's kind of impossible not to echo his smile.

'I'll be sound,' I say with a little snort. 'It's, like, two steps to my front door. Thanks, though,' I add, worried I might have sounded ungrateful.

'Anything for a friend of Isabel's.' His grin widens, and I swear I see Isabel sink a little lower in her seat.

"Kay, er, bye.' I hop out, and scramble to unlock the front door. As I do, I hear the passenger window roll down.

'Eloise?' Isabel asks, her voice small, just as my key turns in the lock. I look back at her, and she honestly just seems horrified that she even spoke. 'I just wanted to say th— Uh, I mean, I'll bring your bike to school on Monday.' She winces.

'Cool, thanks.' I hover for a second in the rain, not sure what to do, and in the end all I can do is give her a weird little wave and dart through the door. I turn to close it behind me, but it's still open just a crack when I hear Isabel let out this guttural groan of frustration through her open window.

And I know I shouldn't – look, *I know*, okay? But it's just so unlike her that I can't help but stop to listen, my fingers round the door handle, my ear close to the gap.

Benji lets out a little chuckle, and she just groans again, the sound more muffled this time, like she's got her face in her hands.

'It wasn't that bad,' he says, his voice soothing.

She doesn't say anything, but I've been on the receiving end of her piercing glowers enough times to know when she's giving one. Benji just laughs again, and there's a moment of silence, just the light pattering of the rain outside, and I think about closing the door, until I hear Benji speak again, softly.

'Come on, I can come back with you to Mum and Dad's. Ice cream and a romcom? Put the window up – you're letting the rain in.'

The sound of the engine starts up, and the car pulls away, and I'm just standing there, the rain coming through the crack in the door and hitting my bare legs, just wondering what the hell that was all about.

CHAPTER FIFTEEN

If I thought that spending time together on the beach might have broken the ice a bit, I couldn't have been more wrong. If anything, it seems to have added a whole other layer of ice. A whole damn iceberg that encompasses Isabel when I see her next. I get the bus into school, and Isabel's there at the gate with my bike.

'Hi.' My voice comes out a little louder than I mean it to, and she jumps.

'I didn't know if you had a bike lock or something,' is all she says in response, practically thrusting the bike at me.

'Er, yeah, it's in my bag.' I take the bike from her, wheeling it into school towards the bike sheds, and I start to speak, hoping that, in the time it takes for me to open my mouth and draw my next breath, I'll find some words – I usually do – but she's already walking away.

Okay, so I see how it is, I guess.

Except I don't really, do I? Because here I was thinking we might actually be, I dunno, like maybe . . . not *friends* exactly, but more like— No, you know what? Fuck it, yes, friends. She'd *called* me her friend. We'd gone paddling together. We'd run hand in hand through the rain. Her brother had winked at me and told me I was exactly like she'd described me. That felt an awful lot like fucking friends to me.

I nod to myself as I decide this, locking my bike and throwing the lock down with a flourish, plus a small kick to the bike for good measure.

'Christ, Lou, what – your time of the month or something?'

'Fuck's sake, Henno, of *course* you're here right now.'

'Aww, sorry to disappoint. Were you waiting for your little girlfriend?'

I spin round, feeling my face contort. 'She's not my— Wait. Who?'

He just shrugs, this irritating smirk on his face. No, it's not a smirk. Isabel smirks. Jay Henno *sneers*.

'Ginger bird,' he says simply. 'The one you've got that weird sexual tension thing going on with. Romantic walks along the beach, holding hands, all that shit.'

'How do you—'

He just bellows out a laugh, so all I can do is walk away.

'Oh yeah, good defence there, Byrnie, nice one.'

I spend the entirety of English literature thinking about that conversation. Pen twitching in my hand as I mull it over. Between Jay glancing over constantly, and Isabel steadfastly looking anywhere but at me, I don't hear a word that Ms Price is saying.

I'm fidgeting, struggling to make it even *look* like I'm paying attention, and Ms Price knows. She keeps shooting me The Look, but I can't seem to get out of my head long enough to do anything about it, and when the lesson ends I see her craning her neck, looking over at me, trying to catch my eye. But between her obviously wanting to call me over for a chat, and Henno's continued sneering, I'm refusing to look at anything but the books I'm shoving into my bag in my haste to escape that classroom. Isabel passes me on her way out, and, well, screw it. If it's this, Ms Price or Jay Henno, I'll take this.

'Isabel!'

She winces when I call out, but she lets me catch up to her, and we both start walking in the direction of the sixth-form building.

Silence. For once in my life, I'm stumped.

'Tell Benji thanks for the lift,' I say after a moment.

'You already thanked him.' Her voice is curt. Eyes trained on the ground.

'Oh, okay. I mean, maybe I'm just double thankful,' I say, forcing a grin. 'Imagine if the world had to see me with my wet hair spiked up like that again.'

Look, I'm trying, okay? Even I can feel how cringe I'm being. But the memory of the two of us breathless and laughing, her doubled over before she reached out to take a photo of my hair, I assumed that might have *some* effect.

It doesn't. She doesn't even fake a laugh. Just keeps walking in silence.

102

'Wow.' My voice turns a little crueller than I mean for it to, but I can't help it. 'Here I was thinking Benji got all the charm in your family. Looks like he got all the basic social skills, too.'

She freezes then. We're standing outside the sixth-form building, but she just stops at the door. When she finally looks up, she's glaring.

'And you're an only child, right?' she asks. 'So, when they were handing out whatever genes make a person infuriating, they just all went to you.'

This, at least, is solid footing. I can't even say I'm mad about it, just relieved not to be frozen out any more.

'Whoa there, Iz, all those words. Save some for the rest of the week or you'll use up your entire reserve.'

For a second, she looks like she might fight back some more, but eventually she just sighs.

'It's okay,' she says quietly. Big words for someone whose tone implies that it's anything but *okay*. 'We don't have to be friends. It's like you said, right? Maybe we can just figure out a way to say as little as possible to each other and still get by. For both our sakes.'

She just turns and leaves, and all I can do is watch as she walks back down the lane and out of the gates. To spend, I assume, her free lesson at home alone.

This definitely hurts more than the insults.

'Wait, so are we mad at Isabel or Jay?' Mel asks suddenly from across the common room. Katie and I are curled up on the

103

comfy seats, but Mel's got what looks like the course material of every one of her subjects splayed out across the table.

'Both, keep up.'

Mel just slumps deeper into her chair, shaking her head slightly as she continues scouring a chemistry textbook like it's got instructions on how to find the Holy Grail.

'Don't worry about her,' Katie murmurs. 'The revision stress has kicked in early this year.' She lowers her voice even more. 'Her dad's on her back again. Best to stay out of her way.'

I just nod, pressing my lips together. That's a plan I can get behind.

'I'll bring her a cup of tea in a bit,' I say as we both watch Mel slowly lower her head until it's resting on the table, and Katie nods solemnly.

'So, okay, lay it out for me one more time. Isabel's ignoring you?'

'Not just ignoring. She specifically told me we shouldn't be friends.'

'That *is* weird. I dunno, she doesn't really give any indication of what she's thinking.'

'Right? It's, like, literally what the hell is going on up there, Iz? What thoughts are rattling around in that overpriced little porcelain head of yours?'

'What about Jay? You said he cornered you at the bikes?'

I groan. 'He called her my girlfriend, said we had some *weird sexual tension thing* going on.'

'I mean . . .' Katie begins tentatively. 'Don't get me wrong – it's a shitty thing to say – but, like, is it news? He's been hurling homophobic slurs at you ever since you swerved him. This is actually tame for him.'

Mel raises her head from the table just far enough to speak.

'He spent all of Year Seven sticking his hand up the back of my shirt to check for a bra.'

'And,' Katie adds, 'he called me *lezza* for all of Year Eight because he asked me out and I said no.'

'Also,' Mel adds, because *now* she's invested, I guess, 'remember when he was literally your boyfriend, and he *still* treated you like shit when he—'

'All right.' I cut her off. *Yes, Mel, I haven't forgotten all the stuff he did when I went out with him, thanks very much.* 'Fine, yes, Jay being Jay is not a surprise. It's just . . . It seemed . . . I dunno, like he was in on a joke I didn't get. And he said something about us holding hands at the beach. You don't reckon he was there, was he?'

'No way,' Mel says, shaking her head. 'You think he'd miss the opportunity to catcall us if he saw us at the beach in our shorts?'

That's a solid point, actually.

'Maybe one of his mates was there?'

'It wouldn't surprise me,' says Mel, finally deep enough into the conversation to lower her textbook, though still not closing it completely. 'It was a freak heatwave in October. Loads of people had the same idea as us.'

I glance at Katie to see what she thinks of it all, but she's hunched over her phone, texting furiously. I give her leg a little nudge with my shoe.

'Still with us?' I watch her blink back into the room as I say it. She locks her phone for a second and looks up.

'Hm?'

'Come on, Katie, who could possibly be more important than your friend in need right now?'

Mel rolls her eyes. 'I wouldn't exactly say you're *in need*. A lad you hate said something a bit mean.'

'That's very rude, Mel, but I'll allow it because you're clearly going through something right now.'

I turn back to Katie, ready to push the question further, but her phone is lighting up with new texts, one after the other.

'Oh, fuck her,' she growls, oblivious to mine and Mel's shared glance of wide-eyed alarm and confused shrugs. When she's done reading, she's back to typing, thumbs flying across the phone in a rage.

I decide to push my luck. 'That wouldn't happen to be Lily you're texting, would it?'

'Lou,' Mel warns.

'What? I can't ask a question?'

I'm trying my best to see what Katie's typing over her shoulder, which might be what Mel's telling me off for, actually, but it's pointless anyway. Katie's so hunched up over her phone it's as if she's trying to crawl into it for the sole purpose of jumping out the other side and throttling Lily with her bare hands. Because it's got to be Lily she's texting. I've never seen her this pissed at anyone else.

'Want to talk about it, Katie?' Mel asks after a moment, which is rich coming from the girl who would rather learn about chemical compounds or whatever than listen to *my* problems, but I can kind of see why. Katie looks like she's about to blow a fuse or something.

She shakes her head firmly before locking her phone again.

'Sorry, Lou. We were talking about your thing. What were you saying?'

'Something something Jay, something something Isabel,' Mel responds before I can.

'I liked you better when you were revising quietly,' I shoot back, but, in the time it takes me to glare at Mel, Katie's phone has started buzzing again, and this time Lily's photo lights up the whole screen as Katie stares down at the incoming call.

'Sorry,' she says quietly, and before Mel and I can frown at each other from across the room, she's up, storming out the door, not quite fast enough for us to miss her shouting, 'I can't *believe* you!' before she charges out of earshot.

'God, we can't even avoid a Lily and Katie blowout when they're not in the same *room*,' I groan.

Mel just shakes her head, sinking back down into her seat and raising the chemistry textbook again. Leaving me to figure out my Jay and Isabel problems alone, I guess.

CHAPTER SIXTEEN

The weather turns quickly after our beach fiasco, the bite of winter setting in hard and fast, and the workload picking up alongside it. Half term comes, offering a moment of peace, but after that's over the teachers seem desperate to have everything tied up neatly before Christmas. Except my brain spends the second half of term barrelling in every other direction but work. Which, y'know. Super helpful. Thanks a bunch, brain, always on my side as ever.

Mostly it's about Isabel.

I can't believe I let myself get hurt by her *again*. This whole thing started because somehow I let a girl I barely knew hurt my feelings. But then she deigned to show me a little bit of decency on one good day, and suddenly I've got the word *mug* written on my forehead all over again. Even Benji's twinkling eyes and easy laughter start to take on a darker tinge in my memory, and I picture the two of them making fun of me the whole drive home, gossiping about every word I said over ice cream and a romcom.

The worst part is that I've still got her stupid annotated copy of stupid *Jane Eyre*. And she's still got mine. So now, even without her tutoring me, I've got to read her annoyingly insightful little notes every time I try and plough on ahead with the work on my own.

'*NB – Victorian class structures remain in place throughout the novel,*' I read aloud in my best Isabel impression at lunch. It elicits sighs and groans from the rest of the table, though how many are at Isabel's expense or at mine for bringing her up *again*, I can't tell. I press on. '*It seems like they move because Jane's station shifts, but only within the confines of the established class system.* And yes, if you're curious, this is squeezed entirely into one margin.'

'I'm not curious,' says Lily.

'It sounds like a good point, to be fair,' Jas chimes in.

'Yeah, sure, it's *intelligent*,' I say tetchily. 'But, like, coming from her? Little Miss One Per Cent?'

'Aren't the one per cent supposed to be the billionaires?' Mel raises an eyebrow.

'Are we sure Isabel isn't a billionaire?' I ask. 'Youse haven't seen her house.'

'Billionaires don't go to Lady of Mercy.' Katie decides to join the conversation, apparently taking a short break from shooting sidelong glowers at Lily, who doesn't seem to have noticed. 'She'd be at Eton or something. Isn't that a boarding school?'

'Eton's an all-boys' school,' Mel says.

'All right, well, if you're all done correcting me, it'd be nice to get through a single complaint without being served an itemised list of counterpoints, thanks, guys.'

'Lou.' Jas leans towards me, her voice low and soft. 'Have you been for a run recently?'

I haven't actually. Not since the beach. I've been too busy stressing about everything to find time. I realise my leg's twitching under the table and the hand not holding the book has somehow found its way to my neck, working away at what used to be a small spot, but has for the past few weeks been an ugly scab. Not any more – it's just blood now. So that's fun.

I'm still formulating a response when Mel kicks me under the table, tilting her head to the left, and I follow her eyes just in time to stuff the copy of *Jane Eyre* back into my bag before Isabel arrives at the table with her tray of food.

The silence, when she sits down, feels like trying to breathe syrup. Everyone's so shocked she's here that nobody says *anything*, and it's painfully uncomfortable.

What is she even doing here? She's been ignoring me for weeks now, since the beach. But it isn't just me she's been ghosting, is it? It's *all* of us. Me and her, we've had our problems, but she's supposed to be actual friends with everyone else, and she's been ignoring them, too.

And yet everyone's looking between me and her, like they're waiting for us to settle some personal beef or something.

Isabel steadfastly says nothing. Not even hi. Not to me, not to anyone else. She just sits down, in total silence, and starts picking at her dinner. So I say nothing, too. Why should I be the one to start a conversation when she's the one who shut it down in the first place?

'How's it going, Isabel?'

It's Jas who speaks finally, her voice not quite as cheerful as I think she means for it to be, but at least it breaks the silence.

'I'm good, thank you.' Another moment of silence. 'You?'

'Oh, you know . . .' Jas waves a hand for a moment, presumably trying to think of something to say that isn't *we were just gossiping about you, actually*.

'Don't mind me,' I say, gathering up my stuff. 'As you were. I'm just gonna go for that run you suggested, Jas.'

I'm out before anyone else can speak. Lunch is half over, but I've already decided to skip my next lesson.

There's blood pounding in my ears, and I need to get it out somehow, need to pummel the restless fury into the tarmac instead of making an absolute show of myself confronting Isabel in the caff.

I struggle through the first fifteen minutes or so of the run – I'm out of practice, and I'm not pacing myself well enough. Everyone keeps talking about the key to finishing a marathon being pacing, but when I feel like this I need to *sprint*, so for a while I'm busy just making sure I'm pulling enough air into my lungs not to pass out. But after a while, when my blood starts to cool and the endorphins take over enough for me to find a comfortable, blissful rhythm, my brain kicks back in again.

What's her play here? Is she realising she fucked up? Crawling back and hoping that, because she deigned to speak to us, she won't need to apologise? Or maybe she's just doing what she told me she would: figuring out a way for us not to be friends but still get by. Keeping the rest of my lot on retainer while making it as clear as possible that she wants nothing to do with me.

And, more importantly, what am I going to do about it? Certainly not confront her. I would literally rather marry Jay Henderson than have to admit out loud to Isabel that she hurt my delicate feelings.

That question takes up most of the run, repeating in my head while I push forward, feet pounding down the gravel of the canal for about half an hour until I hit a bridge and turn back in the direction of school, already feeling my energy flagging. It's not until I'm off the canal, running down that last stretch of road, that I have an answer.

Pretty much the only thing I *can* do is play along. But in my own insufferable way. I can make my disdain known, but I can't let my feelings get all muddled up in it. All I'm able to do is annoy the hell out of her, try and have fun with it, and do my best not to feel abandoned by all of this. Because none of it makes any sense. Not her sudden whiplash changes in attitude, but not mine, either. Feeling abandoned by her makes no sense at all.

The run, at least, helps. I've been keeping a bag of toiletries in my locker since that first day of school disaster, and, by the time I've cooled down and washed up, I'm feeling exhausted but mellow.

*

Problem is, running only helps with the immediate crisis, for a day or so. The Isabel fiasco lasts so much longer than that. The only silver lining is that I get a *ton* of marathon training in.

Over the next week, Isabel slowly warms up again. Like some kind of feral cat learning we're not about to gouge her eyes out every time she looks at us (though I haven't completely ruled that out as an option, to be fair).

But, as time goes on, Isabel's moods become about as temperamental as the shifting weather. It's hard to tell what I'm going to wake up to from one morning to the next. Bitter cold shoulders (most common), warm, inviting smiles (*very* rare) or, from time to time, the swirling excitement of the rivalry I've come to miss, the smirks and glares that raise goosebumps on my skin in the best way.

The strangest part, I think, is how obsessed I am with it all. I *know* we only had one good day. And I should be able to simply write it off, and let it go. Maybe I would if she'd just solidly ignored me since then, but it's the shifting attention that keeps drawing me back in.

It goes like this. For a couple of days at a time, Isabel and I get back to normal. She joins us for lunch, we say borderline cruel things to each other, and it's tense and weird and kind of fun. Eventually, she softens. She'll say something genuinely nice. And then for the next few days she'll freeze me out again – freeze us all out – but somehow I know it's me she's trying to avoid.

I keep a kind of mental tally of when her moods come and go, and I learn that they tend to balance each other out. If she's particularly warm or bold one day, she won't meet my eye the next. So I work to correct it as best I can. I let her come to me some days, and then the next, when she avoids me, I come to her. I stop her in corridors. I sit next to her in the library. I call her over at lunch. Sometimes it even works.

'She's looking for Isabel again.' Katie rolls her eyes over lunch one day. Katie's been a bit snappy recently. And I think it has something to do with the way her and Lily have been throwing daggers at each other when they think we're not looking.

I stop craning my neck to peer round the caff, picking sullenly at my food instead. I don't even try to deny it.

'I don't get why,' Mel adds, barely looking up from her textbook. 'If your terrifyingly detailed Isabel Mood Rota is accurate – and God knows how, but it usually is – then she's probs gone off somewhere to eat dinner on her own.'

Lily looks up from her phone long enough to make a strangled choking sound in my general direction. 'You've got a *rota*?! Having an absolutely normal one, I see.'

'Not like a physical rota,' I grumble. 'Only in my head.'

Lily just scoffs, and I can't even be offended because she's not wrong. Katie, though, seems to be offended enough for the two of us, shooting her a withering glare.

'And you wonder why Jay Henno thinks you're lesbos

together,' Lily jokes, and Katie's on her feet almost instantly, the table rocking with the movement.

'Go fuck yourself, Lil,' she practically growls, and then she's off, blonde hair swinging out behind her. Me, Jas and Mel all just stare after her, until all three sets of eyes fall on Lily, who shrugs.

'I know I might not be the most attentive friend right now,' I say slowly, 'but that definitely wasn't just about me.'

Lily shrugs again.

'Should you, maybe, go after her?' Jas suggests.

'I'm not her keeper.' Lily's trying her absolute best to look unconcerned. She's not succeeding. 'Anyway, I'm busy.' She stands, too, hauling her bag over her shoulder, and before any of us can say anything she's leaving in the opposite direction to Katie.

'Speaking of having an absolutely normal one,' mutters Mel.

Jas tries her best to give us both an encouraging smile.

So, when I say it's mostly about Isabel – mostly her fault that I can't seem to pull it together long enough to get any work done – that's not entirely true. There's also this. Lily and Katie and their constant fights. Mel too stressed about school to care and Jas constantly under strain trying to keep the peace. But *this* means picking sides. *This* means our group – our friendship group that formed in Year Seven, back when we were all too tiny for our new school blazers, when Lily still wore braces, and Katie didn't know how to do her make-up, and Jas was too shy to speak, and Mel was still bringing books to sleepovers, and I was too insufferable to be accepted by any other girls but these because they're *wonderful* – might be in danger of falling apart.

Yeah, I'd rather analyse the new girl's mood swings than think about any of that.

Chapter SEVENTEEN

I've managed to dodge Ms Price pretty solidly for the last month or so, so naturally she catches me on the last day of term.

'Eloise?' she calls.

I'm in the middle of packing up my things. I cringe, looking around in a blind panic for some reason to scarper. I see Isabel hovering at her desk, all her books put away, but still lurking for just a second. When I meet her eye, however, she flees, leaving me to the sharks, I guess.

'Yep?' I call back after too long a pause.

Ms Price motions for me to come over, and she waits a moment for everybody else to file out before crossing her legs, pulling out a seat next to her, which I guess means this isn't a quick chat. I think she knows I've got a free next, too, so I can't even use the excuse of not wanting to be late.

'You've been avoiding me.' Her voice isn't stern, but The Look is unrelenting.

Yeah, well, join the club, miss.

'I haven't skipped any lessons,' is what I say instead.

'You know what I mean. And we both know it's to avoid having this conversation.' She pauses like she might want a response, but I just tug on my hair, feeling the ends where they've turned brittle and dry from the bleach and hair dye.

'How have tutoring sessions with Isabel been?'

This, *this* is what I was avoiding. I shrug.

'We tried a couple of times. We didn't click. She gave me some useful tips I still use, though,' I add, hoping it's enough to keep her off my back.

Eventually, she sighs, shifts forward in her seat.

'Lou,' she says, 'I see how hard you're trying. It's okay that you and Isabel didn't click. Tutoring was an idea, but it's not your only option.' She hesitates for just a second, her words delicate and slow, like she's choosing them very carefully. 'I don't want to tag-team you on the medication front because ultimately that decision is yours. But I'm of the opinion that you shouldn't *have* to try this hard.'

I just shake my head, and, when I finally do speak, I'm mortified to find my voice on the verge of breaking.

'I'm not trying that hard,' I mutter, picking at an already bleeding cuticle on my finger. 'Just letting myself get distracted.'

'When your brain works a little differently, you don't get much of a choice when it comes to *letting* yourself get distracted. You're working harder than any of your neurotypical classmates.'

I hate that word. Neurotypical. I'm *neurodivergent*, apparently. Just a fancy medical way to say insufferable if you ask me.

When I don't answer, watching the blood pool under my nailbed, she sighs again.

'The distractions – are they anything I should be concerned about? Anything I can help with?'

I shake my head again. 'Just friend stuff.'

She nods. 'Normally, if a student were handing in work of the quality you are right now, I'd tell them to work harder. But I need you to work *smarter*, Eloise. It doesn't have to be medication, but you need to find some coping mechanisms to make this easier for yourself somehow. I've already emailed your mum, and I'll be available to contact over the Christmas break if you need anything. But I do expect more from you in January.'

'Mum's been googling like mad. She's got all these ADHD life hacks up her sleeve,' I tell her when my single nod doesn't seem to satisfy her. 'She'll be able to help.'

'That's good. Sometimes the little things really do help. When I first got my diagnosis—' She's still speaking, but I'm too busy processing *my diagnosis* to pay much attention. She's got to mean ADHD, right? It'd be weird if she was talking about anything else. But she's Ms Price. She remembers *everything*. I've never seen her show up to work with one earring on because she got distracted before she could put the other one in (not that I've ever done that or anything). She's always so put together, so on top of things. She was the first person to notice I might have ADHD, which I suppose makes a bit of sense. If she's got it too, then she'd be more likely to see the signs. But still. '—seems ridiculous, but it does work. Every now and then, on a bad day,

I sit underneath my desk to work. Our minds crave novelty, so the strangeness actually helps with focus.'

More distracting than the thought of Ms Price marking our homework underneath her desk – which is saying something, because that's incredibly distracting – is the way she says *our minds*. Like anyone could ever put me and Ms Price next to each other and go, *yeah, seems like their minds work about the same*.

'Wait, miss. Since when have you had ADHD?'

She falters, looking a little taken aback. 'Well, if we're being technical about it, since birth. But I was diagnosed a few years after I started teaching. You knew this, Lou. I mentioned it when I first suggested you seek out a diagnosis yourself.'

Oh. Right. Yeah, I vaguely remember that conversation. I also remember tuning most of it out after she started listing off the numerous examples of me being useless in class.

'I've been where you are, Lou,' she says with a seriousness that brings me back to the conversation a little. 'Except you have the benefit of understanding *why* things are so difficult for you. The next step is to work with that understanding.' She pauses then, and I get the feeling I'm not going to like whatever comes next. 'Can I ask?' she says, hesitant. 'What is it about medication that's so off-putting to you?'

'I can do this,' I tell her, my voice a bit firmer now. 'And I can do it as myself.'

She opens her mouth for a second, closes it, tries again.

'I said I wouldn't tag-team you. I'm not in a position to be handing out medical advice. That's a conversation for you and your doctor. Did they offer coaching at all?'

'Yeah, but the waiting list's massive. They reckon it'll be a few more months at least, and even then it'll only be a few sessions. Unless we go private, which obviously we can't.'

'Right. Unsurprising, given the general state of things. Mental health care's hardly a priority these days, however badly it's needed. But better than nothing, I suppose. All right, well, until then, I think it's a good idea to try to use some of the tips and tricks your mum's found for you. And as I said, I'll be available if you need me. I'll see you in January, Lou.'

I'm out the door pretty much the second she's done talking.

I wonder if Ms Price is on medication. I wonder if that's why she seems so much more put together than I do. She does also spend her life marking essays from underneath her desk and trying to convince me to have opinions about *Jane Eyre*, so I'm not too sure about how much I want to emulate that. But she's right, I think, about having the benefit of understanding. I complain a lot about how having a word for my broken brain doesn't really help, but during GCSEs, I was a mess. And because I'd always been this way, my predicted grades weren't exactly sky high, so nobody thought anything of it. Like, *yeah, she's working herself into the ground to barely scrape a C on a good day, but her target's a D so that seems pretty good.* Everyone else thought I was stupid, lazy, useless, so I assumed they were on to something. My mum did her best, but even she was getting fed up with me, no matter how hard she tried to hide it. Only

Ms Price noticed how hard I was working just to stay afloat. Only she seemed to look at me and think that actually, maybe, I deserved a shot at doing better.

I do want to do better. And not just because I don't want a repeat of that conversation. I'm honestly hoping the break will help – no Isabel, no Lily and Katie bickering or shooting each other frosty looks at lunch. It'll be good for me, I think.

CHAPTER EIGHTEEN

My desire to do better doesn't make it past the first Monday of the Christmas holidays. Or, no, I *do* still want to do better, it's more like the wanting isn't enough to drag me out of bed in the morning. Because I'm apparently incapable of literally anything unless someone's explicitly lit a fire under my arse, and that person can't be me because I *know* me, and that girl's a massive pushover.

This always happens. Why does this always happen? It's past midday, and I'm just lying here. I can't stop thinking about all the things I have to do – first I have to get out of bed, do all the boring little things like get dressed and eat something. Except I can't get dressed until I've showered and I can't eat something until I've brushed my teeth. And once I've done all that, I have to go get my books and my notes and set up on the table downstairs, and *then* there's a whole other infinitely growing list of things I have to do once I'm there, homework to finish and practice essays to write and modules to revise. And I'm stuck here, so paralysed at the thought of doing *all* of it that I'm not doing any of it.

By 2pm, I've even lost the ability to focus on TikToks for more than a second or two, scrolling with increasing speed until I'm no longer sure what I'm even scrolling past. I let out this strangled scream of frustration, half-muffled by my pillow. Not muffled enough, apparently.

'Lou, love?'

I forgot mum was off today. I hear her slippers padding quietly up to my door, and a gentle knock. At my grunt of acknowledgement, she opens it slowly.

I peer over the quilt at her.

'I was about to get up,' I tell her, mortified to hear my voice break.

She doesn't say anything – she doesn't have to, she's dealt with my shit for seventeen years, she gets it. She just steps forward and extends a hand to pull me up. It's amazing how much easier it is with someone else to pull me out of it.

'Better?' she asks.

'Yeah, except I've been lying down for about thirteen hours and gravity just reminded me that I really need a wee.'

'Well, knock yourself out. I'll put the kettle on.'

So as she heads off downstairs, I pelt it to the loo, and since I'm already in the bathroom, I brush my teeth. Two things off the list already. The thought of showering and getting changed feels like pushing it a bit, but hey, two things are better than none. I do manage to grab my school bag on the way down, with all my books and notes and half-hearted revision checklists inside. Whether or not I'll get any of it done is still up for debate, but at least I can stare forlornly at it, maybe that'll make me feel better.

Mum's waiting for me in the kitchen with a cup of tea and a jam butty, but she's watching me with wary eyes as I pull out a chair, dump a pile of papers and books on the table, and proceed to roundly ignore them.

'Revision going well then?' she asks, leaning back against the worktop.

I give her a groan in response, picking at the crusts of the butty, but when I look up at her I'm horrified to feel my face crumple.

She rushes over, pulling out the seat beside me and enveloping me in a hug, and all I can do is sob into her shoulder while I try to warble out some explanation about how overwhelmed I'm feeling. I start with just the current problem: my total inability to function without someone poking me with a stick and shouting through a megaphone that I'm going to fail my exams if I don't get off my arse and do something about it. But at some point I surprise myself by blurting out everything else that's been piling up in the background – Katie and Lily, Isabel, even Jay Henno's teasing, which I hadn't even known was bothering me until it spills out. I think I tell her pretty much everything, but I can't be sure how much is audible.

When I'm done, the kettle has long finished boiling with a soft click, but Mum stays where she is, her arm round me.

To her credit, she doesn't suggest medication again. She knows where I stand on that.

'Okay, so sounds like you've got two problems here. Your friends, and the lack of structure.'

I nod, swiping a sleeve over my face. When she says it like that, it sounds so simple.

'Three,' I add after a moment. 'If you count Isabel as a separate problem to Lily and Katie.'

She nods slowly. She's heard enough of my Isabel rants to know that's a whole other problem of its own.

'Can I suggest a delayed action plan? For the friends. If you have an idea of what to do about it when school starts again, it might help keep you from agonising about it now.'

'Please,' I say with a watery laugh. 'Suggest away.'

Mum scrunches her face up for a moment. 'That was my suggestion. Having a delayed action plan.'

She looks so guilty, I can't help but laugh again, with a bit more genuine warmth in it this time, and she relaxes a little. She gets up, turns the kettle back on, and grabs a second mug for me, too. While she waits for it to boil again, she taps her fingers on the worktop, considering.

'Okay, let's focus on the schoolwork for now. What do you need to do over the break?'

I gesture vaguely to the table full of papers, and she winces.

'That's what I was worried about.'

Five minutes later, she's sitting beside me, a cup of tea in front of each of us, systematically going through everything I need to do over the next week, and I'm practically bursting with love for my mum. Here she is, on her rare day off, making lists and piles of all my revision notes and essays and assignments. Within an hour, she's made a colour-coded, bullet-pointed list. Seriously. I don't know where this shit went when they rolled the genetic dice for me.

'I'm going to email your teachers,' she says proudly, assessing her work.

'You've lost me there.'

'The ADHD specialist said the best way to stay motivated is imminent deadlines and rewards. So I'm going to email your teachers and ask them to set smaller, intermittent deadlines over the next week. You're going to email your work to them in time for the deadlines they set.'

'That's . . . actually kind of genius.' I hate it, but it's genius. I've got to give her that much at least.

'Also, your school's open over the break, yeah? So tomorrow, when I'm at the hospital, you go and work there. I'll put parental controls on your phone if you want so you can't get distracted by twit-tok or whatever. Just use it as a timer. Twenty-five minutes of focus is supposed to be ideal, with five-minute breaks. Even if you only do it two days this week. Two days of real productivity is better than seven days of not quite working, not quite resting. Also, while you revise, read it out loud. It helps if you've been feeling understimulated. And you could run or cycle to school. If you exercise right before working, it helps avoid restlessness.' She looks really proud of herself. 'I've been on the Reddit,' she adds.

Have I mentioned how much I love her?

I don't say anything, just pull her in for another hug, and she squeezes me back for a second. When we pull apart, she keeps her arms round me, holding me at arm's length. 'We can pencil in scheduled freak-out sessions about your friends if you want?'

'Yes, please. Five minutes of anxious spiralling a day keeps the doctor away.'

'You could also, maybe, just try talking to them?'

'Fat chance. The whole problem with Isabel is that she's ignoring me, and Katie and Lily won't talk to anyone about what's going on with them. Mel's on the verge of bursting into tears if you so much as speak to her when she's trying to revise, and Jas . . . Well, Jas just deserves a break. From being our group's resident mediator.'

'God, I do not miss high-school drama,' Mum says with a groan, smoothing her hand over my hair. 'Okay, think you can try to put it out of your mind for a little while at least? You've got that party on New Year's Eve, haven't you? You can all get a bit drunk—'

I gasp, and she rolls her eyes at me.

'*Responsibly* drunk, with parents present, and have a little cry together while you sort through your problems. At least that's always how we worked it out when I was your age.'

That actually does sound like a solid plan, to be fair. Niamh Buckley has this huge house not far from school, and her parents both work for the same company, so once or twice a year, when they get sent off to conferences or office parties at the same time, she throws these massive parties for the entire year.

128

Everyone tells their parents that there'll be adults present, that it'll only be small, that they won't be drinking – though my mum's never fooled by that last one. It's the biggest event of the school year. Just so happens that this one falls on New Year's Eve.

'I think I can do that. Yeah. It'll probably all be fine by New Year's Eve. I can cope until then.'

I let Mum enjoy the rest of her day off then, taking a little day off of my own where we sit in our dressing gowns and catch up on a few weeks' worth of *Corrie*. While we do, I archive our *Gals* group chat. It's been eerily quiet since Lily and Katie went radio silent on each other, and I've already put them all in a little box in my brain to be opened only at New Year.

Then, the next day, she's back at work, and I cycle into school, feeling strange and itchy in the empty building, but miraculously I work. I make my way, bit by bit, through the itemised list Mum made, with the help of the dates and deadlines I added to it when my teachers got back to me. I keep going all the rest of the week, pleased as hell with myself.

I don't text the group chat to tell them how well I've been doing.

CHAPTER NINETEEN

'I vote we lock the two of them in the garden shed tonight. Just chuck 'em a few bottles of wine and let them talk it out until they're friends again,' Jas says.

We're in her bedroom, getting ready for the New Year's party. While she speaks, she doesn't once break her concentration as she applies a perfect flick of golden liquid eyeliner to her lids, eyes fixed on the mirror on her dressing table.

'Seconded,' I say and groan, giving up on my own smudgy pencil eyeliner.

Jas sighs. 'I've just never seen them fight like this.' She turns to me. 'Here, let me do you.' She takes out another bottle of eyeliner, an electric blue that matches the freshly re-dyed ends of my hair. When she comes over to sit next to me on her bed, I turn my face up to her in defeat.

'Well, we've seen Lily like this with everyone,' I say, trying and failing to keep my face still while Jas applies my eyeliner, 'but Katie's like a little puppy round her. I've never known her to get pissed at Lily. I wonder what she did.'

'It might be a bit unfair of us to assume that Lily *did* something.'

'Bless you, Jas,' I tell her as she sits back, nodding at her handiwork. 'But Lily's almost always done something.'

She suppresses a small laugh at that. But then her expression changes to something indecipherable as she looks at me.

'And what about Isabel?'

'What about her?' I ask, suddenly very interested in analysing my eyeliner in the tiny little handheld mirror.

'Are you going to talk to her tonight?'

'She might not even be there,' I say with a shrug.

Jas opens her mouth to respond, and I've never been more relieved to hear shouting from downstairs. Whatever sage advice Jas was about to offer about my Isabel problem flies out the window. The words, 'It's not fair!' can be heard clearly from below, a screech that can only belong to a moody thirteen-year-old. I watch Jas shift into Big Sister Mode almost instantly.

'Jas,' I say as I see her start to stand up. 'You're getting ready for a party – you don't have to be there to break up every fight between Freya and your mum. Freya's her problem. The little ones can be your dad's problem. Isabel's my problem. And Katie and Lily are each other's problem. It's not up to you to fix any of it.'

'I don't mind fixing things,' she murmurs, but at least she doesn't run downstairs. Instead, she moves back to the dressing table, glancing at me in the mirror as she opens her lipstick. 'It's the fighting that upsets me. If I'm there to help, then everyone's less stressed.'

'Unless it can't be fixed. Then you're just stressing yourself out even more.'

She knows I mean Lily and Katie, and there's a long pause as we both consider the possibility that whatever's going on there might never be fixable.

'Should we be worried that Lily never sent anything to the group chat, even on Christmas Day?' Jas asks quietly.

I'm not sure what to say to that. Because – well, yeah – I am worried. But I don't want Jas to be. I'd unarchived the *Gals* group chat on Christmas. My family Christmases are great, but Mum's usually off to work as soon as present-opening's over, and my nan and granddad are great company for Christmas dinner, but they're usually asleep in front of the TV by five. When we're all full of food, lazy and tired and happy, that's when the group chat is most active. But there was the noticeable absence of one person this year that nobody wanted to mention.

'I was at least expecting a picture of her outfit,' I say eventually.

Jas laughs a little. 'Yeah, or a picture of her presents.'

'Never thought I'd miss a selfie of a slightly wine-drunk Lily in a sparkly jumpsuit and a paper crown so much.'

Jas looks so sad when I say it that I have to haul myself off the bed and squeeze beside her on to the little stool in front of the mirror, arm round her waist and head on her shoulder. She deserves a good night tonight. It's not fair that Jas has to play big sister at home and then to all of us, too.

'We'll sort it tonight,' she assures me.

CHAPTER TWENTY

I'm a few beers down. Nothing is happening. Lily and Katie haven't texted the group chat to say they're here yet, but that doesn't mean anything – the way they've been lately, they might have already shown up and been too stubborn to send anything. I'm sitting on my own on the kitchen worktop, taking swigs from a can every time I get stressed about it, which maybe isn't a super-helpful tactic, but I'm doing it anyway.

Jas went off about ten minutes ago to see if she could hunt down Mel, who had apparently arrived, but couldn't find us, and that's when I see Isabel. I assumed she'd been invited – the whole year usually is – but part of me didn't really think she'd actually *come*. Jas seems to have found her first, no Mel in sight, and they're talking by the front door. I see Jas thrust a drink into Isabel's hand, and she takes an immediate swig, but her eyes are roving, even as Jas is talking. She scans the whole room, her gaze shifting over every person she sees, until they land on me. Like it was me she'd been looking for.

But it can't have been me she was looking for because she drops the eye contact immediately. Drops her whole gaze to the ground, reaching up to tuck her hair behind her ears before looking back at Jas, nodding along to whatever she's saying, now with a grimace on her face.

Jas notices, though, flicks her eyes over to where Isabel had been looking, noticing me over here, perched on the kitchen worktop. She stops whatever she's saying, flicks her eyes back to Isabel, and pulls her close, whispering.

Jas has that stern look on her face. Or, well, it's not stern exactly. It's the look only Jas can master, the one that says *I'm sick of your shit so I'm only going to say this once*, but still manages to radiate warmth. It's usually reserved for me or Lily, when we're doing something self-destructive. It's strange seeing it directed at Isabel, and I can't for the life of me figure out why. But she's definitely saying *something* important to her because Isabel goes all pale and tight-lipped for a second, then just buries her face in her hands, nodding slowly. Jas puts an arm round her, talking again.

I try really hard to pretend I'm not watching, but I can't keep my eyes off them for long. This is the best distraction from Katie-Lilygate I've had all night. Jas is saying something with passion now, kind of, like, *pleading* with her. Isabel keeps shaking her head, and Jas takes both of her hands, stooping a little to meet Isabel's downcast eyes. Finally, Isabel gives this little laugh, and Jas breathes a sigh of relief, smiling in response. She lets go of Isabel's hands, which allows Isabel to reach up and wipe away what I'm pretty sure, from here, are tears, but I could be wrong.

They both glance over to me so suddenly that I don't have time to turn away. In a panic, I reach for another beer, focusing on that with as much intensity as I can muster, as if the harder I stare at the pull tab on the can, the easier it will be to pretend I wasn't looking at them at all.

By the time I raise my head, Jas is walking towards me, Isabel nowhere to be found.

'Hey,' I say, and she quirks an eyebrow at me. The casual thing's not working out then, I guess. 'Okay, yes, I was staring. What was going *on* over there?'

She sighs, looks me dead in the eye.

'Lou, I say this with all the love in my heart. You –' she jabs a finger at me – 'and her . . .' She points the same finger vaguely over her shoulder, in the direction of the stairs, I think. 'You're both idiots.'

'Doesn't sound like there's much love in your heart there, Jas.'

'There's a shitload of love. But you *are* both idiots who should just talk to each other because you clearly both want to.'

'She's been *so* weird with me, Jas. She's only got about thirty seconds of friendliness in her before she freezes me out for days on end,' I say, feeling my face contort into a scowl without meaning to.

'Because she's an idiot.'

My scowl deepens, but the way she's looking at me, I can see that shitload of love she mentioned.

'Jas, if there's something you need to tell me here—'

'Not my place.' She shakes her head once, firmly enough to end all argument, but she doesn't look happy about it. 'But it is yours, and it is hers. Which is why I'm saying you should talk to each other.'

I sigh, grabbing two new cans. I'm doing this for Jas. One less problem for her to fix, right?

'Where'd she go?' I ask, making sure my displeasure is evident in my voice, but Jas doesn't care. She's pleased enough for both of us.

'Ran off upstairs somewhere when she saw you watching.'

With another sigh for good measure, I make my way up the stairs.

I find her sitting with her back against the wall, in a quiet corner of the landing. She's just curled up, staring at her knees, when I slump down next to her.

I don't think she saw me coming until I'm beside her, and she jumps a mile. She hadn't been staring at her knees, I realise, but her phone, and I don't mean to look – I don't, I swear – but there's a text from Benji appearing on the lock screen.

You won't know until you try, my lovely.

She tucks the phone away as soon as she's recovered from the shock, and wordlessly I hand her the second beer I grabbed.

She's already finished the drink Jas gave her by the looks of it, so she takes it. Hesitates for a second, then opens it. I see her take a sip, then scrunch her face up. The sight makes me

136

smile, just slightly, and she catches my eye, echoing the smile for half a heartbeat before her face goes stony again. Suddenly she's downing the whole thing.

'You know, I almost thought we were friends,' I tell her, emboldened by the fact that I can't see her face while it's tipped back.

She doesn't answer, just finishes the can and wipes her mouth.

'You've been a real dick to me, but I thought, at the beach . . .'

She nods, just once. 'Yeah, me too.'

And that, more than anything, sets me off. Because what the *fuck* does she mean – '*me too*' – when she's been the one ignoring me?

'I'm a real fucking delight, you know that, Isabel? I'm a goddamn *treat*. I love my friends so much, and for a hot second there I thought you might be one, and then you just go on an absolute mad one for like three straight months. I just can't put my finger on you. It's not like I needed any more drama what with the whole –' I gesture wildly in front of me – '*everything* going on with my friends.'

She nods at that. Even with how off and on she's been with us all recently, she's hung around enough to see at least a handful of Katie and Lily's many fights.

'And yeah,' I continue, 'I know we had this weird rivalry thing going on, but I was kind of into it, you know?'

I hear her choke a little bit then, but I press on.

'Like, I don't know about you, but I was having fun. Eventually.

137

And I thought you were, too. And then I'm left feeling really fucking stupid about it because we have, like, what, one afternoon where we're friend-adjacent, and I was dumb enough to think that might cancel out the fact that you told me *to my face* that you were better than me. And honestly? I wouldn't even be mad about it if we'd gone back to being enemy-adjacent, but we didn't. You just *ignored* me, hence me feeling really fucking stupid.'

At some point mid-tirade, she turns to me, her eyes tired and heavy-lidded.

'You're exhausting, you know that?' she says quietly when I pause for breath, and I fight the urge to scowl again.

'I like that about me. Think it adds a bit of spice to life, y'know? Better to be exhausting than boring. You know what else is exhausting? Exercise. But it's good for you, though.'

I am a bit miffed that she's rude enough to say that out loud. I'm used to seeing it. In the eyes of everyone who isn't one of my closest friends. Sometimes in the eyes of my closest friends, too. But it doesn't bother me much any more. I do like it about me. She doesn't have to. I'm the one stuck in my own head; she can leave whenever she wants.

Although I guess she did. She left, and here I am going off on her about it.

I'm about to get up, to walk away for good, feeling suddenly embarrassed and pathetic, but I can't because she slumps a little further down the wall, laying her head slowly on my shoulder.

I freeze. Like when a particularly unfriendly cat finally curls

138

up in your lap and you're scared to move in case it realises it's made a horrible mistake.

'I like that about you, too.' Her voice is so quiet I almost don't hear it.

Slowly, I tilt my own head, resting my cheek on her hair. It smells like coconut.

'You're a real lightweight, you know that, Williams?'

She laughs, but it doesn't sound genuine. 'I'm a mess, is what I am.'

That doesn't sound accurate. But I also don't really know her very well.

'Join the club,' is all I say, and there's a long pause.

'Sorry. I didn't want to be your friend.'

I wish that didn't hurt so much to hear her say it.

'But now?'

She sighs. 'Now I don't think I can stand the thought of not being your friend.'

And it sounds intense. Or it would if I didn't feel the exact same way. I think I might be drunk, too.

'That's weird, right? From both of us. We really don't know each other that well.'

I feel her shrug.

I can hear someone throwing up in the bathroom, which kind of kills the vibe.

'Come on,' I tell her, hauling myself up. 'Let's get back to the party.' I hold out a hand for her to pull herself up, and she takes it, her face growing pink.

139

I think that means we're friends now. At least until we both sober up.

That's when the door opens to one of the bedrooms we all assumed was locked, and Lily stumbles out, giggling, Jay Henderson's arm snaked round her waist.

CHAPTER TWENTY-ONE

'Oh fuck,' Lily says softly when she sees us.

Jay seems less concerned. He takes one look at Isabel's hand in mine and sneers. 'Hah. We were right, Lil. Right pair of fuckin' lesbos.'

Isabel drops my hand like I've burned her, and I feel myself squaring up to Jay. All five foot three of me, staring up at his towering form. He's skinny, though, and I'm scrappy.

'Wanna say that again?' I hiss.

'Jesus, Lou, stop it.'

I whirl to look at Lily, who doesn't look quite as casual as her voice suggested.

'God, Lil, I knew you had bad taste, but Jay Henno, really?'

'It's none of your business,' she mutters, but she doesn't quite meet my eye.

I'm not sure what to say to that. Because she knows. She knows what a dick Jay was to me when I swerved him. She knows how much I hate him, and she knows all the perfectly good reasons I have for hating him. It's not like Lily's exactly desperate. She's got her pick of lads. So why him?

I'm still thinking about all this when I realise Isabel's pulling me away, and after a moment I let her. Because, fuck, Lily's right. What the hell can I do about it if she wants to start hooking up with an arsehole? It's not like I can stop her.

'That's how he knew,' I whisper as Isabel pulls me back downstairs. I say it more to myself than anything, but I'm surprised when Isabel hears me over the music and noise.

'Knew what?' she asks, faltering, turning to me with one hand still wrapped round my arm.

'About you.' I feel a bit dizzy. That last beer definitely tipped me over the edge of tipsy right into pretty-close-to-smashed territory. 'He said something to me about us holding hands on the beach. She must have been with him ages, just, like, telling him shit about us during pillow talk or whatever.'

I must not be making much sense because Isabel looks alarmed. I see her scanning the room, heading straight for Jas as soon as she spots her in the crowd. Katie and Mel are there, too. Katie's sobbing, Jas's arm wrapped round her. Jas takes one look at me, my face still contorted with rage, and her mouth sets into a grim line.

'Outside,' she says simply, pulling Katie along with her.

We sit on the stone wall of the driveway, shivering in the cold, while Katie tells us through choking tears about her ongoing fight with Lily.

'She hid it from me for ages. Her mum was always ringing to see if she was at mine, and I covered for her every time, but she wouldn't tell me. I knew she was keeping something from

142

me, but I didn't know what. And we'd never fallen out like that before, but we had such a good time together at the beach, and I thought we were okay again, but then when Lou mentioned he knew about our beach trip I figured it out, and when I asked her she told me she'd been seeing him in secret, and I went off at her, told her she should have more sense, that he was a dickhead and—' She pauses to pull in some air, the words having tumbled out of her in a drunken blur.

'Wait, who?' Mel asks, frowning.

'Jay Henno.' I practically spit his name. Jas and Mel stare at me, confused.

'We, uh, we saw them come out of a bedroom upstairs,' says Isabel, her voice hushed and embarrassed.

Katie's nodding through her tears. 'She made me keep it a secret from youse. I hated it, and I kept telling her that if you can't tell your friends you're seeing someone maybe you shouldn't be seeing them, but she wouldn't listen. Then tonight she went off to sneak around with him upstairs, and we got in this huge fight, and she said maybe the reason she couldn't tell her friends is cos she doesn't have good enough friends, and that maybe she's better off with Jay than she ever was being my friend, and she won't talk to me at all now.'

Part of me knows that this is exactly the kind of drunken emotional showdown I'd low-key hoped for tonight. But this isn't how I wanted it to go. Katie and Lily were supposed to bicker about whatever petty drama they'd had, then cry on each other and make up. But Lily's always been headstrong, and

143

Katie's always just adored her, and if Lily decides to stop being friends with her – with all of us – then there's not much anyone can do to change her mind.

'Fuck,' I breathe.

We all hover for a second, Katie's hiccupping sobs slowly wearing themselves out.

'Is he really that bad?' Isabel asks after a second.

'He's not, like, abusive, if that's what you mean,' Mel says slowly. 'But he's not great.'

'We used to go out,' I tell Isabel, not looking her in the eye. 'A couple of years ago, when I was about fourteen. And he'd pressure me into doing a lot of stuff. Some of it I let him do and some of it I didn't. We were only together for, like, two weeks officially, and when I ended it he was so pissed. Told the whole school it was because I was a lesbian, also told the whole school we did lots of things that we didn't do that a lesbian *definitely* wouldn't. So, y'know, get your story straight, but whatever.'

I try to make it sound like it doesn't bother me. Because, well, when I say it all out loud like that, it kind of sounds like nothing.

But Isabel does this weird thing. Her face contorts with anger. And I realise in one swift, strange moment that none of the anger I've ever seen directed at me has ever been real anger from her. Not really. She's given me frustrated glares; she's given me narrowed eyes and smug smirks and hardened steely stares. But nothing like the anger that warps her face now, not towards me but *for* me.

'God, what a *bastard*,' she hisses. 'I knew so many boys like that in my old school. Just walking around being awful, desperately trying to pretend that they're not overcompensating for their fragile masculinity.'

I truly think it's the most enigmatic I've ever seen Isabel. We're all just looking at her – even Katie's stopped sniffling long enough to gape – until I hear this delirious little giggle and realise it came from me.

'I'm sorry—' I choke down another laugh. I'm drunk, and I'm light-headed, and tonight has been a *lot*, and I'm clearly not the only one because even Katie is letting out a breathy, wobbly laugh, and Jas and Mel are grinning at each other in amused confusion.

'Sorry, no, I'm not laughing at you. It's just . . . you really fuckin' nailed him.' I swallow down another laugh and put a hand on her shoulder to reassure her, and she lets out a soft nervous laugh of her own.

It's Katie who falls back down to earth first.

'What if she never talks to me again?' Her voice is small. Jas's arm immediately envelops her, but she's not crying now. She's just looking at each of us, like she desperately needs an answer.

'She will,' Mel tells her. 'She always does. She just needs to throw a bit of a shit fit, but you two are best friends. She can't ignore you for long.'

I don't say it, but I'm not so sure. I love Lily, but she's a sun. She shines bright, attracts as many people as she can, but she

145

does her own thing, and she's proud of it. She doesn't like to be alone, but she doesn't like to need anyone, either. Katie's a planet. She needs Lily more than Lily needs her, I think.

I wrap an arm round her, too, so she's in a little me-and-Jas sandwich, both of us resting our cheeks on her hair.

'She's got to learn how lucky she is to be your friend,' I say. 'So we're going to be there for her if she needs us. If Jay hurts her, we'll be there. But if she has to take some time away to figure out how good she's got it with you, let her. Because you deserve to be treated like you're fucking irreplaceable, yeah?'

She nods, and I close my eyes for a second. When I open them, Isabel's looking at me like I've just figured out the answer to world peace or something.

This, actually. Scrap all the other dynamics, all the other ways she's looked at me. This one's my favourite so far, for sure.

We're still sitting outside, cold and subdued, when I hear the muffled sound of the countdown from inside the house, then the distant fireworks – all over the city, everyone but us is celebrating.

'Happy New Year,' I say quietly.

At first, I think nobody hears me. Jas, at least, seems too preoccupied with Katie, who I doubt can hear anything over her teary little hiccups. Mel, though, gives me a look. It's not stern exactly, but it's frustrated. An *is now really the time?* kind of look.

Well, that's me told, I guess.

But then there's a shuffling beside me, and, before I can react, Isabel's delicate fingers are pressing themselves into my palm.

If now isn't the time for a 'Happy New Year', it's definitely not the time for a 'what the fuck?' So I don't say anything, just look at her in slight alarm.

But she doesn't seem cowed. Just a small smile and a squeeze of my hand.

A quiet, Isabel-esque way of wishing me a Happy New Year back, I suppose.

CHAPTER TWENTY-TWO

Though the sociology textbook is open in front of me, all hope of getting any actual work done went out the window a while ago. Probably when I decided to move from the downstairs table to my bed, but, if we're being honest, I only moved there because I wasn't getting any work done downstairs anyway. Might as well languish in comfort.

It's been a few days since the New Year's party, and the group chat has been dead silent. Lily left the chat sometime after midnight. New year, new her, I suppose, but it's like nobody wants to be the first to say anything about it.

But now all the progress I'd made before Christmas, all the work I'd got done, has come to a standstill. Before Christmas, I had the promise that everything would be resolved, somehow, at the party. But now all the stuff that was spinning around in my head before is picking up speed, collecting debris as it goes. Lily and Katie imploded. The situation is technically resolved, I guess. We know what Lily's been hiding, and she's made it clear she's not our friend any more. But having the issue resolved is no good when the resolution was a worst-case scenario.

Even the Isabel thing has got more intense and confusing. She stopped ignoring me, so that's something. But now I've got a whole scene to play out in my head in excruciating detail, overanalysing every movement, every word, the way she laid her head on my shoulder and the way she told me, hair falling in her face, that she couldn't imagine not being my friend. It's not exactly making peace of mind an option right now.

I give my textbook another baleful look, and just as I'm considering one last crack at it my phone buzzes. I've been texting Jas live updates on my sad attempt at revision.

J: all you can do for now is try and put it out of your mind
J: we can try and parent trap them when school starts again

E: respectfully, since when has putting something aside been something my brain's capable of
E: it has 389428201 tabs open and 17 of them are playing audio

J: i have an idea, hold on

E: open to any and all ideas
E: literally anything pls and thank u

I'm holding on. I wait a few minutes, opening and closing TikTok a couple of times between switching back to check my messages. The next message that comes through, though, isn't from Jas at all, but from an unknown number.

unknown: Hi, so, there's apparently a huge public library in the city centre, we could go there sometime over the break for another tutoring session or even just a revision session for your other subjects if you need a different space to help you focus. Away from all the drama at school, I mean. Or we could work in Starbucks, and I could keep you constantly infused with coffee. I did some reading, and apparently caffeine can be calming for people with ADHD. Sorry, I don't mean to assume about the ADHD. Just that you said something to me a while back about having an attention deficit. But, yeah, it's just a suggestion.

I laugh a little into my phone. I only know one person who would look at that huge block of writing and think, *Yep, it seems reasonable to send this all as one text.*

unknown: Oh, it's Isabel. Sorry. Jas gave me your number.

I laugh again, before switching back to my chat with Jas.

E: Jas.
E: this was your bright idea?

J: you did say *anything*

E: i meant within the realms of sanity

J: oh, well you should have mentioned that
J: sanity isn't something I just assume you're working with ;)

E: so funny xoxoxox
E: but seriously?????????????????

J: Seriously. You should see her revision timetable.
J: she's got A levels down to an art form

I groan, shift my weight in bed a little as I reluctantly switch back to the texts from Isabel.

E: Just so you know, we call it town.
Not 'the city centre'
E: But also that sounds like a solid plan
E: you free now?

She types a few times, stops a few more. Eventually, a new text comes through.

I can be ready in an hour

'You know, I don't think I've ever actually been inside here before.' I notice her jump a little as I approach the table she's sitting at.

She looks round the library for a second, like she didn't actually see it on her way in.

'Me neither. It's nice in here, though. Quiet, but not creepy silent.'

'Yeah.'

It's awkward, I'll say it. More awkward than when we hated each other by a long shot. What do we even say to each other now, if we're trying to be friends? Friends are supposed to say nice things to each other, but that's never been something me and Isabel have been particularly good at.

She saves me from scrambling for another conversation starter by pushing a massive Starbucks cup in my direction.

'Got you this on my way here,' she says, and you'd think she was confessing to murder the way her neck flushes and her eyes drop to the table.

There's something so unexpectedly warm and un-Isabel-like in the gesture that I don't even know what to say, so I take a sip to buy myself some time. I get a mouthful of whipped cream, pieces of gingerbread and sweet, fragrant coffee.

'You got me a gingerbread latte?' I ask incredulously. 'Splurging on the fancy stuff, I see.'

'I didn't know what you liked, but I thought it was appropriately festive.'

I laugh. 'We could all do with a bit more festivity since New Year's Eve, I reckon. Thanks, by the way.'

She smiles then. That smile from the beach. A rare, genuine smile, I think. As warm and kind as the gesture of the coffee, and it just seems to break something between us. Some tension or awkwardness from how everything had been before. If one drunken heart-to-heart couldn't quite manage it, that smile definitely could. I'd missed it more than I knew.

'I have something for you, too,' I say, digging around in my bag for the book, and it takes her a moment to register what it is when I place it down on the table between us.

'Oh, it's okay, you can keep it. I still have your copy—'

'No, seriously, I read your annotations cover to cover like seven times last term. I promise it's safe to take it back.'

I only realise when I sense her embarrassment that maybe I should have been more ashamed to admit that out loud.

'I'm sorry I stopped tutoring you.' Her voice is small.

I just shrug. 'It's not like you had anything to teach me anyway,' I tease, and it reignites something of that glimmer in her eyes.

'Oh yeah?' She cocks an eyebrow. 'So you were just constantly rereading my annotations for what – fun?'

'Actually, I just had to add several notes. I think you'll find –' I reach over and flip the book open to a random page where above her annotations in blue ink mine are in red – 'I have very well-reasoned counterarguments to every single one of your points.'

She lets out this little snort as she holds the book and squints to read the tiny writing.

'This one just says *Sounds wrong. Fuck you.*'

'Well. You were being very rude at the time.'

153

She surprises me by laughing.

'I'll be sure to read every note, and then we'll have been equally rude to each other.'

'That seems fair.'

Once we get started, we spend a chunk of the afternoon comparing the work we'd done in English lit – hers considerably more comprehensive than mine, though I'd never say as much to her – and making a bit of progress on the exam questions we'd drawn up at the start of the year. But a couple of hours in, when I mention something in passing about my overdue sociology essay, she insists that we spend a bit of time just doing independent work.

This is where my focus begins to slide again. Having Isabel next to me means I have to at least *look* like I'm working, but as soon as the conversation fades out the spiralling comes back in full force, and I'm staring at the page, but my mind's not with it. I start to fidget, which makes Isabel glance at me a few times, and that's actually not helping very much, thanks.

I feel her gaze on me as I pick at a scab on my neck. The one that was a zit once, in a past life. I can feel the scab coming away under my fingers, and I know this is going to hurt. I know that it'll bleed, and then tomorrow it'll scab back over, and I know that if I keep doing this it'll never heal, but I don't stop. I can't stop. Once my fingers have found purchase on the skin, it's impossible not to work at it. I try, I always try, as soon as I notice I'm doing it, to pull my hands away, try playing with my pen or my rings, but they always wander back when I lose my focus.

A corner of the scab shifts under my fingertips, just a small piece of it, but it goes deeper than I expected, and I hiss a sharp intake of breath at the pain.

Isabel turns her head sharply at the sound, sees my hand at my neck. I expect her to look disgusted. God knows I am. But she doesn't. She just reaches out and takes my hand in hers, like she's confiscating it. She pulls my hand across the table, and, for just a beat, holds it, her fingers interlocked with mine.

And my brain doesn't go quiet, not exactly. But it does something. It's hard to spiral when my brain's just screaming at me about how *weird* this is, but also nice, which makes it a thousand times weirder. It's not so much that the noise stops, it's more like the noise all turns in the same direction, and it feels almost peaceful. She just smiles at me, and, after a moment, starts playing idly with my fingers, tapping the pads of her fingertips against mine, folding and unfolding each knuckle systematically on the table, satisfying my urge to fidget.

I've never felt more seen by anybody in my life. And I have no idea how to tell her – this girl who hated me only a couple of weeks ago. So, after a minute or so of just watching her, I turn back to my essay, writing with my free hand. And it's amazing, honestly, how easy it is for me to get work done when every part of my brain that isn't focusing on the essay is focusing instead on the warmth of her featherlight touch tapping against my fingers.

CHAPTER TWENTY-THREE

It's like the universe took one stress away and decided to double the other one just for fun. Isabel's here now, all the time. She's just part of the group. One of my people. I mean, she's still Isabel. She has her moments. She's stiff and uncomfortable sometimes, and every now and then she looks at me like she's considering just fleeing the room or even the city entirely, but she doesn't. She stays. Every lunchtime, every English lesson, every free period together. And, yes, she glares, she smirks, she rolls her eyes, but she laughs, too, sometimes. This accidental, contagious laugh that makes me just stare at her, eyes wide, because I can't believe the girl who I've been kind of enemies with this whole time is even capable of making that sound.

So, yeah, that's great. But like I said. The universe. It's got a sick sense of humour. Because, as term starts up again, the January air turning a bitter cold and the workload growing, Isabel lights up and Katie deflates. Lily still hasn't spoken to us since New Year. We see her sometimes, with Jay and his mates. All of them hanging around, smoking by the bike sheds, her hanging off Jay's neck.

I swear she sees us, too, sometimes. She never looks over when Katie's there. But, once Katie's stormed off, I always see her falter, always see her glance over. And I swear she looks guilty.

'What more can we do?' I groan when Jas, Isabel and I have a free together a few weeks into term.

'I don't think there is anything more,' Isabel says. 'You can't force her to stop seeing someone. My friend Caroline, from home, she has the *worst* taste in men. Like, really, my biggest red flag for any boy is that she's interested in him. She's like a magnet for the horrible ones. And the worst thing I can do is tell her that. All I can do is be there for her when they let her down.'

Jas nods. 'We've made it clear we're here for Lily if she needs us. That's all we can do.'

We have. We've sent a ton of messages, both individually and in a whole new group chat we made just to add her back in (she hasn't left that one yet, but I suspect she muted it pretty much immediately). Messages from all of us telling her there's nothing that would ever make us hate her, that if she does ever need us, we're here.

I'll be honest, I didn't feel great about it. It's true, sure, I could never hate her, but I'm still pissed at her, and I do still want her to be held to that. Held accountable for lying to us, for the way she's made Katie feel. The way she's made me feel.

Only Isabel can tell, strangely enough. She doesn't say

157

anything, but I think she sees me sometimes. She sees me coming apart in English, sees me doodling that stupid wonky tree and giving up halfway through and picking at a cuticle instead, my whole body restless and itchy because a few desks down Jay Henderson keeps leaning over to his friends, whispering, turning back to shoot me a seedy grin. Once, during a particularly bad lesson, Ms Price gave me this Look, one that practically dripped with disappointment, and I know it's from a good place, I do, but it wrecked me. But Isabel saw, and she reached over, and took my hand in hers. Just for a second. She didn't even look at me, but it helped.

You'd think it would be better, during free periods, when Jay's nowhere to be seen, but those bring thoughts of Katie, who's listless and mopey all the time. Thoughts of Lily, who still won't answer or even read our texts. I try to remember all the things Mum helped me with over the break, but it's hard to put it all in a little mental box when I'm at school. The more my focus slides away, the more my work slips, the more stressed I become. Then, suddenly, I'm too busy stressing out to focus at all.

It's already at the teachers-calling-home-about-my-work point in the spiral when Isabel suggests another weekend tutoring session in town.

'Dear God, yes,' I tell her. 'I'm flailing out here.'

'I thought it might help,' she agrees. 'And I really liked the city centre when I went with you.'

'Town. Wait. You'd never been before?'

158

She shakes her head.

'You're telling me that you've lived in Liverpool for, what, five months now, and you'd never been into town until you went to the library with me?'

Isabel just shrugs. 'Never had any reason to.'

'What do you even *do*?' I ask, but I regret the question as soon as I say it, realising that the answer is, probably, nothing. It's not like she has any friends except us – and even we barely counted as friends until recently – but we've never invited her out anywhere outside school except the beach.

We haven't really been doing anything outside school since Christmas, to be honest. I dropped by Katie's once or twice with Ben & Jerry's to binge old seasons of *Schitt's Creek* with her to cheer her up. Jas let me stay over a couple of times when my mum was on nights. Mel came over once to try to test each other on some of our revision, but she got fed up pretty quickly with how unfocused I was. But we haven't really *gone* anywhere. And suddenly, looking at Isabel as she struggles to answer the question, I feel bad as hell about it.

'I go to school,' she says with another shrug that doesn't seem quite as casual this time. 'Then I go home, and I watch Netflix or read or FaceTime some of my friends from home, or Benji comes over, or I go for a walk along the canal. I'm not, like, sitting in my room perpetually alone or anything,' she hastens to add, correctly interpreting my expression. I try to stifle it. I don't want her to think I'm only her friend because I pity her or something.

'Well, good job you've got me then,' I tell her, slamming my product design coursework folder closed. It had only really been opened for the sake of appearances anyway. I hadn't actually got any work done since I sat down, and I only took product design because it felt like it'd be a piss-take. 'You haven't done any of the big tourist spots yet, have you? The Cavern Club is, like, *right there*.'

'I actually don't care all that much for the Beatles.' She sounds a bit guilty, like she's just insulted my family.

'Neither do I.' I roll my eyes. 'But that's not the point, is it? The point is that next time you FaceTime your posh little London pals, you get to tell them you saw the Cavern Club, which you can only see in Liverpool because Liverpool is amazing, so fuck them and their London Eye or whatever.'

She laughs, shooting a nervous glance down at the books I'm now packing back up.

'Okay, but then we go to the library,' she insists. 'Ms Price loves you, but she's nowhere near as nice to the rest of us, and if she finds out I've been distracting you from work, she'll kill me.'

I've got to admit, after the whole *asking Isabel to tutor me debacle*, it's kind of nice to hear that I'm still Ms Price's favourite.

'One tourist attraction,' I concede, swallowing the desire to look smug about it. 'One hour of work.'

She shakes her head, still laughing. 'One tourist attraction, one afternoon of work. It can be an extended project.'

I pretend to consider for a moment, before holding out my hand.

'Deal,' I tell her. 'First thing Saturday morning.'

She reaches out to shake my hand, unable to suppress a grin.

CHAPTER TWENTY-FOUR

We make a list. Isabel loves a good list.

That first Saturday, we meet at Central Station, the two of us bundled up against the cold with coffees in hand – though hers, for some ungodly reason, is iced. Seriously, she's wearing two sets of gloves, cradling this iced coffee with both hands, tilting her head down to take a sip every now and then.

'So Cavern Club is first on the list,' I tell her as we set off. 'Just to say we've done it.'

She lets me lead her, and I take an unnecessarily long route, meandering through the older part of town where the buildings tower over us, all intricate pale brickwork, the grandeur of the nineteenth-century architecture offset with bright signs for the bars and restaurants within.

This is all just part of the tapestry of my life. The background noise to being a teenager. But there's something about showing someone round your home as a tourist. You see it through their eyes. And Isabel might have been as judgemental as she liked when she first moved here, but even she can't deny the beauty of this city.

'This area reminds me of parts of London,' she says as we wander along. I've never been to London, but I'm not sure I agree with her.

'Because it's beautiful?'

She nods.

'That doesn't mean it looks like London. That just means it doesn't look like what you thought you knew about Liverpool.'

Isabel frowns, considering.

'You're expecting some brutalist shit-hole, right? Because that's what everyone's told you Liverpool looks like. *It's grim up north*. We're just industrialists, working-class scallies with not enough time or money or culture to appreciate beauty. But the beautiful parts of Liverpool have always been here. They were here for Liverpool's downfall, the unemployment and the underfunding. They were here for the rise of the Beatles, and Liverpool's shift from industrial city to this trendy little cultural hub. They were here when Thatcher fucked us over, when the world turned its back on us, decided we were all unemployed scumbags, poverty-stricken leeches on government funding. And they were still here when we rose from the ashes. When we were named European Capital of Culture, they were here for the sneering and the laughing from people who went, *Liverpool, really?* and they helped us prove them wrong. With a little bit of funding and a whole fuckload of history.'

I pause for breath, and she's just staring at me. Looking at me with these wide eyes and a flush in her cheeks that might be from the cold, but wasn't there a minute ago.

'You really care about this city, don't you?'

'It's home,' I tell her simply.

There's a moment of silence, and she drops her gaze as we continue walking.

'You're right,' she says eventually, her voice quiet. 'I made assumptions. I'm sorry.'

We haven't even got to the Cavern Club yet, and I'm already counting this as a successful day. Isabel Williams admitting I'm right? And admitting I'm right about Liverpool being beautiful to boot?

I decide not to push it, going for more light-hearted topics as I pull her down Stanley Street, a bit less Gothic grandeur in exchange for some personal anecdotes. Here's the drag bar we sometimes manage to get into without being ID'd. Here's the gay club that one time got shut down because – rumour has it – they put poppers into the fog machine. She nods along as I talk, and she seems to be drinking in every word. When we arrive at the Cavern Club, though, she seems significantly less enthused.

'So this is just . . . where the Beatles performed, right?'

'I mean, that's what it's most famous for, yeah, but it's older than the Beatles. It's an icon of the music scene. Everyone who's ever made a significant contribution to music has played here. Look—'

I drag her over to the Wall of Fame, point out the bricks carved with the names of musicians and bands that have performed at the club. Queen, the Rolling Stones, Status Quo.

This, at least, seems to suitably impress her, and we snap a few pics in front of the wall. I watch with satisfaction as she sends them to the group chat she has with her London mates.

'Okay, now we go to the library?' she asks finally.

I'm all buzzed now. I've given my rousing speech on Liverpool's beauty, and I feel like some kind of Scouse Braveheart. I want to show her more.

'We had a deal!' she argues when I shoot her a guilty look instead of agreeing.

'Well, yes, but hear me out.'

'This is not a good sentence coming from you.'

'No, but hear me out! Because I have an even better deal where we'll get even *more* work done!'

'But . . . ?'

'*But* we spend all of today sightseeing. So we can spend *all* of tomorrow in the library. A whole *day* of work, not just an afternoon. That's a better deal, right? If you're not busy tomorrow, I mean?'

'The library's closed tomorrow.'

Of *course* she has this information locked and loaded.

'What kind of library closes on a Sunday?'

'Most of them, Eloise.'

'Well, fine, Starbucks then. I work better with background noise anyway.' I see her start to argue, and hurry to get my point across, grabbing her arm in my excitement. 'Please? I promise I'll work *so* hard in Starbucks.'

For a second, I'm not sure she'll agree. She's just staring at my hand on her arm, and there's a pause that stretches on for so long it's almost uncomfortable. But, when she looks back at me, it's with a momentarily shocking earnestness, before she rearranges her face into a long-suffering eye-roll.

'Where next then?'

I take her to the Docks. We walk well into the afternoon along the railings that edge the Mersey, littered with padlocks, through the red-bricked arches and the white stone steps and the black ridged metal of the bridges. Here, I tell her, is where that one scene from *Captain America* was filmed. There, on that bench, is where I had my first kiss – grim, do not recommend, though the blame for that falls more on the boy than it does on the bench itself. Here, the Maritime Museum – which Isabel won't let me go into yet because she says she'll end up spending all day there – and there a little collection of souvenir shops selling touristy trinkets, which she insists we go into, and we both buy little matching Liver Bird key rings. At that, I drag her along to the Liver Building, too, even if it is a bit out of the way, because I can't let her own a key ring of it without having actually seen it.

'Legend has it,' I tell her, and she's already laughing at my attempt at a husky, serious, storytelling voice, 'that if the birds ever flew away from their perch, the city would crumble.'

She's staring at me while I speak, the way she does sometimes when she thinks I'm not looking, and when I turn towards her she glances away quickly, eyeing the pale building that looms over us with amused consideration. I watch her gaze flicker over the two stone birds perched, as if ready for flight, on the domed towers at either end.

'I think they're in love,' she says simply after a moment, before turning to me and cracking up at the expression on my face. 'Look at them,' she insists. 'Star-crossed lovers, chained down and kept apart. What if they were never intending to fly away? What if they were only going to fly to each other?'

'You really want to risk the whole city sinking into the Mersey for two –' I bite my lip, struggling to contain my smug grin – 'lover birds?'

She cracks up, but amid her laughter there are cries of, 'Oh God, that was awful,' and, 'I hate you,' but I can't help laughing, too, now that I see how easily that laughter just falls out of her these days. After all our stony silences, I'd make all the cheesy puns in the world just to hear the sound of it.

CHAPTER TWENTY-FIVE

I feel kind of guilty, really, about how easy it is to put Lily and Katie and everything else that bothers me out of my mind when weekends roll around. It's like, Monday to Friday is stress, and schoolwork, and friend drama. It's feeling like I'm going to crawl out of my skin from the restless buzz of it all rattling around inside me. But then Saturday comes, and I'm exploring this beautiful city with a girl who seems to hang on my every word, and who, with every day we spend together, gets funnier, louder. Like I'm seeing her become a little bit more herself each week.

We keep going with the set-up I suggested outside the Cavern Club. Saturdays, we explore, then Sundays we make camp in the back corner of Starbucks, upstairs where it's a little quieter, spreading out notes and revision over the biggest table we can get. Isabel's a big help. In the mornings, we do our 'tutoring sessions', but then, in the afternoon, we work on our other subjects.

She times me in frantic bursts, takes my hand when I'm fidgeting, traces repetitive patterns into my palm, taps my fingers with a quick, insistent rhythm. Sometimes she'll make to-do lists for us both, with rewards of coffee or snacks or a three-minute break where we split headphones and listen to each other's music. Honestly, I'm pretty sure she's been googling *tips to help your loved ones with ADHD* or something, which would be annoying if it wasn't a) helpful as hell and b) kind of cute, if I'm being truthful.

'I feel like I benefit *way* more from our study Sundays than you do,' I tell her one weekend, each of us sipping on iced lattes, despite the bitter cold outside. The first time I mocked her for it, she made a compelling argument for iced coffee being too delicious to be dictated by the weather. 'Like, ninety per cent of the work you do is about making sure I do work.'

She smiles round her straw before she answers.

'I'm good. Unlike some, I actually, you know, do my homework and revision over the rest of the week.' And there it is, that smirk, those narrowed eyes. They still come out sometimes. It's better now that I know it's all in good fun, though.

'Oh, sorry I'm too busy being cool and popular to be an absolute nerd like you.'

She kicks me under the table.

'Oh yeah? So cool and popular you've spent every weekend this month hanging out with an *absolute* nerd?'

'Charity project. Ms Price didn't mention it, but part of this tutoring session was so that I can put *helps nerds less fortunate than herself* on my personal statement.'

'Well, you can inflict your charitable nature on someone else because I'm set. Being a nerd will get me into university, where

I'll have ample opportunity to be cool and popular while you . . . I don't know, retake your A levels?'

I clutch my chest like she's wounded me.

'Genuinely low blow there, Iz. Who hurt you?'

'You. You literally just called me a nerd,' she points out, laughing.

'I never said it was a bad thing! Just nobody gets everything, right? Like, you can be cool, fit or smart. You can be two of those things, but never three.'

'Wait, so are you saying I'm—'

'Well, you're definitely not cool.'

And I sit back and watch as her face, neck and ears all turn a frankly alarming shade. I suppress a smirk as she sinks into herself in embarrassment, her neck seeming to just melt into the collar of her jacket.

She stammers for a few moments, which is hilarious, and I watch her face flicker from one expression to another as she cycles through her options of how to react to that.

She skips past earnestness entirely, and falls on snark, eventually working hard to restructure her expression back into that familiar smirk and steely gaze.

'So, if those are the three options, and we've already established you're cool . . . maybe you're smarter than I originally thought?'

And I know she's joking because for one she's grinning, and second have you seen me?

I bite my lip, drag my eyes up and down her like I'm flirting, and I swear she goes bright red again in an instant. I honestly didn't think it was even possible for blood to rush to a person's face as quickly and as completely as that. I raise my eyebrows, grinning.

'You sure about that?' I ask, and she makes to kick me again, but I dodge, leaning towards her on one elbow, chin in hand. 'Because I *swear* the first time you saw me you complimented my hair like you couldn't physically stop yourself.'

She actually chokes a little on her coffee, but that blush is getting borderline unhealthy, and I don't want her to have an aneurysm or something, so I lean back, still smirking, but decide to change the topic.

'I, for one, am glad you're such a nerd. Me, my grades and Ms Price all thank you for it.'

She laughs, still a bit flustered. 'It's all good. I get something out of it, too.'

I just raise an eyebrow at her.

'I mean, getting a personal tourist guide round Liverpool. I help you on Sundays because you help me on Saturdays.'

And she seems to really mean it. I'd never thought about it that way. I was having so much fun, I'd never considered how grateful she might be for it.

After a few weeks, I can't imagine spending my Saturdays any other way. We really milk the city for all it's worth. We go to the Maritime Museum, the Museum of Liverpool, the International Slavery Museum. She learns more about Liverpool and its history than most people who have lived here their whole lives. We move on to galleries then, the Tate, the Walker Art Gallery. And, when they're done, I show her round the Baltic Triangle, the expensive hipster area with exposed brick and low ceiling beams and bougie coffee art in neon-lit cafés, just to snap some photos of her in front of the graffiti art of angel wings that every Scouser has at least one of on their Instagram.

My favourite, though, has to be the Mersey ferry.

'This was a really bad idea!' she yells out over the biting wind on the almost empty ferry.

'What?' I yell back.

She laughs, pulling her little knitted hat down further, and a strand of hair, whipped up by the wind, gets caught in the hat. I reach over and pull it free, and for once – I'm not sure why, but maybe it's just the fact that I can't see her blush, her cheeks and nose already pink from the cold – she doesn't drop her eyes. She just looks at me, her gaze intense. Her big brown eyes bore right into me, and I get lost in them for a second. Eventually, a fresh gust of wind nearly blows my own hat off, and it breaks the spell, but something's still there, something that makes my skin tingle and my stomach squirm.

It's in pursuit of that feeling that I wrap an arm round her waist, resting my head on her shoulder as we look back at the city skyline against the flat grey of the February afternoon. The city is beautiful from here. But my eyes keep being drawn back to the silhouette of the Liver Building. Up close, those two domed towers, their birds chained eternally to their tips, look so far apart. Rows of windows and pale brick separate them.

But from this angle, far away, there's a weird twist of perspective in which they're almost touching.

I don't think I can ever unsee them now through Isabel's eyes. Two birds in love, kept apart.

I'm not sure why, but I hold her a bit closer.

CHAPTER TWENTY-SIX

'You doing okay, Lou?'

I look up with a start at Mel's question. We were just sitting in companionable silence, various assignments spread out in front of us. I hadn't realised Mel was thinking about anything other than her revision. That's pretty much *all* she thinks about these days.

'Huh? Yeah, fine. Why?'

'You're spacey.'

'What's new?'

'Not Lou spacey, though. You're not even fidgeting. You're just . . . staring out the window.'

'Oh.'

I was thinking about Isabel, actually. Having two days of the week where I don't have to worry about Lily helps a lot, but it's not like the other five days are a walk in the park. So I try to just focus on those two days when I can. This free period used to be the one I'd spend with Lily and Mel, so instead of letting myself obsess over that, or how it makes me feel that Lily's still a noticeable absence, I'm trying to plan where to take Isabel next weekend.

'No, I'm fine. I'm good, actually.'

'Makes one of us,' she murmurs, mostly to herself. Then she thrusts a handful of flashcards at me. 'Can you test me, please?'

I take them slowly. 'Are *you* okay, Mel?'

She looks at me like I'm wasting precious flashcard time. 'Fine, I'm fine.'

'Yeah, you sound real fine.'

'I'm just stressed.'

'You're going to be okay. You've done more work than all of us combined, and we don't even have real exams this year.'

'You don't. I have to take the UKCAT this summer if I want a shot at studying medicine. And we might not have any A levels this year, but *everything* we learn is going to be in our actual exams at the end of *next* year, which means we have to remember it all, which is objectively worse.'

'Okay, you make some compelling points. And I don't want to, like, diminish your stress or anything, but if you're working yourself too hard now you risk burning out before the end of next year.'

She seems to genuinely consider that, which feels like progress.

'Can you still test me, though?' she asks quietly after a moment.

I sigh, shuffling the cards. 'All right . . . Jesus, okay, er, define the term *standard enthalpy of combustion.*'

'It's the enthalpy change, or . . . heat change at constant pressure when one molecule . . .'

She trails off, and I follow her gaze to the door where Lily's just walked in.

It shouldn't be a surprise, really, we know she has this period free, but usually she's with Jay. They skive off half their lessons these days, and they're rarely even on school premises.

But she's alone when she walks in. She doesn't look at us, even though we're the only ones in here. She just walks straight past, falls with a little thump into one of the ratty armchairs in the corner and opens up a textbook.

There are a tense few minutes of silence during which Mel and I just look at each other, and Lily steadfastly looks *not* at us. Mel, ever the pragmatist, breaks first.

'Why are you here, Lil?'

And, well, Jesus, Mel. I know Mel, and I know how she means it. She's blunt, she likes to be clear and communicate precisely, and she doesn't mean to be rude, I know she doesn't, but Lily is also prickly right now and *honestly* Mel should know better than to spook the skittish feral cat that Lily seems to be channelling.

'What?' Lily snaps, slamming her book shut. 'You mean in the *shared* common room? As if I don't have a right to be here, too?'

'Lily, calm your tits. You know that's not how she means it. We just want to know if, maybe, you came in here to make peace? You've avoided us for so long that—'

'Oh, because it's my job to come crawling to you two to make peace, is it?'

She stands up, taking a few strides towards us, and I realise she looks, well, *bad*. I mean, at first glance she seems perfect

– she always does: her make-up is flawless and her hair is clean and shiny as always – but her baby hairs are sticking up. It happens when she's stressed sometimes. She has this nervous habit of putting her hair up in a ponytail only to immediately pull it down again, and, after the second or third repetition, that's when the baby hairs start to stand on end. There's something else, too, something subtle: she's skinnier, tired-looking.

But, while I'm taking all this in, Mel is bristling with anger. Woe to anyone who interrupts her flashcards, apparently.

'Actually, yes. You're the one who snuck around, and you're the one who stopped speaking to us.'

'*I* stopped speaking to *you*?' Lily laughs, but it's a sharp, cutting sound that I really don't like. 'Good one. As if you didn't all make it *so* clear that you thought I'd done something awful. Loved those condescending messages you all sent after New Year, really I did. *Hope you're okay, Lily, even though you've been a piece of shit. Please talk to us, Lily – we all forgive you for being awful. Hope your bad choices don't bite you in the arse like we all know they will because we're all so much smarter than you.*'

I roll my eyes at that. I don't mean to, but it's so like her to take genuinely well-meaning messages and interpret them in such a horrible way. She clocks it, her eyes zeroing in on me before she narrows them for just a second, and then she's off. Storming out the door, reaching up to tie her hair into a ponytail as she does.

'Yikes,' Mel says softly. And I think about tearing into her for how she handled things, but it's not her fault. Mel should have known how Lily would take that, but Lily should have known how Mel meant it. It's all just a bit fucked.

'I think you might have a point about burnout,' Mel says quietly after a moment. 'Shall we, er, go to the caff?' she adds, her voice tight.

'You go,' I say, and I'm surprised to hear how drained my voice sounds. 'I think I need a minute – I'll catch up.'

She nods, clearly unsure what to do. Mel's not exactly the cry-on-my-shoulder type, and I would never ask her to be. So she just packs up quietly and leaves.

I sit there for a few minutes, ragging my hands through my hair in the empty common room.

I don't know why it *bothers* me so damn much. Lily and I didn't even spend a lot of one-on-one time together. Katie was Lily's best friend, and we all knew it, and we all accepted it. I have my other friends. I even have Isabel now, so I'm technically at a net-zero loss on the friend front. And I should be fine with that, but I know it doesn't work that way. I miss Lily.

I love all my friends, I do. Isabel's new, and she's all-encompassing at the minute. I'm learning she's this whole different and wonderful person underneath it all, and that's exciting, but she's not Lily. Mel's the smartest person I know, Jas is the kindest, and Katie's the most loyal. But Lily? Lily and I are the same. We're both angry, and we both know we should do better. We're both impulsive and a bit self-absorbed and honestly kind of annoying, but we *get* each other. Because we're the same, we both know that just because we mess up sometimes doesn't mean we're not trying, doesn't mean we don't care deeply for the people that might get hurt or bulldozed over in our wake. We see that in each other even when most people might not because *we're the same.*

And I think part of me is pissed at her for forgetting that. And another bigger part of me is pissed at myself for forgetting it, too. She hurt me by sneaking around with a lad who made it his mission to make my life miserable. I know that, she knows it, but she's flawed. I know that about her, and I love her. I reacted badly, flipped, froze her out for a while. But I'm flawed, too. We're both hurting, and we can't seem to come back from it, but that's what we *do.* We come back from it. We're supposed to be the same.

'Fuck,' I hiss to myself, my fingers tangling in my hair.

'Hey.'

I glance up at the sound of the soft voice, and there's Isabel, taking a tentative step into the common room, a Styrofoam pasta pot in each hand. Looking at me with those wide brown eyes that make me think she's weighing up whether to give me a hug or pelt it out of the room.

'Hey,' I say back, my voice a bit strained, but she takes the response as confirmation that she can stay, and pads over to the seat next to me, handing me one of the pasta pots.

It's the veggie pasta, the one she knows I like, and that seems to send me over the edge.

'Do you want to talk about it?' she asks when my face crumples.

And I shake my head, because how am I supposed to explain

179

to perfect Isabel Williams that I miss having someone who was fucked up and who I loved anyway because she did the same for me? And how am I supposed to explain that if this thing that Lily did, this thing that seems to have cast her out of her friend group forever, is so unforgivable, then surely that means something I do eventually will be unforgivable, too?

So I just choke down a sob and force a smile, and she's not buying it, I can tell, but she echoes the fake smile anyway.

'*Okaaaayy,*' she says. 'Do you want to talk about something else instead?'

I nod, a bit too enthusiastically, and her smile turns warmer.

'So what's next on the tourist checklist for this weekend?'

'I'm . . . not sure, actually. I've been thinking and I honestly reckon we're out. There's only so many tourist traps in Liverpool. We're a chronically underfunded city, you know.'

She laughs a bit at that, and it helps a lot.

'Well –' she picks at her pasta, not quite looking me in the eye – 'I've been thinking, too, and actually I was wondering if . . . You've shown me tourist Liverpool, but what about your Liverpool? Your favourite places. The places that a tourist might never think to visit?'

'I love that,' I say, and she does look me in the eye then, and she's beaming. I beam back and try really hard not to think about all the things making me sad and stressed, and just focus on how happy I can somehow make Isabel by granting the smallest request. 'And I think I have an idea already. Of where to take you next weekend.'

I do have an idea, and I'm already letting myself feel excited. Nothing's changed. All the shitty things have stayed shitty, and I'm just gonna have to be okay with that because at least the good things are getting better every week. This – distracting myself with Isabel and our weekends – has been working so far. It should keep on working. I just can't let myself focus too much on Lily. That shouldn't be hard. After all, I don't know if you've noticed, but not focusing is kinda my special skill.

And, well, if I'm maybe neglecting the other parts of my life to chase this new distraction, so what? So what if I haven't been on a run in weeks, or I don't spend as much time with my other friends any more? This is working for me.

Chapter TWENTY-SEVEN

Isabel's biting back a laugh, but I'm still posing like I'm unveiling some grand work of art: big beaming grin, and arms extended in the direction of the O2 Academy. It's closed right now, and pretty unspectacular from the outside. The remnants of Friday night still lingering, plastic cups left outside, cigarette butts on the ground.

She's not exactly succeeding at biting back that laugh.

'Excuse me.' I readjust my pose, struggling to arrange my face into an expression of seriousness, and placing my hands on my hips instead. 'This, I'll have you know, was the scene of the best night of my life.'

She just eyes the outside of the building, an eyebrow raised in scepticism.

'It was where I saw Frank Turner live. My first real gig. And by real I mean I wasn't sitting in the very highest seats of the Echo Arena with my mum to see Carly Rae Jepsen. It was, like, my first standing gig.'

She smirks, and I do kinda miss seeing that. Don't get me wrong – I really like our new dynamic. I like that she belly-laughs around me now, that she smiles more openly, with eyes wide instead of narrowed, but I miss the way that smirk tugs at me.

'Okay, I love that you're sharing this, but do we need to be standing outside the building for it?'

'Picture it,' I say, and I feel her shoulders shake with giggles she silences as I lean in close. 'I've just turned sixteen, I'm hyperactive and undiagnosed, I'm stressed about GCSEs, which I'm failing, and I've got a lot of steam to let out. Then suddenly I'm in the basement of this place. And I'm listening to Frank Turner play, and I'm in a sea of bodies that just *pulse*, and I'm jumping with them – I can't not. Everyone's moving, and it's amazing. I'm drenched in sweat. I've just dyed my hair blue, like all blue, not just the ends, and I'm so sweaty there's actually faint blue streaks trickling down my face. Nobody cares – there's condensation dripping from the ceiling. Everything is good.'

'Sounds . . . kind of gross.'

I laugh. 'Yes. Completely disgusting. But brilliant.'

'I think I get it. Closest I have to that is when I went to see Girl in Red live a while back. It was . . . a much, *much* more relaxed vibe than what you're describing. But it was similar, too, that feeling of getting lost in a sea of people. *My* people. Because of course most of the audience were qu—' She cuts herself off almost comically. 'Uh. Quite, um. Quite into it.' Her eyes widen and her hands fly up to her ears, pushing back phantom hair that was already thoroughly tucked back. 'So, uh. I mean, are you running out of places to show me then?'

It's clear she wants to move on, and I can't for the life of me figure out why, or what just happened, so I play along.

'Running out of places? What do you mean? I haven't even made you walk the full length of my old delivery route from when I was a papergirl back in the day. I'll have you know that was the best ten quid a fortnight I ever made.'

Isabel just raises an eyebrow.

She's right. It's been a few weeks now since we made the shift from tourist attractions to the Grand Lou Byrne History Tour, weak March sunlight just beginning to thaw out our frozen hands. But, I'll be honest, I just don't have that many big meaningful spots. I took her up to Chavasse Park, showed her where we hang out in the summer, the Starbucks tucked away underneath where Jas and I used to go just for the sake of it when we first got old enough to be allowed into town on our own.

I took her to the minigolf in Liverpool One where we went for Katie's birthday last year, and where we'd all cheated horrendously by the end of it. Isabel, incidentally, steadfastly refused to cheat during our game, and I treated her to a Barburrito for her prize after she won. I gave her a tour of Concert Square, pointed out the clubs that check IDs, but don't scan them, allowing us to use our terribly made fake ones to get in. I showed her where you could buy a quad vod – four shots of vodka with a WKD mixer – for £5. She looked both horrified at the prospect, and impressed at the price, so I'd call that a solid win for Liverpool. I took her to the record shop

184

where I go to browse sometimes, despite not owning a record player. But now here because, well, yes, I'm running low on places to show her.

'I still haven't taken you to one place, but I was saving that for last.'

'Sounds like we've reached last,' she points out.

I don't want to think about that. I don't want to think about what we're going to do once our weekend traditions end. I don't want to figure out if we'll still have any reason to see each other outside school. I don't want to deal with all the problems I should be dealing with when I'm not planning out these trips. But hell, she's right. And, if this is going to be our last weekend, then fuck it – let's go out with a bang.

'Fine, okay, we'll go to my favourite street in the whole city. And we're doing it all.'

Isabel beams back at me, and I link my arm through hers and guide her to Bold Street.

She stops, huffing, about halfway up the stairs, and I try to stifle a laugh.

'What kind of café's up about three flights of stairs anyway?' she gasps, clutching the bannister. The stairs are a bit steep, to be fair. I'm grateful for the rest myself, and I've got thighs of steel.

'The cute, independent, vegetarian kind,' I tell her, my voice teasing. 'Sorry it's not Pret or some other London corporate bullshit.'

'We have independent cafés in London.' She rolls her eyes, but her voice doesn't sound quite so cutting when she's still gasping for breath. 'Wait— Are you vegetarian?'

'Have you ever seen me eat meat?' I ask slowly, watching with amusement as she considers. 'Trying to be vegan, actually. I'm not doing great at it, but I'm getting there.'

And her look of confusion melts into something that I can't place at first, until I realise that, as she's finally catching her breath, she's now letting out a small airy laugh.

'What?' I ask, feeling a bit out of the loop. I watch as she shakes her head, tries and fails to stop giggling.

'Sorry,' she sputters through another laugh, then presses her fingers to her lips, shaking her head again. 'Sorry. It's just . . . between the iced coffee and being a vegetarian, you're just so— For a str— No, sorry, it's fine.'

Isabel's almost got her giggling under control by now, and instead a look of complete horror is settling on her face, which is reddening by the second. I'm dying to know what she'd been about to say, but she looks so embarrassed about it, I can't imagine it's anything good. I suppose I can only be grateful that she's making massive strides by *not actually* saying it.

'Come on,' I say, rolling my eyes a bit. I grab her hand and pull her along with me as I start back up the stairs again. 'Let's go, you absolute crank.'

By the time we're in the café – The Egg Café, it's called – ready to order, the blush of embarrassment that tinged Isabel's cheeks on the stairs has redoubled, and it only seems to get worse every time I look at her. It isn't until I reach for my phone to pay for my order that I realise I'm still holding her hand. I drop it – I kind of have to, to pay – and she seems to sort of deflate a little. And I wonder vaguely, as I step aside to let her order, whether it's a good deflate or a bad deflate. Like, whether me touching her made her so uncomfortable that she could only relax when I let go, or whether she liked being touched by me so much that she missed it when I stopped. And then I'm wondering, less vaguely now, and with considerably more concern, why this is even something I'm wondering about.

'This is nice,' she says when she steps aside, too, the pair of us clutching our little slips of paper with our order numbers on them, and for half a second I think she might be answering my panicked internal question. But she's looking up, her eyes roving the high ceiling of the café, and I realise that she means the place is nice.

'Yeah, it is,' I say, guiding her to a free table and looking around, too, as if I'm seeing it for the first time through Isabel's eyes. The low wooden beams, the light that pours in from high panelled windows. It's a bit rustic, but not like it's trying too hard, and the place seems filled with people to match. Not fussy hipsters like you'd find in the Baltic Triangle, but people who look as if they could either be planning an art project or a protest march in equal measure. It's weird, because Isabel normally comes across so uptight, but she seems to fit right in here somehow. Like she's suddenly more at ease than I've ever seen her.

Once our food arrives, and I'm tearing through a frittata, and she's picking at a plate of cheese on toast, we reassess the day's activities. We're both a bit knackered, to be honest.

Isabel begins listing places. 'Okay, so we saw the Cat Café, which we will absolutely be coming back to when we can book a table. And we did that vintage clothes shop with a silly name. *Moo*, maybe?'

'*Cow*,' I tell her, thinking of the two truly hideous bold-print vintage button-down shirts I bought from there, and the other three that Isabel had to physically restrain me from buying because we both know I can't afford that many vintage shirts. But they were magnificent, even if Isabel wholeheartedly disagreed with that assessment.

She nods. 'Then that cute fair-trade giftshop,' she says, uncurling another finger like she's counting through the places we've been.

'*Shared Earth*,' I say, and she nods again.

'St Luke's?' she asks as she counts off another finger. I roll my eyes.

'How many times do I have to tell you? *Nobody* calls it that. It's the bombed-out church. Which, honestly, should have been on the tourist list rather than the personal one. I can't believe I forgot it.'

'Well, I'm glad we went there in the end. It was gorgeous.'

188

'Not the end yet,' I point out. 'We've still got News From Nowhere.'

Her face lights up. 'The bookshop? I saw it when we passed.'

'Yep, I love it there. You got enough energy for one last place?'

'You *know* I love a bookshop, Eloise.'

I laugh because I didn't, actually. I mean, I could have guessed, but I'm still learning new stuff about her every day. And I try not to worry about whether I'll *keep* learning new stuff about her after today.

I know it's stupid, okay? I know we're friends now, and I'll still see her in school, and there's nothing necessarily stopping me from just inviting her over even if we've got nowhere to go. But I think part of me already suspects that she'll just clamber right back into her shell once we don't have a good reason to meet up, and that I won't have what it takes to draw her back out again.

I really, really don't want that to happen.

'Okay, well, eat up then. And maybe let's get some more coffees. Because I don't know about you, but I plan on spending a *lot* of time in there.'

Her smile turns beaming and silly and joyous, and I can't take my eyes off her. It's hard to believe there was a time when I thought she wasn't capable of a smile like that. Like, I'd seen Benji and thought those two couldn't possibly be related – he's much too happy. And, in my defence, they're still nothing alike. Benji's smiles come easily and often, and Isabel is still more

189

often sullen and tightly wound than not. But she's certainly *capable* of that kind of unabashed joy, and honestly it's all the more rewarding for how rare it is. Making Isabel smile like this is an achievement. One that I enjoy striving for, every chance I get.

CHAPTER TWENTY-EIGHT

If I thought Isabel looked at home in the Egg Café, that's nothing compared to how she is in News From Nowhere. It's only a small shop, but they use the space well. The walls are lined with bookshelves piled high, the floor space filled with tables and displays.

I linger near the front of the shop first, scanning the racks of independent zines and newsletters, mostly just to give Isabel a chance to get her bearings, figure out where she wants to go. She takes a moment to scan the new-release fiction near where I'm standing, but it's not long before she gravitates further in. Mostly I watch her, a small smile that I can't quite hide on my face while her eyes rove over the displays. I follow her and find a spot at the centre of the shop. This, I decide, is the best way to let her make the decision on where in the shop to go.

As I'm rifling through a little box of badges, though, she hovers close to me instead. I keep thinking she's going to choose a shelf or a corner to go off and examine, but she doesn't. She just stands with me, and I keep seeing her eyes flicker towards the corner of the shop. It's a little dance she's doing where her eyes will fly over there, she'll turn her head away, and a second later tear her gaze away, too. She'll try to occupy herself with something else, then eventually her eyes will be dragged back there.

I try to make it look like it's my own decision, and it kind of is. The particular corner she's glancing at contains part of the politics section, which I always like looking through, so I wander over. When she follows, her attempt at disinterest practically radiates desperation, and I try not to pay attention as I pull a book about rebellion and resistance off a shelf. She parks herself in front of a shelf just a little to the left, her body tilted slightly away from it, but her eyes betray her with the way they rake hungrily over the spines of the books.

I do a poor job of pretending not to read the big sign above the bookcase, and an even poorer job of concealing my surprise when I see what it says: *LGBTQ+*

From my sidelong glances – which Isabel seems oblivious to, too wrapped up in her own attempts to be inconspicuous – I see smaller signs dotted along the shelves denoting specifics. The shelf she seems to be examining so thoroughly declares itself to be lesbian fiction.

Oh.

Hm.

Well.

That's, er . . . I mean. That's. It's a surprise, I think. It's definitely something, for sure.

And maybe it doesn't even mean anything at all, really. Lots of straight women read lesbian fiction. I'm sure lots of lesbians read straight fiction. I read lots of books about American teenagers – doesn't make me American, does it? But then there's some other stuff, too. The way she mentioned being around *my people* when she went to see Girl in Red, a singer I googled in the toilets after and found out is basically synonymous with lesbianism. The way she always seems to hide some part of herself, always shutting down when she thinks she's said too much, shown too much.

And then there's the way she stiffens whenever I touch her. The way she stares at me sometimes. The way my heart races when we lock eyes. And okay, maybe that last one is more on me than it is on her, but there's definitely *something* there, right? Like, sure, I know it's a classic straight girl thing to be all *oh my God, she's defo into me* when a friend comes out, but is she, maybe?

But she hasn't come out. I've got way ahead of myself. She's just browsing a shelf that might mean nothing, but, even if it does mean something, she clearly doesn't want me to *know* that if the way she's been stealing sneaky glances at it is anything to go by.

She's flicking through this one book with a yellow cover and what look like two girls in Regency-era dresses, and she's finally too engrossed in it to be checking over her shoulder to see if I've noticed. I can't help but watch her. Her hair is pushed behind her ear on one side, allowing me a glimpse of her profile, the rest of her hair cascading, shiny and straight, over her other shoulder. Her mouth quirks up into a small smile at whatever she's reading, and she's focusing so intently that I see her eyes flickering over the page, infinitesimal changes in her expression as they move, a small deepening of a frown here, a widening of her eyes there. I want so badly for her to buy this book – she's clearly enjoying it – and I'm terrified that she won't if she's worried about what I'll think.

She goes to turn the page, and in doing so glances up at me, and I panic, turning my head and scanning the shelves in front of me. I watch as she scrambles to put the book back.

'No, you should get it!' I call out, louder and more flustered than I mean to, and she looks startled, jumping a little with the book halfway to the shelf, her eyes wide.

'I just mean that it seemed like you were enjoying it. And you're gonna have to queue up with me anyway, because I'm buying this.'

In a panic, I reach up and pull out the first book that looks vaguely familiar, something from the gay fiction section about superheroes. I realise when I do why I recognised it, actually. I've seen it in a few lists of recommendations for teen fiction with ADHD representation.

Isabel's watching me, her brow furrowed in confusion.

'Love me some gay superheroes,' I say with a shrug.

She looks a bit puzzled, even as she holds the book close, the cover pressed to her chest as if to hide it.

'Have you ever seen the film *Pride*?' she asks after a long moment. The question catches me off-guard. Is . . . is this her coming out?

194

'I love that film,' I tell her. 'I have to be careful not to watch it when my period's due otherwise I'll start sobbing my eyes out at "Bread and Roses".'

'Not the ending?'

'Oh, I don't need to be hormonal to cry at the ending.'

She laughs a little, but it's still tinged with nervousness.

'Well, you know the bookshop in it? The one they own, and they run LGSM out of – Gay's the Word?'

'Yeah?'

'It still exists, in London. It's my favourite bookshop in the world. Maybe even my favourite place in the world. And this kind of reminds me of it. I think News from Nowhere might be a new close second.'

Okay, so no coming out. The conversation was about the bookshop part of the gay books, not the gay part. Totally cool. Not like my heart started pounding or anything when she started speaking. There's no logical reason to feel *disappointed* that she didn't just come out to me.

'You can buy the Pits and Perverts T-shirts here, too,' I say instead. 'You know, the ones from the film?'

'I already have one,' she admits. 'And they're not *from* the film. They're from the actual history of the place. LGSM was a real thing, and so was the benefit concert—'

She never can resist correcting me, can she?

'I *know*, Iz. You think I don't know the history of my people?'

She gives me this look. This weird, indecipherable look that might be confusion, but could also be about a dozen other things.

'*Your people?*'

'Socialists! Or at least the labour movement.'

She laughs a little, but her smile is inexplicably sad.

'Do you wanna stay a bit longer?' I ask, unsure what to say. 'Or we can just go pay for these now.'

She seems willing enough to leave, the mood having deflated somewhat, and once we've paid, and we step back outside, we're done. There's nowhere left to show her. But I really don't want the day to be over. Especially not like this.

'I'm knackered. Do you wanna come back to mine? We can just get a takeaway and watch Netflix or something.'

And, for just a second, she looks surprised, but it's only for a second. Once it's passed, the small smile she'd given me turns instead into a big, beaming grin as she nods.

Which, I won't lie, makes me wonder if she *does* like me. I think the thought might make me happier than it should. Maybe it's just an ego trip or something. I dunno. But I'm matching her smile, and taking her free hand, and pulling her back towards the station, a warmth spilling out from my belly and inching its way all over me, right down to my fingertips, clasped in hers.

CHAPTER TWENTY-NINE

Isabel leans back on the kitchen worktop where I'm trying to empty vast cartons of takeaway food on to plates, mostly because she doesn't strike me as the type to eat out of Styrofoam if she can help it. It's wild to think how out of place she seemed here even just a few months ago. Maybe she's just relaxed since that god-awful first tutoring session, but maybe some of it *was* just in my head. If she's bothered by the dirty dishes in the sink or the floor that's peeling where it meets the corners, she doesn't show it now. Instead, she mostly just seems to be watching me.

'Can I at least help carry some of it?' she asks, eyes fixed warily on the poorly balanced plates.

'Only to let you feel useful,' I say graciously.

I pile us both up with plates before showing her upstairs, clambering on to my bed in a tentative little dance so as not to knock the food over. Isabel's better at it than I am. Delicate is kind of her middle name.

I can feel her trying to be subtle as she takes in my bedroom. We've never been in each other's rooms before. The way her eyes rove around now, though, makes me wonder what she sees in it. The room's small and cluttered, but if it bothers her she doesn't show it. It bothers me a little. I've never exactly been the tidiest person – I'm not some sort of feral goblin or anything, I'm clean enough – but seeing the room as Isabel must see it is . . . a little embarrassing. There's so much clutter in here I wasn't even aware of. Things tend to fade into nonexistence for me pretty much the second I put them down, so unless I'm actively using it, half the crap in this room exists on a different plane of reality to me. But with fresh eyes, I'm suddenly hyper-aware of the empty cans of energy drink clustered in the corner of a shelf, the pile of not-quite-dirty not-quite-clean clothes on the back of the chair. The bag of clean laundry that I keep forgetting to put away and have just been pulling clean socks from for the last week or so.

It's not all bad, though. I watch her take in the walls, plastered with posters and gig tickets and photos, smiling at some. There are photos stuck to the wall over the bed that had become so thoroughly invisible to me, it's like I'm seeing them for the first time. Trinkets that I never found a good space for just littering whatever open surface I left them on one day, and I'm suddenly remembering just *why* I needed that tiny ceramic frog so badly I emptied my bank account for it. The world becomes background noise so easily to me, but with Isabel here, I'm seeing everything, full-colour, for the first time in ages.

We fall into silence for a while as we eat, and I think about putting something on, a film or something on my laptop, but she still seems to be intent on drinking in every bit of my bedroom.

'You play?' she asks after a while, nodding towards the cheap acoustic guitar gathering dust in the corner.

'For a while, I got really into it, then just gave up when I wasn't getting any better.'

She rolls her eyes as she takes another bite of food, and I laugh.

'It's an ADHD thing.' I feel the need to explain for some reason, as I pick at a spring roll. 'You get these hyper-fixations, things you obsess over for a bit, and usually they fade after a while, or you find a new one and that takes over.'

'What other ones have you had then?'

'Embroidery,' I tell her, pointing at a little crate of hoops and fabrics and threads. 'I absolutely did *not* have the patience for that.'

She laughs out loud. 'I can just picture you swearing at a needle because you can't get the thread through.'

'Like a fucking sailor,' I agree with a grin. 'Also, video games.' I point to the pile of second-hand discs next to an ancient PlayStation. 'And, very briefly, whittling, though I was terrible at that, and it did not last long.' I pull a little lump of wood out of a bedside drawer, and she presses her lips together, examining it.

'It's a very lovely, um . . .'

'Cat. It was supposed to be a cat.'

A bubble of laughter escapes her then, and I try to act offended, but it doesn't really work.

'Marathon training's been my most recent one. It's also the longest I've stuck to something for a while, but I haven't trained much since Christmas so who knows any more? I do sometimes worry that basically my whole personality is just a collection of hyper-fixations that I pick up over the years.'

Isabel chews thoughtfully for a moment before answering. I like it when she does that. Really considers what she's going to say. It always makes me feel safer, like she's not just shooting back a knee-jerk response, but that she really means whatever she's about to tell me.

'It's not,' she says finally. 'Your personality is so much more than that. You're snarky, and you're confident, and you're fiercely loyal. You're more than just your hobbies.'

I know I don't have that easily flushed complexion Isabel has, but even so I feel my face grow hot and itchy under the weight of what she's saying. I wonder if, for the first time, she's the one making me blush.

'Well, what about you?' I ask. 'I feel like you know me inside out, but shouldn't that go both ways?'

She shrugs, looking uncomfortable. 'What do you want to know?'

Everything. 'Anything,' I say, fighting to keep my voice casual. 'Like, I've shown you everywhere I've ever been in this city. I've shown you where I hang out with my friends, the spot where I first kissed a boy, the spots I've kissed some other boys after that.' My nose scrunches up with mild disgust at the memories, and a nervous laugh escapes her.

'I can't really add anything of my own like that,' she says, her voice even quieter now. And she's not looking at me, staring instead at her crossed legs and the now empty space of bed between us. 'I've never kissed a boy.'

'Oh,' I say, suddenly feeling guilty for bringing it up, but somehow unable to drop the subject. 'Don't worry, it's not like you're missing out on anything. It's all a bit meh. Honestly, the best thing to do is just to get the first one out of the way so you can be, like, *okay, that's what that was like, time to move on with my life*, you know?'

The words kind of tumble out, and her eyes flit up to me for a second, a small crease forming between her eyebrows.

God, I wish I could stop speaking. But, well, fuck. Because all I can think about is the things I might have learned about her today and maybe, somewhere in the back of my mind, the things I might have learned about myself, and *fuck, fuck, fuck, I'm an idiot*. I am. I know I am, but I can feel the words on my tongue, and even as I'm thinking how utterly moronic they are I know I won't be able to stop myself from saying them.

'You can try with me if you want?'

Yep. Truly an idiot. But, in the second after I say it, I don't think I care any more. Because her eyes have widened, those big brown eyes huge and intense and so wonderfully fixed on me.

She only holds my gaze for the briefest of seconds, and, when she drops it, she focuses instead on her hands in her lap where she's picking at a loose thread in her tights.

'It doesn't mean anything,' I tell her, not entirely sure why I'm pushing this. 'I've kissed loads of lads, and it's not really anything. It's just a thing you do. But it isn't all magical and life-changing like it is in books. It doesn't feel like anything, really.'

Her frown only deepens at that, and, when she finally looks up, I kinda wish she hadn't. Her eyes are indescribably sad, and, well, I wish I hadn't been the one to break that to her, but it's true. Kissing isn't nearly as big a deal as we're made to believe. All the boys I've kissed, I've liked well enough. But, when they did kiss me, it was still just . . . someone else's tongue in my mouth, which is a bit gross if you think too hard about it. If you don't think too hard about it, then it's just kinda something you do.

'It's not a big deal, I swear.'

I reach out and take her hand, mostly to stop her picking at her tights before she gets a hole in them. But when I do her eyes widen, and her face gets lovely and pink and embarrassed, which reminds me that I'm the one with the confidence here, so I should use it.

I lean in towards her, and it's a bit awkward closing the space between us because we're both cross-legged on the bed, so I laugh a little – because what else do you do when things get awkward? – but she doesn't. In fact, I don't think she's even breathing. It makes the whole situation feel suddenly serious and tense, and I hesitate just before my lips find hers because the tension in the room right now, heavy and thick, makes me wonder if this is maybe the stupidest idea I've ever had.

But then she closes the rest of the space between us, sharp and fast, and I only have half a moment to be proud of her for making the jump before I realise she's moved too quickly, and I've lost my balance. I reach out and grab the back of her shirt to steady myself, but I can't think of much else because she's not just kissing me, she's *kissing me*.

Like a fucking pro.

And maybe it's just the shock of the way she dives at me, but I'm sort of winded by it, and my breathing becomes more like gasping. She seems to notice my lips part before I do because, as soon as they do, I feel her tongue just lightly sweep across my bottom lip.

Something in me just clicks awake.

Like there are nerve endings I didn't know I had, and every single one of them has just been lit on fire, and I feel the burn of it everywhere her skin and lips and tongue touch me, and I feel it in her warm breath and, *oh*, is this how it's supposed to feel when somebody kisses you?

She pulls away, just a little, and I can already tell she's overthinking this. I can practically see the thought bubbles appear in the way she stiffens, calculating if the tongue was a step too far, if her hand on the small of my back was too much, and I can't bear the thought of finally finding this crack in her shell only to watch her plaster over it again in embarrassment, so I act fast, without thinking.

My hands, still clutching the back of her shirt, wind themselves into her hair instead, pushing her mouth back to mine, and everything is more frantic this time. I feel her breath hitch as her mouth opens wide and messily on to mine, and I pull her towards me, maybe a little too hard, our legs intertwining as the two of us fall back on to the bed, her arms catching her just in time, propping her up on top of me.

Somewhere, in the back of my mind, I notice the plates topple over, hear one fall to the floor, feel another spill egg-fried rice somewhere on the bed, but I genuinely do not care. I'll happily spend hours picking each individual grain of rice out of my sheets later because, right now, all overthinking seems to be entirely abandoned. Right now, Isabel's kissing me with *purpose*. With ragged breaths stolen between kisses that we draw from each other in fierce, hungry lunges. With one arm propping her up, her other hand is no longer tentative now, but grasping, at my face, my neck, my waist, and I feel the ghost of her everywhere she touches. My fingers stay tangled in her hair, as if keeping her close to me is the only thing in the world that matters right now. More important than drawing breath is making sure that I can pull her back to me once the breaths have been drawn.

I'm not sure how much time has passed when she does pull away. My only measurement is the chafing of my lips and the swimming quality my thoughts seem to have taken on for lack of air. But when she does, extending her elbows so that she hovers over me, close enough to get a good look at, but too far to kiss again, she's someone else entirely. I can't tell you how good it is to see her like this. Every inch of stiffness and every knot that makes her Isabel are just entirely undone. Her face and neck and chest are flushed, not in her usual pretty pink blush, but in a dark and blotchy redness that matches the redness of her lips, now chapped and parted and panting for air, and her hair is tangled and falls in messy strands down to where I lie. She's beautiful, I decide. And not just in the prim and meticulous way she tries so hard to be, but in a raw and wonderful way. Better, even, than seeing her come undone like this, I think, is the possibility that maybe I did this to her.

Even as I consider all of this, she seems to be spiralling again. Her eyes are growing wider and her breaths, instead of calming the longer we're apart, become shallower, more panicked. She pushes herself up from the bed, and I scramble upright a bit.

'Isabel—'

But she cuts me off, shaking her head.

'Sorry,' she says, frantic as she searches for her coat and her bag. I watch as she runs a hand through her hair, tries to smooth it down, but is met with resistance in the form of some tangle or knot. This seems to be the last straw for her, and her face just crumples.

'Sorry,' she says again, and her voice cracks at the word, but she's already gone, hair and bag flying out behind her as she turns and runs downstairs.

I feel like maybe I should stop her. Or say something. Or

maybe I should be processing something that I haven't quite sussed yet.

But I don't do any of those things. All I do is sit there, on the bed, thinking about how she tasted like cinnamon.

CHAPTER THIRTY

E: you clearly want space and I'm trying to give it to you I swear

E: it's just

E: why do you taste like cinnamon?

E: sorry I just really have to know

It's been a day. That's how long I held out after she ran off. Less than a day, actually. It's Sunday afternoon. And her silence has been killing me.

I'm going to go ahead and assume we're not doing our usual study session today.

She still hasn't answered the cinnamon question.

E: do you still want space?

E: I'm thinking yes but I'm trying not to assume

E: also I'm not sure why

E: I hope you're ok

E: I didn't do anything to upset you did I?

The little typing bubbles appear. Finally. Then they disappear again. A few times, actually.

I: No, Lou. No, of course you didn't, I'm sorry.
I: I'm really sorry.

And more than the apologising and the double texting – which are alarming because neither are things that Isabel particularly enjoys doing – it's the fact that she calls me Lou that concerns me. Something really must be off.

So I phone her. It almost rings out, but she answers it at the last second.

'Isabel?' I ask, but she doesn't speak at first. She just kind of gasps a few times. And I realise she's crying.

'I'm so—'

'I swear to God, Isabel, if the next thing to come out of your mouth is another apology I'll come over there and – and – I dunno. I'll apologise all the way back. That'll show you.'

She makes this weak little snuffling sound that I think might be a laugh-cry.

'I am, though,' she says after a moment, her voice low and flat.

'Why? For what? You didn't do anything wrong.'

'Yes, I did. I tricked you, Eloise, and then I—' She gives a sort of hiccup, and her crying redoubles. 'God, I'm awful. I'm so sorry.'

Then she hangs up. Just like that. No time for me to respond, but enough to hear one more gasping sob before the line goes dead.

I'm on my bike before I can even think about it. I'm not even sure what's happening, or what *has* happened. I just know that I had a realisation – about Isabel, about myself – and I pulled a classic me and made a stupid impulse decision to *act* on that realisation, and now Isabel's crying? Perfect, composed, put-together Isabel is having a meltdown of some kind because I did something stupid. So I don't get to have a meltdown of my own yet. I don't get to sit and worry about what it means that the best – maybe the only good – kiss I've ever had was a) with a girl, and b) with a girl I was supposed to *hate*. I have to fix whatever mess I've made here.

'Isabel!' I've tried ringing her phone, but she's not answering, so I settle for just calling out her name between pounding on the front door. If she doesn't let me in soon, there's a worryingly high chance that one of her posh neighbours will call the police on me.

When the door opens, my fist freezes mid-pound, and Isabel's staring back at me, red-eyed, her puffy face warped into such an expression of slack-jawed surprise it would be almost comical if it wasn't so unsettling on someone who is usually so perfectly composed.

'Hi,' I say, lowering my fist, awkwardly pulling the sleeve of my hoodie over it as I dance in place a little, waiting for her to respond.

She just blinks back at me.

'I told you I'd come round and apologise right back at you,' I add when that's all she gives me, aiming for a charming smirk that I think just comes out a bit wobbly through all the nervous energy. 'Can I, y'know, come inside?'

Her bloodshot eyes are still fixed on me, wide and wary, but she nods as she steps aside to let me in, swiping the cuff of her jumper over her face when she thinks I'm not looking, as if that'd hide that she's been crying.

There's an awkward moment then, where the momentum of my frantic bike ride, my big gesture, kind of dissipates, and what's left is me standing there while Isabel stares at the floor, fidgeting with her sleeves, shifting her weight uncomfortably, filled with a kind of restless energy that feels like my wheelhouse, but looks *all wrong* on her.

'Isabel,' I say, taking a step closer, but she's still just standing there, looking around as if desperate to find something to focus on that isn't me.

'Why are you here?' she asks after a second.

'Well, I was looking for you so your house seemed like the most sensible place to start. Next option was to roam the nearby streets with a bell, so,' I tell her with a shrug. She almost cracks a smile at that. Almost.

'No, I mean why are you *here*, Eloise?'

'You sounded upset. And I couldn't figure out why. And I want to help.'

She looks like she might cry again. And we're still just standing in her hallway, the two of us about thirty centimetres apart beside her front door. The house is eerily quiet, and the silence seems to settle into my bones when she doesn't answer. It's the only reason I hear her breath hitch before she speaks again.

'I'm a lesbian, Eloise,' she says eventually, looking literally anywhere but at me. 'As in, I've always *been* a lesbian. I mean, I've known for years. I came out when I was about fourteen, and I've never hidden it since. Until I met you. Because it was so *obvious* how flustered I was around you. And it's been so *strange* being back in the closet again. But I couldn't bear to tell you. Even when we became friends, and it started to feel like lying, because I suppose I thought that if you knew I was a lesbian you'd be more likely to figure it out. And I couldn't stand the thought of that.'

It's the most words I think I've ever heard spill out of her in one go, but she only pauses to pull in another shaky breath, eyes still fixed on the floor, before more tumble out.

'So I think I'd rather you just think I'm rude or awkward than know that the real reason I act so nervous around you is because of *that*. I was mostly just hoping I'd get over it eventually, and we could stay friends, but I was terrified that if you realised before then, maybe you'd start avoiding me, and honestly I just couldn't cope with that.'

When her eyes glance up at mine finally, they're wide and nervous, and her eyebrows are tipped expectantly, but I can't give her anything that she wants.

'Wait, what?' is all I can say. She lets out this groan of

211

frustration that reminds me of the day Benji dropped me off at home, and things start clicking into place a bit.

'God, Eloise, for someone whose mind moves a hundred miles an hour, how are you not getting this?' She takes another deep, trembling breath, and her next words come out slower, more deliberate. 'I've tried. I've tried to ignore it, I've tried to repress it, but it hasn't worked. I really like you, Eloise. Against all my better judgement. And I should have told you before I threw myself at you. It was predatory and wrong, because you thought I was just an awkward straight girl who didn't know how to kiss, but I didn't say I'd never kissed anyone. I said I'd never kissed a *boy*, and I knew it was pretty morally grey as far as half-truths go, but then you were so close to me, and I couldn't imagine telling you to stop, and I—'

She starts spiralling again towards the end there, and I instinctively step towards her, reaching up and taking her face in my hands, startling her quiet.

'You didn't trick me. It wasn't predatory. It wouldn't have been, even if I'd had no idea. But, as it stands, I did figure it out. Kinda. Or at least I suspected, before the kiss.'

'Then why did you kiss me?' she asks, and her voice sounds almost pleading.

'Wanted to,' I tell her, my voice quiet. My eyes glance down at her lips completely accidentally, but I see her notice. My hands are still cupped round her face, and the moment I realise that all I'd have to do is just barely twitch my thumb and I'd be able to run it along her lips, it takes every ounce of effort not to.

'You're not into girls, though, are you? It's the first thing I ever heard you say, when we met. Something about being a raging heterosexual and a bit of a— Well, you said you were straight.'

I try not to laugh at the unfinished sentence. I vaguely remember it being something about me being a bit of a slag, actually.

'Well, sometimes we get things wrong. Sorry we can't all be massive overachievers and figure it out when we're fourteen. Which is very *you*, by the way.'

She laughs, and I actually feel her face grow warm under my hands.

'Are you out to your parents?' I blurt suddenly, and she looks taken aback.

'What – yes. They're not home right now anyway. Why?'

I draw her face to mine, and I feel all the tension in her melt away when she realises what I'm doing. She gives this sigh almost as soon as our lips touch, and an arm snakes its way round my waist, and I feel it more acutely than I think I've ever felt anything.

When we pull apart, she rests her forehead on mine.

'Okay,' I say, my voice breathy and pitchy, and she lets out a small laugh. 'So I take back everything I said yesterday about kissing not being a big deal. That's what kissing should be like.'

She pulls back slightly, just enough to look me in the eye, something indecipherable in her expression.

'I can't tell you how sad it made me when you said that. Like you just didn't know it could be any better.'

'I mean, you've met some of the lads I've been with, right?'

She smiles, just a little, before hooking her finger through the belt loop in my jeans, pulling me close again.

'I guess it's my job to show you it gets better then,' she murmurs, and her voice is low and serious, and honestly it's doing things to me.

She's kissing me again like she did the night before, deeper and more intentional than a moment ago, her whole body pressed against mine, one hand still pulling me towards her by my belt loop, the other hand on my waist.

Which, you know. Might just be the sexiest thing that's ever happened to me.

'Where,' I ask, giving a shaky laugh between jagged breaths when she pulls away, 'the fuck did that come from?'

And she laughs, too, a little light-headed, breathy laugh, before her expression turns to one of horror.

'Oh my God,' she says, and I see the panic in her eyes. 'That was a lot, sorry. I – I just. I can't believe I did that.'

I laugh again, but reach out and pull her close by the waist, leaning my forehead against hers, hoping this might cut the spiral short.

'I don't know how many times I have to tell you to stop apologising,' I say, my voice measured and deliberate. 'But let's be clear that of all things, never apologise for whatever that just was.'

She lets out a kind of hum, and I can't tell if it's embarrassment or contentment. I can't resist raising a hand to touch the pinkness in her cheek, which deepens when I do.

'Just a bit overeager, I think,' she says after a moment, her voice low and sheepish. 'Been dreaming of kissing you for a while.'

'You kissed me yesterday,' I tell her, suppressing a smirk, but she shakes her head.

'Doesn't count. I didn't think it was real.'

'It was.'

I see her raise a hand to her head, and I know before she's even halfway there that she's back to her nervous habit of tucking her hair behind her ears, so I reach up and stop her hand. Then slowly, tentatively, I tuck the strand of hair behind her ear myself.

She's just staring at me. 'How did you not know?' she whispers after a second. 'Look at me. I melt into a puddle whenever you touch me.'

'Isabel,' I tell her, doing my best to implant some seriousness into my voice. 'I didn't even notice myself melting into a puddle. How was I supposed to notice you doing it?'

CHAPTER THIRTY-ONE

'So, what about all the times you just suddenly froze me out?'

We're in Isabel's bedroom, which is exactly as tidy and minimalist as I'd have expected – everything is neat little lines and corners, the tightly made bed, the books arranged into colour-coded columns on the bookshelves, the framed art prints of Renaissance women cutting perfect straight lines into pale stretches of wall. I'm almost nervous to sit on her bed, but Isabel went first, so here we are now. Perched on the end of her bed, me tense because I don't want to mess up the neatly arranged duvet, her tense because . . . Well, because she's Isabel. She seems happy, though. Constantly suppressing small smiles when she thinks I'm not looking.

'It was never sudden, Eloise,' she protests. 'There was always a logic to it.'

'Uh-huh, what logic?'

'Like. Okay, so after the beach. It was *so ridiculously* obvious how into you I was—'

'It absolutely was not.'

'It *was* to anyone paying attention. I just spent the whole day fawning over you. So I shut it down for a while. Thought I'd throw you off the scent.'

'Yeah, and give me whiplash and a stomach ulcer while you were at it.'

'Well, I didn't think you'd care!'

'I . . .' She's got me there, actually. 'Yeah, I didn't think I'd care, either. But I did. A lot. I just didn't understand why.'

'And then, all through last term, I'd say something stupid, look at you for too long or, I don't know, say something so obviously *infatuated*, and I'd panic. Hide away. We were barely even friends – you obviously weren't going to take it well if you figured it out.'

'*Obviously*,' I tease.

She sits up straighter then, shifting her weight to better look me in the eye.

'Can you seriously keep a straight face and tell me you would have reacted with anything other than disgust?'

I struggle to keep a straight face at the best of times, but I work to maintain as serious an expression as possible as I lean in now.

'Isabel,' I tell her, speaking slowly and clearly, 'when we went to the beach, I spent a good ten minutes just staring at your shoulders. Like, physically restraining myself from reaching out and touching them. I was in it from the start, too, Iz. And if you hadn't been so defensive, we might have both figured it out a bit sooner.'

She looks like she might cry. I realise this is maybe the longest stretch of her earnestly meeting my gaze in all the time I've known her. It's not a challenge, not a glare; her eyes are fixed on mine as if by looking away, even for a second, she might miss something vital, and the thought terrifies her.

'I'm sorry we wasted all that time,' she says eventually.

I am, too. If I'm being honest, I'm furious at myself. Because I reach out now, and I take her hand, entwine her fingers in mine, and this warmth floods through me, a held breath and an electric pulse that set my heart racing, and I can't believe I didn't notice it sooner. Didn't realise what it was sooner.

All I can do to show her that is lean forward again, take the hand that's not holding hers and place it on the back of her neck, smile into the kiss as I feel goosebumps there. I wonder if there should be more agonising on my part. Some confusion over whether or not this feels right. But nothing has ever felt more right than Isabel's hand on the small of my back, feeling her nerves melt away after a moment, getting to be the person she relaxes for as she pulls herself closer to me.

We hear the voice call out only half a second before the bedroom door swings open.

'Iiiizzzzz—'

And honestly it's more hilarious than it is embarrassing. Isabel scrambles away just in time when the door is thrown open to reveal Benji Williams standing there, fist still half in the air like he hadn't expected the door to open so easily at his knock. His face is frozen in shock, mouth hanging open a little.

It's so clear how the scene must look through his eyes. Isabel's

218

bright red, drawing into herself and away from me as unsubtly as she possibly could, smoothing down her hair as if we'd been doing anything more intense than a single, slow kiss.

This is the first time I've truly seen the resemblance between them, actually. The easy, carefree smile Benji wore last time I saw him looked so unlike anything I'd ever seen in Isabel's expression. But, right now, they're a matching set of wide-eyed horror.

'I'll, um.' Benji's voice pitches, and I try and fail to muffle a snort of laughter. 'I'll come back later then.' He turns on his heel, closing the door behind him.

Isabel buries her burning face in her hands, and I bury my face in the crook of her neck, still laughing. When she just groans, I wrap an arm round her, kissing her neck softly between peals of laughter, and, by the time she's removed her face from her hands, she's suppressing a grin, too, even though her face still radiates warmth.

'We need to go downstairs and tell him nothing happened,' she says anxiously.

'What if we left it open to interpretation? It'd be funnier.' I grin, but her face is back in her hands, and, when I still can't help but laugh, she throws a pillow at me, which only makes me laugh harder.

'Come on,' she mutters after a moment, and I promise I'm trying not to smile as she takes my hand and leads me downstairs.

Benji's sitting on a stool at the kitchen island, rolling a bottle cap up and down on the marble worktop, and he seems to be torn between embarrassment and smugness when he sees us, the strangest mix of emotions I've ever seen on a person's face. Isabel approaches, head bowed, hand still in mine, and while her dad potters around, putting some shopping into the fridge at the other end of the room, she turns to Benji, eyes narrow.

'You saw nothing,' she hisses.

'All right, Iz,' he murmurs, eyes all twinkling mischief now. 'No need to bring out the big guns. I actually saw nothing. It all looked innocent to me. Apart from, you know, the obvious guilt.'

'Oh.' She lets out a little huff. 'Well. That's okay then.'

'I feel like I should add that it's on me,' I chip in, voice still low to avoid being overheard by their dad, who still hasn't noticed our arrival. 'I probably should have timed my big romantic gesture better.'

Benji's eyes widen just slightly, and so does his smile.

'*Romantic gesture?*' he gasps, but he doesn't do such a good job of keeping his voice low.

'Isabel!' We all turn to face Mr Williams, who is basically an older, balder version of Benji, that same wide smile, though with fewer dimples and more lines, and those same joyful eyes. It's kind of hard to imagine the uptight, tense Isabel I knew for so long growing up surrounded by such easy smiles. 'Who's your friend?'

He closes the fridge door, taking a few strides over to me, hand extended. I drop Isabel's hand and shake his instead.

'Er, Lou,' I tell him. 'Friend from sixth form.'

He tilts his head, frowning just slightly.

'Eloise, Dad,' says Isabel, and his frown dissipates, eyes widening in recognition.

'Ahhh, Eloise. Of course. *The* Eloise.'

'I must be,' I tell him, before turning to smirk at Isabel, who's reddening again.

Benji reaches over and throws an arm round her. She tries to shrug him off, but he's relentless.

'We've embarrassed her,' he croons.

'When aren't you embarrassing me?' Isabel mutters.

'It's lovely to meet you, Lou,' Mr Williams says after a moment, before turning back to look at Isabel, eyebrows raised. 'We may need to have a chat about having girls in the house when me and Mum are both out. Of course, you can always have friends over, but you know the rules for girlfriends.'

'Oh my God, Dad.'

Isabel looks like she might just turn to steam and never return to mortal form. Even Benji gives an embarrassed little wince on her behalf.

'Dad, really? A bit of tact? We don't even know if they're a couple yet.'

'Sorry!' Mr Williams raises his hands in defence. 'You were holding hands!'

'Straight girls hold hands all the time—' I point out, but then trail off.

I'm realising for the first time that I'm not quite the authority on *straight girls* that I thought I was. Maybe there's a whole list of things I assumed were totally normal for straight girls to do that never were. But, before I can consider that too deeply, the implications of the interaction begin to sink in, and I turn back to Isabel, unable to keep the shit-eating grin off my face.

'Wait. Your whole family knows you *like* me?' I ask, and she groans, throwing her hands over her face. 'How did everyone but me know?'

Benji lets out what can only be described as a giggle. This light, completely gleeful peal of laughter in the face of Isabel's complete mortification.

'How did you *not* know?' he asks, and I should feel mocked, but I'm not even entirely convinced he knows *how* to mock someone.

'Thought she hated me for ages,' I tell him with a shrug. Even Mr Williams chuckles a bit at that.

'Classic Iz.' Benji shakes his head, still smirking.

'Come on now, Benji.' Mr Williams's voice is soothing as he turns back to continue putting the shopping in the fridge. 'Be nice. They got there in the end by the looks of things. Good timing, too – Caroline and Wil are coming up soon, aren't they?'

Isabel's face darkens then. It's sudden and strange, a whirlwind flashback to last-term Isabel, her face just shutting down and devoid of any emotion.

It strikes me as a bit odd, as I see it, that I've barely heard anything about Caroline and Wil. But, from the look on her face, there's definitely been something big bubbling away in the background that I don't know about.

'Uh, touchy subject there, Dad,' Benji stage-whispers.

'Oh?' Mr Williams looks as confused as I feel. 'Sorry, darling, everything all right?'

'Yeah,' Isabel grumbles. 'Just Caroline. She's being . . . She might not come up to visit. We're still working it out – we're not sure yet.'

'Well, let me know what she decides. Catherine's been talking about coming up for the Easter holidays, too, so if a guest bedroom is free that saves her having to get a hotel.'

'She's been dodging when I ask,' Isabel says begrudgingly. 'So I don't know how long it'll take her to let me know. Just tell Aunt Catherine she can have a guest room. Worst-case scenario, Wil and Caroline can share the other spare room.'

I'm still reeling from the *other spare room* comment, but, when Benji shoots Isabel a sympathetic look that I don't understand, I'm struck by a realisation. I think Isabel and I have been doing the same thing these past couple of months. She's been using me, I think, the same way I've been using her. Or we've both been using our little Isabel-and-Lou weekend bubble to avoid our problems.

I realise how long it's been since I've spent any time with my friends outside school. A few months ago, my first thought after kissing Isabel for the first time would have been to gather the gang and relay the whole experience scene by scene to them. But none of them even know.

Isabel's got her own problems to deal with, separate from me. I want to share her problems, though. And I want her to share mine. I don't want us to be in a bubble any more.

CHAPTER THIRTY-TWO

Step one of bursting the bubble, I decide, is coming out.

Before I leave her house, Isabel and I talk about it. She keeps insisting that I don't have to, that I'm allowed time to figure myself out fully before I owe anyone an explanation, but I really don't think I need to. I'm not coming out as gay, or bi, or whatever. I'm not in any rush to pin it down. I'm just coming out as someone who's dating Isabel. Someone who's fallen for a girl. Whatever that means for me, in the long run.

When Isabel's in front of me, when she's close enough to kiss, and that warm, exciting feeling fills my stomach, it's so obvious that it isn't a big deal. Of course I like girls. There's nothing in this feeling worth agonising about. Nothing confusing about how Isabel makes my heart race. The only part of it that doesn't make sense is that it took me so long to figure out.

It's after Benji drives me home that things get murkier. At first, I'm not even nervous, just excited to share this new part of me with Mum. But then I get a text telling me she had to stay at work a few extra hours, and I start overthinking it.

What do I even tell her?

Maybe I got this all wrong. Maybe you're not even *allowed* to come out until you've got a label. Like, is it possible to come out when you don't know what you're coming out as?

Hi, Mum! Guess what? I'm [static sounds]!

It makes sense to say bi. It does. Me kissing one girl doesn't automatically make me a lesbian. But, then again, all it took was me kissing one girl to know that I've never – not once – really enjoyed kissing any of the boys I've kissed.

So that's something to consider.

When I was at Isabel's, it didn't feel this deep. I kissed her. I liked it. I wanted to do more of that. But here alone it's like . . . I'm re-evaluating my whole life. I'm learning I've always been a slightly different person than I thought I was. It's not a bad thing. It's just strange. And it's a bigger deal than I expected it to be.

It turns out there's all these things I do that are stereotypically gay, too. Like being a vegetarian. Like the blue hair and the oversized shirts. Also, my cartilage piercings – they're gay, apparently. Isabel filled me in on all this back at hers. She told me how ironic it felt that she'd fallen for the gayest straight girl she'd ever met. But how can I be stereotypically gay if I didn't know I was? I've been a vegetarian for years. And I always thought my hair and fashion sense was, okay, a bit weird, sure, but very uniquely *me*. The ear piercings were mostly because my mum wasn't there to stop me, and they were on offer if you got a bunch done at once. But now I'm finding out my decisions have always been somehow predestined by this realisation that I'm only just having?

Finding out I had ADHD was like this, too. But in that case, the label, helpfully, came first. Yeah, okay, I rejected it for a while – Ms Price mentioned it to me, then when I ignored it, she mentioned it to my mum, who dragged me on to a waiting list kicking and screaming. But when the assessment came around, the doctor asked me all these questions, and mum came prepared with old school reports, a notebook full of examples. Between the two of them, I watched my whole childhood get tipped upside down in the doctor's office like it was someone's ratty old handbag and they could've sworn they'd left their keys in there somewhere. Every action, every memory, got picked up and held against the light and came back a little different. Oh, *that's why I did that*. I still get those moments, months later. I'll be thinking about something harmless, like when I got kicked out of dance lessons as a kid because I was 'disruptive' while I had to wait for the older kids to finish practising. Or that time I burst into tears in primary school because the teacher gave us too many things to do all at once and I didn't know where to start. It's just a constant bombardment of lightbulb moments, revisiting each memory with a new name for it.

I feel like I should be doing something similar right now (is this why I was so obsessed with Kristen Stewart in *Charlie's Angels*? Is this why I got so upset in Year Three when April Miller made a Valentine's Day card for some boy?). But it's so

226

much harder when there's not a clear-cut answer. No clean and simple word for what I am.

The house gets dark around me while I'm turning all this over in my head, and I end up just lying on my bed, staring at the ceiling, waiting to hear the sound of the door unlocking that means Mum's home.

I play it out in my head. I think about telling her I'm bi. And the mum in my head just smiles and makes some joke about how I've doubled my chances of marrying rich. And then I think about telling her I'm a lesbian. And the mum in my head just smiles and makes some joke about how at least she doesn't have to worry about me getting pregnant.

Either way, by the end of it, my mum loves me. Same as she always has. Nothing's changed.

That's just it, isn't it? That's what feels so strange about it. But it's also what finally reassures me as I hear Mum's key in the door. It's what makes me finally relax, my mind eventually slowing as I hear her shuffle upstairs and get in the shower.

Nothing's changed.

Whatever I've learned about myself, whatever it means for me that I fancy Isabel, it's always been true, hasn't it? Just because I didn't notice it doesn't mean it wasn't there. Like the birthmark on the small of my back that Mum keeps taking the piss out of me for only noticing last year.

So maybe it doesn't matter if I take a while to figure out exactly what I am. Because what I am hasn't changed, and it isn't going to change in the time it takes me to figure myself out.

I hadn't realised how anxious the whole thing had been making me until the feeling lifts. But, when it does, it feels really good to take a breath, and make my way out on to the landing as I hear Mum moving between the bathroom and her bedroom. It feels really good that I get to share this with her. Even without a concrete label to give it.

She finds me hovering outside her door when she leaves her bedroom again, jumping a little in surprise when she sees me.

'Hiya, love,' she says when she recovers. 'Thought you'd be asleep by now.'

I just shake my head, following her as she pads along in her pyjamas and slippers back to the bathroom.

'Still awake,' I tell her, fidgeting in the doorway of the bathroom when she makes a beeline for the sink.

'What did you do?' Mum asks, watching me closely as she plucks her toothbrush from the holder. She's got one eyebrow raised, and she's pursing her lips to hide a smirk.

'Nothing,' I say, sounding guiltier than I should.

She assesses me for another second.

'No new piercings, no *visible* tattoos. You're not pregnant, are you?'

I snort, pressing my lips together. 'Definitely not.'

'All right. Shouldn't you be in bed then?'

I nod, but I don't move, just continue lurking, watching her yawn while she squeezes a little blob of toothpaste on to her toothbrush.

'Mum?' I ask just as she starts brushing her teeth. She hums her acknowledgement.

'I kissed a girl,' I blurt out.

Bad timing on my part. There's a moment's pause, a silence that stretches on too long, before she tilts back her head to ensure the toothpaste stays put as she murmurs her next words, a little garbled.

'Course you did, Katy Perry.'

I roll my eyes. Outdated music references aside, I don't think she's being dismissive on purpose. I don't think she knows there's anything real to dismiss. She probably thinks I'm messing with her, and she's being chill. I hurry over to where she's standing, squeezing between her and the sink, pushing myself up to sit on the rim in front of her so that she's looking me in the eye.

'I kissed Isabel, Mum. I think I've liked her for a long time.'

That seems to register a bit better.

'Hm,' she murmurs over her toothbrush, seeming to consider, and I hold my breath for a long moment. Eventually, she taps me a few times, and though it takes a few nudges, I finally realise what she means, hopping off the sink so she can spit.

'Well,' she says, after a moment, 'it would explain why you two were so obsessed with each other.'

I don't take my eyes off her. 'So, you're okay with that?'

'Well, I only met her briefly, but she seemed nice. Very pretty.'

'Well, yes, but you're okay with her being a girl?'

'She's not a Tory, is she?'

I bark out a laugh, part humour and part giddy relief. 'No, Mum, she's not.'

'Good, good. Can never be too sure with those London types.'

For a second, I think that's it. She's ready for bed, and the conversation's done. But then Mum sits down on the edge of the bath. Even through her exhaustion, she smiles at me and pats the spot next to her.

'So tell me more about her then.'

And I do. I can already feel the bubble expanding, just a bit, as I tell her about our weekends together. I can feel Isabel becoming part of my Real Life as I tell my mum about the way she blushes so easily, especially for someone so intent on hiding her emotions. I tell her about Benji and Mr Williams, who are very different from Isabel, but seem to complement her so well. I tell her that I think I've been falling for Isabel for a while. Longer than I ever realised. Maybe as long as Isabel's been falling for me. Mum's smiling the whole time, a small, tired, warm smile.

'It sounds like she's good for you,' she says when I'm finished.

I hug her, tight.

CHAPTER THIRTY-THREE

With that sorted, there's school. I think Isabel would have been content to lie for me. Stay hidden a bit longer so I can come out in my own time. But I don't want that. I don't think she would have enjoyed it much, either, really.

It's less scary, the thought of being out at school. I think that's because I don't owe the school an explanation. Once my friends know, people will just see me and Isabel together, and they'll make their own assumptions. Some of them will probably be wrong, but I don't care much either way, as long as I don't have to faff about explaining it.

My big idea was to start aggressively necking or something just as the first bell goes, where enough people can see it for word to get out, letting the gossip mill do the work for us. But Isabel helpfully pointed out that this maybe wouldn't be very fair to, y'know, my best friends in the whole world who *maybe* deserve, like, an actual conversation about it or something, I guess. So I text the group chat and ask them all to meet me a bit early in the common room on Monday. Everyone but Lily agrees, but that isn't new.

Isabel's looking at me with desperate eyes when I arrive.

'Thank God,' she says with a sigh. 'They've been grilling me for information.'

'Yeah, Lou, you cannot just send *Isabel and I need to tell you guys something*, then show up late,' Katie whines.

'Well, if you let her actually talk,' says Mel, 'then she'll tell us now.'

'Lads, let her speak in her own time.'

'Thanks, Jas,' I say with a small laugh, throwing my bag off and pulling out a chair next to Isabel. Three pairs of eyes bore into us, and I watch with a small smile as Isabel ducks her head a bit, tucking the hair behind one ear.

'Er, so.' I let out a long exhale. 'Jesus, Iz, how do I even do this? You've got more experience with this than me – you say it.'

She smirks, nudging me with an elbow. 'Exactly – you need the practice.'

I groan. '*Soooooo*, I learned something new about myself.'

Isabel giggles, but presses her fingertips to her mouth guiltily when I shoot her a look. *Fine, fuck it.*

'I'm probably gay,' I say simply.

'Probably?' Isabel asks quietly.

I groan again. 'All right, Ms Semantics. I *definitely* like girls. I *probably* don't like guys. I'm not straight, that much I can confirm. Oh, and I'm not straight with Isabel. Almost forgot that part.'

It's almost worth the struggle of finding the right words just

232

to watch Katie gasp so hard she swallows her chewy, choking for a second, and Mel's eyes widen so much I'm actually worried they might fall out of her head. Only Jas seems calm and collected, leaning back a bit in her seat, arms folded, a smug smile playing across her lips.

'Fucking *finally*.'

Excuse me, what?

But Jas is looking at Isabel, who's turning pink.

'She, uh, she knew I liked you.'

I look between them, head spinning in two different directions like some kind of cartoon character.

'*How?* Since *when*? I didn't even know!'

'That's because you're an idiot,' Jas says, her eyes warm. The words remind me of something, though.

'New Year's Eve?' I breathe after a moment. Isabel's blush deepens, and Jas nods.

'I confronted her. It was so obvious that you were obsessed with each other. She admitted it, I told her to talk to you, she caught you staring and ran away. You went and talked to her. Turns out you didn't talk about the *right* thing, but you got there in the end.'

'I don't think I can be given the blame for this. I had *no* idea I was even into girls, let alone Isabel.'

'Oh, please.' We all turn to look at Mel. '*Isabel looked at me today, what does that mean? Isabel said something mean to me – excellent, I'm gonna think about it for three days straight.* In hindsight, yeah, it was obvious as hell.'

Isabel's trying so hard to smother a laugh that it comes out as a sort of whimper, her hand pressed over her mouth.

Katie raises a hand. 'I had no idea – if that helps.'

'It does, Katie, thank you,' I say, nodding, ignoring Isabel still struggling to contain herself.

'Katie had her own drama to deal with,' says Mel. 'Doesn't mean it wasn't obvious, just that Katie didn't get a moment to notice it.'

'Oh, like you knew,' I scoff. 'I saw the shock on your face just now.'

'Hey, I said in *hindsight*. I know a lot of stuff, but I never claimed to be a dating expert.'

And maybe it's just the giddy relief of all of this, but I can't keep from laughing at that, and the others seem to relax, too, the formality of the meeting over as the bell rings and everyone grabs their bags, chuckling. They all give me and Isabel a hug before they leave, telling me that, joking aside, they're happy for us – and mostly happy that they don't have to listen to me whine about her any more.

When everyone else has gone, though, Isabel's still beside me, and Katie hovers, indecisive, by the door.

After a moment, she turns back, her face all scrunched up with determination.

'Me too,' she says to us, her voice low. 'But I'm not ready to tell everyone yet.'

I try to swallow my shock for her sake. She seems way more nervous about it than I was.

'Secret's safe with me,' I tell her, at the same time as Isabel says, 'Lily, right?'

I look at Isabel in horror. Like, suddenly I'm the one with tact?

But she's looking at Katie, and Katie's looking back at her, and there's so much understanding between them.

Katie just nods once, her chin dimpling for a brief second as her lower lip wobbles.

And suddenly it all makes sense. She's in love with Lily. Of course she is.

'Oh, hun.' I pull her into a hug, and she holds me tight for a second. I think of all the years she's fawned over Lily, the way Lily thrives off the attention. How hurt Katie must have been when she started seeing Jay. How hard it must have been, the double knife edge of having to keep Lily's secret from her friends on top of keeping her own secret from Lily. I hug her harder.

This is my second chance to expand the bubble.

'Let us come over tonight,' I tell her quietly. 'You can have a vent in private, yeah?' I feel her nod, and, when I let go, she wraps Isabel in a quick hug before she turns and flees the common room. Isabel looks like she's just been blessed by the Pope himself.

'You're in,' I say to her, grinning. 'You're one of us now.'

'I'm pretty sure I was in already. You were the only one who hated me.'

'I . . . All right, you got me there. But now you have special girlfriend privileges. So that's gotta mean something, right?'

235

Her expression shifts into something unreadable. It's almost funny: she's just full-on malfunctioned for a second. Then, when she blinks back into existence, it stops being funny.

'Girlfriend?'

Oh. Er. Shit.

'I mean, are we not? I just thought because – I mean, it's not like we're *dating*, in the traditional sense. Like, we didn't just go on a first date and get to know each other. We know each other already, and then we kissed, and I mean – there was a speech, Isabel. A speech! You gave a *whole* speech! I thought that was— Are we not?'

It isn't helping my stammering buffoonery that the whole time I'm trying to speak, Isabel's getting more and more flustered.

'I'm sorry,' I say, taking a step back towards the common-room door. 'I shouldn't have assumed.'

But my movement triggers something in her. Her frozen embarrassment thaws just in time for her to act on instinct and reach out to grab my hand before I can retreat any further.

'No, don't be sorry,' she says, her voice laced with panic. 'I just wasn't sure, that's all.'

I struggle for a second. 'You gave a speech,' is my only feeble response.

There's a long pause, and then, to my surprise – and I think hers, too – Isabel laughs.

'You're never going to let me live that speech down, are you?'

'I'll consider it if you agree to be my girlfriend,' I say with a smirk, emboldened by her laughter.

'Of course I'm your girlfriend, Eloise. I'm sorry, I thought I'd made it clear back at my house that I'm . . . well, that I'm in deep. Have been for a long time. I just wasn't sure that you felt the same.'

I shrug, trying not to let it show how happy that makes me.

'I keep telling you: you have to remember the kinds of lads I've dated up until now. I don't know the rules for an actual relationship.'

'Maybe there are no rules,' she says, pulling me a bit closer in the empty common room. I feel my head swim a little with how close she is, and it reminds me again how good this feels. How sure I am of Isabel.

'I can work with that. I'm no good at rules.'

'So, girlfriends?' she asks, leaning in close.

I nod, a bit too energetically, considering how close she is to kissing me, and we bump heads a little, but she doesn't seem to mind. She just laughs a little into the kiss.

We're both late to English. Neither of us cares.

CHAPTER THIRTY-FOUR

'I'm sorry I wasn't paying enough attention to see it coming,' Katie says sheepishly, already in her pyjamas as we all settle in on her bed, backs against the wall, facing the TV while it plays some cheesy romcom that none of us are really watching.

'Don't be.' I wave her apology away. 'You had a lot going on. We were both dealing with our own stuff. I'm sorry I haven't been exactly on it with figuring out how you're feeling, either.'

She shakes her head. 'You came over a few times to watch *One Day at a Time* and pretended not to notice me cry – you carried out your friend duties.'

'I've been there,' Isabel says after a moment, her voice still a bit timid, as if she's not sure whether she's intruding on some sacred in-group moment. 'When Elena wears a suit to her quinceañera? It gets me every time.'

'How did I not know either of you were gay?'

'Lou, you were the most oblivious straight girl I've ever met. Even *while* you were mooning over Isabel.'

I throw some popcorn at her, but it's such a relief to see Katie being herself again. She's been so closed off since all this Lily drama started, but tonight with me, her and Isabel, she's coming out (no pun intended) of her shell again. Maybe even more so than before.

So, naturally, I push my luck.

'How long have you liked her?' I ask, after a moment of silence has passed. 'Lily, I mean.'

For a second, I think she might not answer. She just hangs her head, staring at her hands picking at her fingernails in her lap, and I feel an elbow dig into my side.

'*Ow?*'

When I turn my head, Isabel is glaring at me, like I've just said something completely tactless. I only have time to shake my head at her like *what?* before Katie answers, and we both turn our attention back to her.

'I think since Year Seven? Right from the start, really. But I obvs didn't know, like, what it was. I just knew she was my best friend, and all girls feel like that about their best friend. And then remember the summer after Year Ten? She went on holiday to Spain with me and my mum and dad, and we were always in our bikinis, and she was just so . . . I mean, okay, I'll say it: she was proper fit.'

I can't suppress a snort, and it gets me another elbow from Isabel, but Katie seems unfazed.

'And that was when I was like oh, okay. So this isn't normal, right? Up until then, I was, like, yeah, every girl thinks her best friend is the prettiest girl in the world and, yeah, y'know, every girl would probably kiss her friend in a *totally no homo hundred per cent besties* kinda way if they could, right? But then I literally could *not* stop staring at her boobs.'

I snort again, and this time Katie giggles, too. She stops staring into her lap, and her face is pink with embarrassment, but she's looking up at us with this kind of giddy amusement in her expression that I haven't seen for a long time.

'Yeah, that's when I was, like, this is not a heterosexual thing to feel.'

'Definitely not,' Isabel agrees after a moment of apparent indecision on whether to further chastise me for my lack of sensitivity, choosing instead to allow herself a smile, too.

'I can't believe you've had to keep it quiet for so long,' I tell Katie once the giggles subside.

She shrugs. 'It felt gross. Not the liking girls part, I mean – I accepted that quite quick – just the . . . I dunno, *leering* after my best mate part.'

'That's definitely a thing,' Isabel says, jumping in. 'The predatory lesbian trope has *not* done us any favours.'

'It's different, though, right?' I ask, and they both look at me as if maybe, as the brand-new baby gay, I don't get an input here, but I charge in anyway. 'You looking at Lily's boobs and going *oh no, I fancy her* is NOT the same as some lad staring at her boobs and forgetting there's a person under them. You're not *objectifying* her is the difference. You're still allowed to find someone fit.'

'That's . . . actually very true.' Isabel's voice has an unflattering amount of surprise in it.

'I'm very wise,' I tell her, leaning in close while I radiate smugness.

'I'm very happy for you two,' Katie interjects, 'but I'm going to need you to be a thousand per cent less couple-y while I'm talking about my tragic five-year crush.'

I'm hit with a brainwave. 'What if we got you on some dating apps?'

Katie rolls her eyes. 'I've got bigger problems right now than finding a *new* girl to break my heart.'

'O ye of little faith. We'll find you the most wonderful girl in the world to *mend* your broken heart. What's your type?'

She hesitates, then winces as she gives her answer.

'Lily,' she says, like she's embarrassed to even be saying it.

'We're going to need a slightly wider range than that.'

'You don't have to, Katie,' says Isabel. 'It's okay to take some time to get over her before moving on.'

Katie nods slowly. 'I think I am. Getting over her. You know how I know?'

I shake my head.

'I'm *pissed*. I'm . . . I'm so angry at her. At first, I was just heartbroken. But now I'm starting to get past being sad that she'll never like me back, and it's making all this room in my head to be furious that she didn't treat me better. Whatever else I felt, she was my friend, and she treated me like some lovesick puppy she could play with.'

I, for one, believe Katie when she says she's pissed. I can hear it in her voice, a rising anger that seems strange in her. But it does something to me, hearing that anger turned on to Lily. Gives me this uncomfortable gnawing feeling in the pit of my stomach. All I can think about is how stressed Lily looked in the common room with me and Mel.

We never ended up telling Katie about it. It seemed like too much to handle, and I immediately threw myself back into the Isabel bubble to distract myself.

'I know she treated you badly,' I say, 'but I . . . I can't stop wondering if she's been trying to reach out.' My fidgety hands betray the guilt I feel as I say it, picking at a bleeding cuticle.

Isabel reaches out a hand, featherlight, to still mine.

'What –' Katie's voice still hasn't lost that angry edge – 'by muting the group chat and avoiding us at school?'

'Well, okay, solid point, but—'

'I don't care how she feels right now. I just want my friends back.' Katie deflates as she says it, and she looks so sad it knocks my follow-up argument right out of the window. 'I might have lost Lily forever, but I was always so scared youse were only friends with her, and I just tagged along. And these past few months have kind of proved it. This is the first time I've hung out with anyone in ages.'

'That's not on you, Katie. We've all been kinda . . . fractured since January. I've been dealing with the whole *figuring out I like Isabel* thing. And we've been leaving you to deal with the Lily fallout, and Mel to deal with revision stress, and Jas to deal with trying to keep us all holding on at once, and it's not fair.

242

We need a girls' night. But . . . maybe we can figure out what to do about Lil after.'

Katie's lip wobbles a bit as she nods, and she dives in to wrap both me and Isabel in a sideways hug.

'I'd really, really like that,' she tells us.

CHAPTER THIRTY-FIVE

It takes some wrangling – and many promises to Mel to test her on her revision to make up for the lost evening of work – but we manage to arrange a pub night the next Friday, all of us (minus Lily) just spending a long night eating burgers and drinking cheap cocktail pitchers.

I've missed this. A lot. And, from the way everyone seems to unwind as the night goes on, I think the rest of them have, too.

I forget, sometimes, how well Isabel already gets on with my friends. It was only me she had a problem with at the start, after all. But it surprises me, still, how seamlessly she's fitted into the group now that we're a couple.

I catch Jas a few times shooting us a warm smile whenever Isabel takes my hand. Or whenever I lean across to push Isabel's hair back. Which I do often. It's insane how much of a thrill it gives me, just touching her. After all those months of hating her, of thinking she hated me, when the lightest touch or the smallest glance would set my stomach squirming. It still feels unreal that I'm able to reach out so casually now, place a hand on the small of her back, respond to an infuriated glare with a quick kiss – which is my favourite thing to do. I honestly wish I'd thought of it when we were first cultivating our little rivalry because it leaves her hilariously flustered. I'd have seriously won every round of our verbal sparring matches if I'd known to do that from the start. And, from the way she still blushes at my touch, I'm guessing she's feeling the same.

'Could you two be a bit less in love, please?' Mel groans, pouring herself another glass of strawberry daiquiri. 'It's actually quite painful to watch.'

Isabel's complexion switches rapidly from the flushed pink my hand on her back has elicited to the furious red of embarrassment.

'Soz that you're jealous,' I tell Mel, shrugging.

'If you think I have time to even *think* about wanting a relationship, you've seriously misunderstood how stressed I am.'

'Quick,' I tell her, not missing a beat, 'tell me one feature of the chloroplast that allows protein to be synthesised inside the chloroplast and why it's different to other parts of the cell.'

Her eyes widen, but she fires back her answer almost instantly.

'DNA. Because the DNA molecules in the chloroplast are circular, but nuclear DNA is linear.'

'I have no idea if that's right, but you answered fast enough so I'm guessing it is.'

Mel laughs, and it's the first time in ages I've seen her visibly relax. Isabel, however, is just staring at me.

'Where,' she asks slowly, 'is that energy for *your* revision?'

I shrug. I've been falling behind again in school, and Isabel has definitely noticed. Thing is, I can't juggle it all, right? I ignored *everything* for a while to focus on Isabel. And Isabel in turn helped me with school stuff because it was an excuse to spend time together. But then I neglected my friends, and my hobbies, and my whole life for a bit. And now I'm trying not to do that. I'm working on being a good friend again. And okay, so I haven't had time to be a good student, or to get much marathon training done. But hey, isn't it supposed to be a thing that *anything is better than nothing and doing something is more important than perfect*? Or something along those lines.

And seeing Mel relax is worth it in that moment. Even if Isabel is still giving me a bit of a Look. Even if that Look isn't doing anything for the little ball of anxiety that tightens in my stomach when I think about mock exams next term. Even if the Look feels, somehow, like Isabel is seriously disappointed in me.

Mel shakes her head. 'I can't believe you have my practice questions memorised.'

'I can. I think I know your flashcards better than mine at this point,' Katie says, laughing.

Isabel looks like she might still say something more, but I feel her phone buzz in her pocket beside me, and when she takes it out her eyes widen.

I catch a glimpse of the screen before she hurries to stand up. Her friend Caroline is FaceTiming her.

'I'm going to take this in the toilets,' she says quickly. 'Sorry, I'll be right back.'

Jas looks at me when Isabel flees, and I just shrug.

'Mystery friend from home,' I tell her. 'Something weird going on there – haven't had a chance to ask her about it yet.'

'Is she okay?'

It strikes me that I don't know. She's my girlfriend so I should know. Shouldn't I?

'I think so?'

Jas looks worried.

'I'll ask when she gets back,' I reassure her.

'Speaking of weird friend things,' says Mel. *Oh no.* 'Lou, we never ended up telling everyone about Lil in the common room.'

Oh great. This is not a conversation I want to have right now. But there's that uncomfortable guilty feeling in my stomach again. And, no matter how Katie might react, it does feel important.

'She did seem really weird,' I admit.

'Like she was looking for a fight,' Mel adds.

'I . . . dunno. I think she was on edge, and we fought because she was feeling defensive, but I can't help thinking she was gonna try and talk to us before everything blew up.'

'I've seen her around, the few times she's actually been at school,' Jas adds, looking worried. 'She doesn't seem as . . . vibrant as usual.'

'Obnoxious, you mean?' Katie mutters.

'We go on Easter break next week,' Jas continues, ignoring Katie's comment. 'If she's not answering texts, I don't know how we can talk to her outside school.'

'Yeah, I don't think she'd appreciate us showing up at her door.'

Mel smiles a little as she says it, as if she's imagining Lily's face if we all just turned up at her house. It is quite funny. But then everyone falls into silence after a moment, as if we're all trying to find a solution and coming up blank. I'm sick of devoting all this energy to unfixable problems. I'm sick of worrying and stressing and hoping. Isabel's upstairs, taking what looked like an incredibly stressful call, and she's someone I *can* help. Someone I can show up for and not be shot down.

'I'm going to check on Isabel,' I announce, the quiet already becoming uncomfortable.

Jas smiles. 'Good idea.'

I'm half expecting Isabel to pass me on her way back – she's been gone a while – but I just keep walking until I hit the toilets. There's a few girls taking selfies in the mirror, a couple of stalls being used, and I just stand there like a lemon for a second, wondering if maybe I should call out, until I hear her voice.

'Caroline, don't be insane – that's literally the whole point.'

She's muttering in a stall at the end of the room. Something about her voice makes me not want to interrupt. She sounds close to tears. When I slip quietly into the stall beside her, I can't see her feet. I wonder if she's tucked up on the seat, hugging her knees.

There's a moment of quiet, and I hold my breath. I think Isabel might be, too, but she must have grabbed her headphones on her way up here because I can't hear what's got her so tense.

'No,' she says after a moment, voice strained to the point of breaking. 'If that was the point, I'd be coming back to London. You think I don't miss home? But you're coming *here*, to see where I live, to meet my new friends, to meet—'

Somebody cuts her off, and she lets them.

'You know Eloise can't afford the kind of hotel you're thinking of in York for, what, two weeks?'

Oh. They're talking about me. Feels a little rude to assume what I can and can't afford, but I mean she's not wrong. I'm not sure I could even afford a Travelodge for two weeks.

'Maybe you could just come to Liverpool!'

Whatever Caroline's saying has Isabel breathing heavily. She starts speaking a few times, but can't seem to get more than a sound out before stopping.

'I am *not* embarrassed about my girlfriend, Caroline,' she hisses eventually.

And, well, it should be nice. It *should* feel like she's standing up for me. But there's just something a little too defensive in her voice. I hadn't even considered that she was embarrassed about me, but now I'm not so sure.

'Fine, don't come. It's fine. Let Wil come on their own. I don't care.'

But she's full-on crying now. So I'm not sure I believe that, either.

There's a long pause then, with only a few sniffles and murmurs of agreement from Isabel, but whatever Caroline's saying must have taken a more soothing turn because the sniffling starts to subside after a while.

'I haven't forgotten. I *know* what I said about this place, but I— No, of course I still miss London. What kind of a question is that? I'd be there with you right now if I could, but— I just want you to . . . No, I know. It's fine. I'll see you next time I visit. Tell Wil I'm excited to see them. Yeah, okay. Bye.'

It shouldn't hurt as much as it does, to hear that. Isabel shit-talking Liverpool to her friends isn't news – I overheard her doing that on the very first day we met – but the part about how she'd be in London right now if she could cuts more deeply than I'd like. I know the girls would say I'm being dramatic, that Isabel's just smoothing over an argument with Caroline. And she's defending me, right? She's arguing with her friend because she cares enough to fight for me. That's something, right?

I sit in silence as I hear Isabel unlock her stall, spend a few moments at the sink, then leave. When I get back downstairs, she announces that her friend Wil is coming for Easter break. She tells the table excitedly that their train gets in next Friday night, asking if there's a time when everyone's free to meet them.

She doesn't mention Caroline.

She must know that I was in the bathroom at the same time as her, but she doesn't ask me what I heard. I don't tell her, either.

I just take her hand under the table and hope it's enough.

Chapter THIRTY-SIX

'Eloise! Is that Eloise?'

I hear the voice before Isabel's front door even opens, and I'm holding back a laugh as I stand on her front step, hearing a conversation on the other side of the door.

'Don't embarrass me,' comes Isabel's voice.

'Would I ever? Come on, I want to meet her!'

The door opens, and Isabel is standing there, red in the face, with the lankiest person I've ever seen standing behind her, a lilac silk shirt, unbuttoned almost to their waist, looking absolutely stunning alongside their dark skin and bright green hair. They're leaning all faux-casual against the wall, like, *oh, there's someone at the door? I hadn't even noticed.*

'Hi,' Isabel says, her voice low and embarrassed.

'Hi,' I say back with a grin. 'Who's your friend?'

'Oh, me?' The person behind her – who I already know is Wil – jumps to attention, a hand on their chest. 'Well, I'm just Isabel's bestie, recently bumped up to top spot, actually.'

'There was never a top spot,' says Isabel grumpily as she steps aside to let me in.

'No, no, it's fine. Caroline's loss is my win. And you must be Eloise? Excellent hair.'

'Lou is fine,' I say, laughing. 'Only Isabel calls me Eloise. And right back at you, with the excellent hair, I mean.'

'I know,' they sing-song, twirling one of their curls round their finger. Their hair is a vibrant sage green that complements my blue wonderfully, but they haven't half-arsed it like I have: they're green right down to the roots.

'All right, shall we go?' Isabel says, not really asking before grabbing Wil by the wrist and pulling them out of the door with her. Isabel, I'm coming to learn, really does carry her Little Sibling Energy around everywhere she goes.

'What's the plan?' I ask.

'Well, Wil's here for all of Easter break, so I thought we could give them some of the Liverpool grand tour you gave me?'

'I'd like to start with the gay bookshop, please,' Wil says, leaning an elbow on each of our shoulders as we begin walking towards the station. 'And I've been informed that there's a drag bar that doesn't ID?'

I grin. 'That can be arranged. Iz, you really hung on my every word back when I was showing you around, huh?'

Isabel's face reddens as she fixes her gaze on the ground.

'It was interesting,' she mutters.

'She *luuurrrvveeddd* you,' Wil teases, and Isabel elbows them in the stomach, hard.

It's . . . easy with Wil. Much easier than I expected. I knew that Isabel's argument had been with Caroline. Whatever was going on, Wil had no part in it, but I guess I just made my assumptions anyway. Caroline, from the little I've been able to piece together, sounds exactly like the kind of person I'd have expected to be friends with Last-Year-Isabel. The Isabel who was better than me, better than this city. Wil, though? They're more like Benji than I expected. And, to be honest, a lot more like me.

'So, what ended up happening with your friend Lily?' Wil asks as we settle in on the train into town. Isabel just widens her eyes, giving Wil a little kick.

'What? I'm making conversation! I'm not allowed to make conversation?'

Isabel just stammers something about it not being either of their business. And it's weird. She seems genuinely embarrassed. Not just grumbling little sister being teased for fun, but, like, she's really ashamed to have confided in Wil about this.

'It's okay that you told them,' I tell her, frowning. 'The girls are your friends, too. You're allowed to talk to people about things that happen with your mates.'

'*That's* what *I* said!' Wil raises their hands.

'I suppose,' Isabel concedes.

I'm a little worried that she's been feeling like this, but it doesn't seem like a conversation to have in front of Wil, so I just reach out and take her hand for now, hoping it's enough to reassure her.

'Not much has happened, really,' I tell Wil. 'We spent the

last week or so of term trying to come up with an action plan, but she's barely been in school, so it's not like we could approach her. We're hoping she'll be back after Easter. Exams are coming up so she's gotta come into school sometime.'

Wil shrugs. 'Sounds like she's just been a bit of a shitty friend.'

'No . . .' I look at Isabel, who's staring at the ground again. 'I mean, we're pissed, but she . . . It's not unforgivable. She got in with a bad lad – it happens.'

I'm not even sure what makes me say that. Up until recently, I've been firmly on the *hold-Lily-accountable* train, but I'm suddenly feeling defensive. Like the idea of Isabel and Wil gossiping about Lily being a 'shitty friend' is suddenly making me bristle.

I wasn't lying when I said Isabel has every right to talk about this. That part isn't the problem. It's this irrational feeling that she's judging Lily somehow. Even after everything, that feels wrong to me.

'Jay's got a way of being . . . manipulative,' I say, dropping Isabel's hand to pick at a cuticle. 'Not on any major level, but I think – I think there's more to it. She seems really off recently.'

Wil, to their credit, leans back a little in their seat and seems to genuinely consider this.

'Remember Heather?' they ask, and I frown a little, until I realise they're talking to Isabel, whose face reddens just a little.

'Who's Heather?' I say, looking between the two of them.

'An ex,' Isabel mutters.

Okay, trying to ignore the little swooping in my stomach at

Isabel having exes. Those are a totally normal thing for a person to have.

'She broke up with Isabel a few years ago, and, like, *immediately* started dating our other friend Alexis. So naturally we were all furious. It was clear she'd been cheating – emotionally cheating at least – and it's just bad form, right? If you go to the same school as your ex, still run in the same circles or whatever, you just, you wait a polite amount of time before you go public with someone new. But . . .'

Isabel's face has been growing increasingly red throughout this little monologue, but when Wil says *but*, I see her expression switch to realisation, like she's connecting a few dots.

'Oh. Yeah. No, we found out that Alexis had been really cruel to Heather. Convinced her that I was just with her out of pity or something. Then, when she'd got her to break up with me, she did the same for all of our friends until she'd completely isolated her.'

'Oh,' I say. 'Okay, yeah, I see the comparison.'

'Yeah, like, Heather's behaviour looked bad on paper. But sometimes there's a twisted kind of logic to it. If something similar is happening with your friend, maybe it's just important to show her you still care.'

I nod, thinking again about Lily's face that day in the common room.

Isabel looks at me, all concern. 'Maybe we don't think about Lily until break's over,' she suggests quietly. 'Maybe we take your mind off it a bit, until there's something concrete we can do.'

I nod. I'd like that very much.

And mostly the day is wonderful after that. Wil apologises for bringing the 'vibe down' and immediately takes off on a million more cheerful conversations.

As promised, we do News From Nowhere, then I take Wil to the vintage shop because they've already showered me with compliments for the bright yellow shirt I'm wearing, one of the ones I bought when I took Isabel there, which Isabel absolutely hates.

Mostly we wander. It feels more aimless than it did with just me and Isabel, but Wil has more of a relaxed air about them, a feeling that as long as you're walking it doesn't really matter where you're going – you're still getting an experience out of it. Isabel, though, is excited to be able to point out buildings and landmarks that I pointed out to her, and I realise how little time it's been since we started getting to know each other. We fell for each other so fast, so completely, I forget, until we're outside the Liver Building, that it's only been a couple of months since the last time we were here.

We're just getting started, Isabel and I.

We're in Starbucks. I think that's one of the laws of thermodynamics or something, right? All teenagers wandering aimlessly round a city will, inevitably, find themselves sitting in a Starbucks before the day is out.

The plan was to get just enough coffee in us to provide the energy we needed to do a little more sightseeing, but I don't

257

think we're sticking to that any more. Isabel and I finished our iced lattes a while back, and Wil is starting on a second Frappuccino.

'Someone's in high demand,' they tease as Isabel's phone buzzes incessantly. It's been going off all day.

'I'm ignoring it. It's probably Caroline seeing our Insta posts and becoming suddenly very apologetic about the whole thing.'

'Hm. Well, I for one would like to see what Caroline looks like while apologetic.' Wil grins as they reach into Isabel's pocket, sliding her phone out seamlessly. 'Oh, uh. Not Caroline,' they say with a grimace, offering the phone back to Isabel.

She reads for a moment, becoming increasingly more panicked as she does.

'Oh crap!' Isabel locks her phone. 'My aunt's train is due in any minute. I totally forgot. I, uh . . .' She hesitates, eyes flickering between me and Wil.

'I've met Catherine,' Wil says, hands in the air, 'and it's bad enough that I have to spend the next two weeks under the same roof as her. I have no interest in meeting her at the station. You go. I'll keep Lou company.'

Isabel's worried gaze flicks back to me.

I shrug. 'That sounds good. I'm happy either way.'

She looks oddly relieved, and she darts in for a quick kiss before turning to leave. She only gets a couple of steps away before hesitating, spinning back round, hair fanning out behind her and phone still clutched to her chest.

'I forgot. My dad invited you to dinner. With my aunt, I mean. Sometime this week, if you'd like?'

'Me? Sure. I like dinner.'

She smiles, a tight, anxious kind of smile, and then she's gone.

'*Woof.*'

I look over at Wil, eyebrow raised.

'I'm just saying,' they say with a shrug. 'Couldn't be me. Catherine's a lot. You've met Isabel's mum?'

I nod. I've only met her once, after me and Isabel started dating, and she's a bit scary if I'm honest.

'She's like an older, richer caricature of Mrs Williams.'

'I'm lovable,' I say, feigning more disinterest than I actually feel.

'You are, you really are. But I'm not sure Catherine's capable of experiencing love.'

I snort, pressing a guilty hand to my mouth to stifle it.

'That's an Isabel thing!' Wil points at my hand excitedly.

'Huh?'

'The thing you just did, with the fingers over the lips, like you can shove the giggle right back in. *You* got that from your girlfriend. She does it all the time.'

I pull my hand away from my mouth, and I realise they're right. I think it's supposed to be cute that I'm picking up Isabel-isms. But I've never been embarrassed about my laugh before.

I don't like that feeling. I don't like it at all. It's not me. I'm always the one being shushed at the cinema. I'm always the one getting glares for being too loud in the restaurant. Sitting in

259

detention for laughing too hard at a whispered conversation in class. I used to be proud of that.

If Wil notices that I've suddenly got all introspective, they don't show it. They're busy moving the straw around in their Frappuccino, seemingly trying to mix together the last dregs of cream and coffee to a specific consistency.

Wil's not what I expected when I pictured Isabel's London friends. They definitely haven't picked up any Isabel-isms over the years. But they complement each other somehow. Wil is loud and affectionate and warm. Isabel is hushed and embarrassed and collected. They don't match, but they slot in together perfectly.

I hesitate, wondering if what I want to say is too much.

'You know, it never used to make sense that Isabel liked *me*, of all people,' I say eventually, biting the bullet. 'We just seemed too different. But the more I meet the people in her life, the more it starts to make sense, actually.'

'That's because you've only met the good ones,' Wil says with a chuckle. 'Me and Benji, right? The rest – uh, well . . . the rest aren't quite our kind of people. But they are Isabel's.'

I'm not sure what to say to that. 'Like Caroline?'

They press their lips together, raising their eyebrows a little.

'Exactly like Caroline. But she's just . . . She epitomises the problem. She's one of Isabel's best friends, always has been, and *God*, she's awful. But she's not the only one. Isabel's got a ton of friends like that. Cruel, pompous, rich arseholes that Isabel fits right in with. Not because she's cruel or pompous herself, but because . . . there's nothing Isabel hates more than not fitting in.'

It shouldn't surprise me, really. I know Isabel now. In fact, I know her well enough to know that I don't know her all that well. She hides so much beneath the surface, keeps so much inside for fear of embarrassing herself. I've seen more of her these past few months than any of my friends have, and even I've barely scratched that surface. It shouldn't surprise me that she's the same way with the Carolines of the world, but it does.

'I overheard part of the call,' I say. 'When Caroline told Isabel she wasn't visiting.' I'm not sure why I'm admitting this to Wil, when I haven't even said it to Isabel, but they're nodding as I speak.

'Isabel said she thought you might have.'

So, okay, both Isabel and I are nil–nil on the communication front then, I guess.

'I haven't caused any problems there, have I?'

They're shaking their head enthusiastically before I've even finished speaking.

'Dear God, no. If you think you might have the power to cause problems between Isabel and Caroline, I'm begging you to do so. But I don't think anyone does.' They take a long sip of their drink while I process that. 'Don't take it personally,' they add after a moment. 'Caroline is just . . . very particular. She's been calling me *too much* since Year Seven. And I used to be shy. If Caroline doesn't like you, consider it a badge of honour. Not to armchair therapise or anything, but I honestly think that most of the reason Isabel's *the way that she is*, is because Caroline set the bar for what counts as *too much* for Isabel, like, underground.'

It's a harmless comment. They're trying to reassure me. But I can't get Isabel and Caroline and her sea of other Caroline-esque friends out of my head. All that day, and over the next few days, whenever I go to say something stupid, do something impulsive, be loud or obnoxious or just, honestly, *myself*, I keep thinking about Isabel's bar for what counts as too much.

I can't help feeling that I – my specific brand of insufferable, the parts of me I've always been so proud of, so reluctant to smother for anybody – crossed that bar a long time ago.

CHAPTER THIRTY-SEVEN

I think I might be sick as I ring the doorbell. I went on not one but *two* runs this morning. I got back from the first one, showered, sat down, and immediately got back up and out again. But my heel still bounces up and down as I wait for Isabel to answer the door.

'Eloise, darling.' It's Isabel's mum who answers.

Great. Excellent. Totally not helping with the likelihood of being sick.

Isabel's mum has *technically* never been anything but polite to me. But she is objectively, overwhelmingly, terrifying.

'Hi, Mrs Williams,' I squeak. 'Sorry I'm early.'

'No, of course, don't worry about it. Isabel's upstairs if you'd like to join her. You can get dressed for dinner up in her room if you like?'

I can't help glancing downwards for a second, and Isabel's mum doesn't change her expression as she follows my gaze. Well. That seemed pointed. I hadn't thought there was anything wrong with what I'm wearing.

In any other situation, I would really, *really* enjoy seeing the face she'd pull if I looked her in the eye right now and said, in my coolest, most innocent voice, 'But I'm already dressed. Is there a problem?'

But I'm not in any other situation. I'm trying to impress Isabel's stupid posh mum and her stupid posher auntie, and I feel my stomach fill with cold shame at the suggestion.

'Will do.' I force a smile. 'Thanks, Mrs W!'

I'm practically legging it upstairs before she can respond, bursting into Isabel's room to find her sitting on the bed with Wil. They both stop and look up in alarm when they see me.

'Is there something wrong with my clothes?' I ask, my voice coming out so strangled it almost feels ridiculous.

'What?'

'Your mum's expecting me to get dressed for dinner. I thought I already was.'

Isabel bites her lip, but Wil just rolls their eyes.

'Lou, angel, you look fantastic.'

There's a moment of hesitation before Isabel speaks.

'I mean, there's nothing *wrong* with what you're wearing . . .' she says eventually, and there's definitely a *but* coming. 'But –' *there it is* – 'it's just that you might feel a bit underdressed. Nobody's going to judge you, obviously. It's only so you don't feel uncomfortable.'

I see my own sceptical look mirrored in Wil's expression. They just raise an eyebrow at her.

'I'm serious!' she protests. 'What you're wearing is *fine*. It's

264

just . . .' She jumps up, hurrying over to her wardrobe. 'Here's what I'm wearing for reference.'

She pulls out a dress, this silky green thing that just keeps coming as she unspools it from the wardrobe. It hangs down to the floor when she holds it up to show me.

I look down at my own outfit. Doc Martens (they're nice, though! They're clean, at least), jeans, a T-shirt with a boxy vintage shirt over it. When I was getting dressed, it seemed like a good idea. Button-down collared shirt, that's formal, right? But the more I think about it now – the obnoxiously bright paisley print, the boxy oversized fit – it's all wrong.

'Maybe . . . maybe you can borrow something of mine?' says Isabel.

I don't need to flick through the hanging clothes to know that everything I've seen her wear so far is a million miles away from something I'd be comfortable in. There's absolutely nothing in her wardrobe that's *me*.

'Wil?' I ask, my voice getting a bit pathetic now. 'What are you wearing?'

Wil gives me a look of horrified indignance.

'Bless you, Lou, but I am *not* going to this dinner.' They look me dead in the eye, raise a feeble fist to their lips and give a weak cough. 'I'm *sick*.'

That, at least, gets a little laugh out of me. But Isabel brings it all crashing back down because, while Wil and I have been talking, *she's* apparently been rifling through her stuff.

'How about this?' she asks, thrusting a blouse at me. I've seen her wear this to sixth form. It's pretty on her, all cream silk with a huge bow that ties round the collar, balanced out by the slightly puffy sleeves, the cinched waist.

I couldn't picture myself wearing it. *Ever.*

'It's not ideal,' she says, though I can tell her reservations don't come from the same place mine do. 'But I mean, if you don't want to wear any of my dresses – and that's fine, I've never seen you wear a dress, and you don't have to – it's just this is about as formal as I can do, otherwise. I have some suit trousers you could borrow, too. They'll be a bit long on you, obviously, but—'

Wil lays a hand on her shoulder. 'Isabel, love of my life, look at your girlfriend's face right now. I've known her less than a week, and even I could tell you she will not be comfortable in that blouse.'

I don't know what to say, so I just try to thank Wil with my eyes. Isabel, though, looks pissed.

'I'm just trying to help,' she mutters.

'Well, okay, let's say you're right, and that Lou will feel totally underdressed in this restaurant. Let's say you are *genuinely* just looking out for her feelings.' The scepticism in their voice implies everything I don't want to think about right now. 'In that case,' Wil presses on, 'don't you want something she'll be comfortable in?'

They hold up a finger, darting out of the room for just a second, leaving me and Isabel, eyes fixed on each other. In the moment of silence that follows, she gnaws on her lip.

'I don't—' she says, then stops herself. 'You—' She hesitates again.

Wil's back before she can say what she needs to say, holding up two long-sleeved collared shirts, each with a bold pattern.

'This seems a little more you,' they say, smiling.

I nod enthusiastically as I reach out to take the midnight blue one, metallic stars and constellations dotting the fabric. There's even a little matching golden collar chain attached, pulling the whole look together.

'You having boobs might be a bit of a problem,' Wil adds as I take it. 'But I tend to prefer oversized, so it should be just snug enough to look polished on you. And you've got Isabel's trousers to choose from – mine definitely won't fit. They were not made for people with hips.'

They're right – the shirt itself doesn't button down to the bottom, my hips stretching the fabric too taut, but a pair of Isabel's high-waisted trousers hides that well enough.

I'll be honest, I feel . . . really good. No, I'll say it: I feel stunning. I look amazing. Almost amazing enough for me to try to dismiss the suspicion that Isabel's gaze keeps flitting anxiously down to my Doc Martens as she changes into her floor-length dress.

I'm almost feeling confident by the time Benji knocks at Isabel's bedroom door, stepping in and breaking into a beaming smile when he sees us both, Wil stretched out lazily on Isabel's bed echoing his expression.

'Well, don't you both scrub up nicely?'

'This isn't prom, Benji.' Isabel rolls her eyes. 'No pictures, please.'

He laughs. 'No pictures, promise. Mum, Dad and Catherine are downstairs, ready to head out when you are. I'll drive you two if you want? Dad and Catherine will go in Mum's car.'

'Works for me, thanks,' I say, and Benji shoots me another grin.

'Loving the look, Lou. But, uh, hang on—'

He dives out of the room, and comes back brandishing a blazer and an enormous grin.

'It'll definitely be too big,' he says, 'but I'm pretty, uh, narrow, so it won't be comically large or anything. It's a sore point, but it's fine, moving on. The oversized look is big right now. Don't give me that look! My girlfriend is really into *America's Next Top Model* and it's kind of impossible not to binge it with her. Just try the damn thing on.'

I laugh, but I take the jacket, and, when I roll the sleeves up, it actually kinda looks pretty badass.

'Thanks, Benji,' I tell him, beaming. 'How come your girlfriend's not here tonight?'

'Oh God, I would not put her through meeting Catherine. If Mum and Dad ask, she's got uni deadlines, okay?'

This dinner is starting to feel more and more like a bad idea. A realisation that's only confirmed when the three of us head downstairs, leaving a very smug-looking Wil on Isabel's bed, and are greeted by the best-dressed people in all Liverpool.

Isabel's mum and aunt both flick their eyes down to my Doc Martens a couple of times when they think I'm not looking.

CHAPTER THIRTY-EIGHT

'You'll have a Bordeaux, Eloise?'

Never in my life has such a seemingly innocuous question struck such fear into my heart. A Bordeaux – that's wine, right? Red, maybe? I've never tried red wine. I've had a few glasses of the rosé my mum likes to drink; it can't be that different, can it?

Catherine is watching me. Waiting for my response. So I force a smile, give her an overly enthusiastic nod, and she turns to the waiter.

'We'll have two bottles of the Château Montrose,' she tells him. Her perfect French accent sounds even more intimidating than her perfect King's English.

'Do you know what you're having?' Isabel asks me quietly while this is happening.

'I'm leaning towards the ratatouille,' I murmur. Mostly because it's one of only a handful of vegetarian options, and because it's the only one I'm confident I could pronounce. Y'know. Because of the film.

'I think that's a side,' she tells me. 'What about the—'

She definitely says something. Those are almost certainly words.

'Mm, yeah, that sounds delicious,' I say.

'Do you read much, Eloise?'

Isabel's head snaps up at the same time as mine, both of us wide-eyed at Catherine in the wake of the unexpected question.

'I read a lot as a kid?' I say tentatively, and she purses her lips. 'I still love books. I just, I don't get much of a . . . My attention span isn't what it used to be,' I finish with a nervous little chuckle.

The lip-pursing is becoming extreme.

'She's doing English literature A level, Aunt Catherine. We're in the same class.'

'Oh, so you like the classics then?'

'Love 'em,' I say too loudly. 'Jane Eyre, she's like my main man. Or, I mean, Brontë, I guess. Jane isn't real. Just, er, in our hearts.'

Thankfully, the waiter is back, pouring out wine, giving me time to full-body cringe at whatever that just was. I thank the guy filling my glass and immediately reach out to take a nervous sip. It's vile. I take another just in case. Still vile.

'So, if you aren't finding the time to read, what about other hobbies then?'

I wasn't expecting follow-up questions. I'm busy fumbling desperately for something to fidget with that isn't in Catherine's line of sight. My fingers find a loose thread on the trousers, pulling at it like if I unspool enough thread, I'll find some secret escape plan at the end of it. I remember, with a little nauseating swoop of guilt, that these trousers aren't mine to destroy, so I switch to my cuticles instead. Which isn't much better, really, since I'm pretty sure Isabel doesn't exactly want my bloodstained fingertips all over her nice trousers either.

'Are you ready to order?' the waiter asks.

Catherine is looking at me, waiting for an answer, but so is the waiter.

'I'll just have the ratatouille,' I say with a tense smile. Again with the lip-pursing from Catherine.

I clear my throat nervously once the waiter is gone, and take another big gulp of my stupid wine.

'I, er, I run,' I say after a long, embarrassing silence.

'You run?'

'As a hobby, I mean.'

'Would that be considered a hobby? Or simply keeping fit.'

'Catherine,' Benji says, his smile taut and thin and so *unlike* him, 'Lou's training for the London Marathon. That's more time and effort than I've ever put into any hobby.'

'But you're so busy with university, dear,' she croons. Then back to me. 'Well, you'll have to be careful with all that training. It's quite hideous when girls nowadays become so muscular. Ladieswear is not flattering to *biceps*.'

'Oh, no worries,' I say with a little chuckle. 'I run with my legs. So, y'know, the biceps are fine.'

I watch Benji smother a chuckle with a cough. But Catherine just gives me this look. This, well, this *sneer*. And it's shocking, in that moment, how much she reminds me of Jay Henno. Worlds apart in most ways, sure. But this moment, this look, it's everything he represents. A sneer, a laugh, a snide comment

271

designed to undermine. To remind you that you're lesser. That people like them come out on top every time.

'So what about university then, dear?' she fires back, but I'm still reeling from the anger that's roiling in my stomach at her sneer.

'Oh, I don't think that's a concern. I'm pretty sure they don't make you deadlift at university. Unless there's some secret working-class university that sends you down into the mines for class credits. That'd wreak havoc on the biceps.'

I offer the sweetest of smiles. She does not offer one back.

So, turns out that red wine isn't just there to make you grimace every time you take a nervous sip. It also, apparently, gets you a bit drunk when you take a few too many nervous sips.

It also turns out that Isabel's aunt is not quite as charmed by my sweet smiles and witty repartee as her niece is. Or used to be, at least.

'I . . . need to pee,' I announce while we wait for dessert. (Disastrous decision to order pudding if you ask me. Not a single person at this table wants to be here a second longer, but yeah, sure, keep up the pretence over thimble-sized servings of crème brûlée, why not?) The announcement gets me some displeased looks, but, as I push my chair back, Isabel stands suddenly next to me.

'I'll be right back,' she murmurs to her family as she hurries off to the bathroom with me in tow.

When we get there, I turn to her. 'Can you believe her?' I

ask, giggling. 'Fucking *you should consider learning to play piano, guitar is unbecoming.* Like, who does she think she is? Lady—'
I stop myself mid-giggle because Isabel's pulling a face at me that I'm really not liking the look of. 'Everything okay?'

'You could have tried a little bit harder out there, Eloise.'

'A little bit— Did you hear how she was speaking to me? I *tried* to be polite, but she made it very clear polite was not on the menu tonight.'

'She just gets very protective of me, that's all.'

'Protective? What's she protecting you against, poor people?'

'She was being . . . a little out of line, yes, but she's still my *aunt*. And you're drunk.'

'Oh sorry. I was playing a game where I took a sip of wine every time your *aunt* insulted me.'

'You *what?*'

'Jesus, Isabel, I'm joking. I'm just . . . I'm nervous.'

'I'm not sure I believe that. Nervous people don't act so . . . so . . .'

'So what?'

'Obnoxious, Eloise! You're embarrassing me!'

A long, painful stretch of silence follows that. It's only punctuated by a small knock on the bathroom door.

'Uh, Isabel and Lou? Are you in there?' Benji's voice is muffled and tentative from the other side of the door.

'Eloise,' Isabel says quietly as I reach over to open it. Benji is looking very nervous about his position outside the ladies' bathroom.

273

'I was wondering if either of you had maybe come down with terrible stomach problems and needed to be driven home as a matter of urgency?'

I pretend I'm not holding back tears as I smile at him, mime clutching my stomach.

'How did you know?'

We don't even go back to the table. Benji makes our excuses for us, and me and Isabel wait outside.

'Eloise—'

'It's fine.'

'It's not. I'm sorry.'

'It's fine – I get it.'

'No, it isn't fine, but you *know* I didn't mean it, Eloise.'

Do I?

'I know.'

'I don't think you're obnoxious. She was being obnoxious. I just. I get easily embarrassed – you know that about me.'

So, noted: she's back-pedalling on the obnoxious thing, but doubling down on the embarrassing thing.

'All right.' Benji is already loosening his tie on the way out of the restaurant. 'I don't think Mum bought it, we may both be in for a bollocking later, but for now we're free.'

'I know,' I tell Isabel as Benji not-so-subtly notes the tension before stepping quietly into the car. 'Really, I understand. It's okay. I'm sorry I didn't make more of an effort.'

It's all I can think to say because it's so much simpler than what I mean. *I'm sorry that even my best efforts weren't enough for your family.*

'Thanks.' She gives me a small smile.

'So, ladies,' Benji asks, eyeing us nervously as we both climb into the back seat, 'whose home are we dropping Lou off at?'

'Mine, please,' I say.

When we get there, I kiss Isabel goodbye. Reassure her one more time that it's fine.

'Hi, love!' Mum calls out as I throw my keys on the table, pulling off my shoes. 'Dinner go well?'

I don't answer, just chuck my shoes half-heartedly in the direction of the shoe rack and slump on to the couch. She sits a little more upright as I do, brow furrowing.

'That bad?'

'*Mmmph.*' I groan into a cushion.

'Well, look, none of my boyfriends' families ever liked me, but it never made much of a difference. In fact, I think it made them like me more.'

I pull my face out of the cushion, choosing instead to curl into a foetal position beside her, careful not to look her in the eye when I speak.

'Mum? Am I too much?'

She hesitates for a moment before she wraps me up in her arms.

'Yes,' she says eventually, and I do look over at her then, my face warped in horror, but she's smiling. 'I love that about you. It is *always* better to be too much than not enough.'

'I don't think everyone agrees with that.'

'Then the people who feel that way aren't enough for you. That's their problem.'

But that's it, isn't it? I don't want to be Isabel's *problem*. I just want to be enough.

Chapter THIRTY-NINE

Isabel doesn't mention dinner again.

I see her the day after next. And she seems fine. She does. At least, there's nothing specific that I can point to that says she doesn't.

Wil, thankfully, is impossible to feel tense around. Jas especially takes to them when we all go out as a group, the two of them just twin balls of sunshine that light each other up from pretty much the moment they meet. Katie seems to brighten in their presence, too, and even Mel relaxes – just a little – over the Easter break, with time to catch up on revision and sleep.

But Wil leaves when the holiday ends. Summer term starts, and the vibe feels – oddly – just like it did last year. And, just like last year, I'm back to having two problems: Lily and Isabel. Again.

The situation has shifted, in both cases. Last year, the Lily problem felt on the verge of some big explosion, like everything was a minefield we needed to tiptoe through. But the worst case has already happened, the explosion over with. Now we have to figure out how to clean up the debris. Reach out and put the pieces back together, with Lily still intact.

And, well, with the Isabel thing . . . Nothing's *wrong* exactly. Not really. It's just that things don't exactly feel right, either.

'What's eating your knickers?' Katie asks, absent-mindedly laying her leg over my knee to stop it bouncing up and down in the empty common room.

'Just feels weird,' I say with a shrug. 'The empty school.'

It's not a total lie. The school *does* feel bizarre as hell today. A ghost town of a school. The younger kids are in, mostly, and I'm sure there's plenty of people *not* skiving today, but there are enough people absent to feel a noticeable shift in the atmosphere.

'Not something to do with Isabel?' Katie asks, nudging me a little with her leg when my knee starts bouncing again.

'No?' I shoot back too fast. 'No, defo not. Why would it— What?'

'Uh-huh. Sounds convincing. You two have been weird recently. What's up?'

'Have we?' I ask, and it's a genuine question. In that moment, it feels really, *really* important to find out whether what I've been sensing has been more than just a bad feeling on my end.

She shrugs a little, apparently not picking up the intensity of the question.

'You both just seem a bit off this week.'

'Off how?'

She shrugs again, removing her leg from my lap.

'I dunno, just off.'

'Okay, but, like, in what sense?'

'Jesus, Lou, I don't know, do I?' she snaps. 'But you seem to think something's up so if it's that big a deal why not do something about it yourself?'

'All right, what's crawled up your arsehole and died today?' I regret it as soon as I ask it, actually. I know exactly why she's in a bad mood. 'Sorry,' I mutter after a second.

'Yeah, me too,' she sighs eventually. 'I mean, I'm right, but I'm sorry I'm being right with that tone of voice.'

I snort a small laugh, and she gives me a sad smile. The ensuing silence is the heaviest quiet I've ever known in this common room. We're early on in the school day, sure, but that's not why it's so empty. And we're both painfully aware of the reason.

'You're sure you don't want to go today?' I ask her after a moment, punctuating the quiet and eliciting a small groan from her. 'Just you and me?'

'I am *really* sure, Lou. Sorry.'

'No, don't be sorry. I don't mind. Just, if you change your mind.'

'I won't. But can we please not talk about it any more?'

'Okay, okay,' I say, but it doesn't last long.

'Where . . . is everyone?' Isabel asks when she arrives about a minute later, pulling out a chair beside us like she's somehow afraid of spooking the silence. Poor Katie barely looks up, just keeps scrolling through Instagram on her phone, barely stopping to look at anything she scrolls past.

'Ladies Day,' I murmur to Isabel quietly, as if Katie's heart might just break if I say it too loud.

'Huh?'

Isabel's clearly not cottoning on to the whole *being tactful* thing.

'Grand National? Today's Ladies Day at Aintree racecourse.'

'The . . . like, horse racing?' She seems so utterly confused by this. I just nod slowly, unsure what part she's not getting. 'And half the school is at . . . Aintree racecourse?'

'Well, not right now, but most of the girls skive off in the morning to get ready. It happens every year so the teachers just kinda turn a blind eye.'

'It's that big a thing? Horse races?'

'Yeah, I mean, I don't think anyone actually cares about the races, but everyone gets all dressed up and makes an afternoon of it, yeah.'

'Oh.' She looks like she's processing. 'Huh. That's . . . unexpected. Not the kinda crowd I thought would be the Grand National's main clientele.'

I don't know why it makes me bristle so quickly, but it does, my hackles raised, and I sit up a bit straighter in my seat.

'Why? Scouse birds not classy enough?'

'No!'

I hadn't really believed it, not completely, but she says it so defensively it makes me think that maybe she did mean it, after all. I don't like it. I don't like it one bit, this feeling in my stomach, this acid sitting ready to roil and burn at the smallest imagined slight from Isabel.

'I just meant teenagers. Scouse or not. Thought it was like a stuffy old lady thing. Boomers in their fascinators, you know?'

'Why not?' Katie asks then, and we both look at her like we'd forgotten she was there. Her voice is small and sad. 'Who loves an excuse to get dolled up more than a teenage girl?'

'Fair enough . . .' Isabel concedes. 'So, why aren't you guys there?'

'Jas has the flu,' Katie murmurs.

'Mel hates it,' I add.

'And the races were kinda always mine and Lily's thing so . . .'

'Ah.' Isabel nods sagely. 'Not feeling it this year.' It isn't a question, but Katie gives her a small nod anyway. We all avert our eyes a little when her lip wobbles.

'What about you, though?' Katie adds after a moment, her voice suddenly far too chipper to be believable. I look back up at her in surprise.

'What do you mean?'

'Why aren't you going?'

I shrug, glancing away again.

'Can't exactly go on my own,' I mutter.

What I don't say is that I also didn't like the idea of leaving Katie on her own. Because the only thing worse than being left out of something is when someone tells you explicitly they're missing out on it, too, to babysit you.

'You should go. Isabel can take my ticket.'

'Oh, I couldn't—' Isabel starts, but neither me nor Katie miss the way her eyes light up for just a second.

It's then that I realise the opportunity we've got here. My turf. A true Scouse bird tradition, but her style. Formalwear and fascinators, horse racing and high heels. It's like a little slice of Hampstead right here in Liverpool. It's perfect. It's exactly what we need. I lock eyes with Isabel, and maybe the distance between us isn't quite as bad as I'd feared because we have this whole exchange with just a glance. Her looking up kind of shyly from behind her hair, like she's afraid to be too excited about it. Me kind of pleading back to her. *Can we have this? Will this be what we need?* Her small smile tells me everything I want to know.

'Only if you're absolutely sure, Katie,' I say after a moment, but Katie – who has just watched that whole thing go down – just rolls her eyes.

'Just go, ye crank.'

I beam, then try not to look too happy about it.

'I mean, we don't have to, like, go now. We can stay for a few lessons at least.'

'Babe, I know how long it takes you to fake tan. You need to have started three hours ago. Just fuck off home and have a glass of Prosecco for me while youse get ready, will you?'

This time I don't try to hide my grin, pulling Katie in with a hand on each cheek to plant a kiss on the top of her head. She makes a face.

'You're sure the teachers won't mind?' Isabel asks, nervously reaching up to tuck her hair behind her ear.

'Iz,' I say, taking her hand to drag her out of her seat, 'look around. How many girls over the age of fourteen do you see in

282

this school right now? The teachers absolutely do not mind. Plus,' I add, already towing her towards the door, 'we're sixth-formers – we're basically adults now!'

I don't think she's entirely convinced, but she laughs anyway when we're out of the sixth-form building and, her hand still in mine, we run through the school gates.

Since she refuses to ride on my handlebars (yeah, okay, Isabel, sure it's a *massive health hazard*, but it'd look sick as fuck, wouldn't it?), we walk as far as hers, where she sneakily makes sure her parents aren't in before darting in to grab an outfit and some make-up. Then it's the train back to mine, and the real work begins.

CHAPTER FORTY

'How do you still look hot right now?' Isabel shouts over the music blasting as loud as my little speakers will go – it's her playlist, full of the kind of moody Sapphic music she loves that isn't quite my speed, but it makes her happy – and her face lights up with laughter when I do an overly dramatic catwalk across my bedroom in only my underwear. Every inch of me is slick with fake tan, and I pretend to flip my hair in response, despite it being held tight to my scalp by rollers.

'It's my superpower,' I say with a grin.

She's partway through curling her hair, and I watch as she turns the curler off, sets it down carefully on the heatproof mat, then walks, slowly and deliberately, over to me. When she kisses me, so deeply and intense my head swims, it takes me a moment to react, reaching up to grab her hands.

'The tan!' I squeal, stopping her before she can touch my arms, and she laughs, biting her lip.

'Sorry, sorry,' she says softly. Then her face turns serious, her eyes searching, and my stomach swoops at the sudden tension. 'What if I touch you somewhere the tan won't show?' she asks, her voice a low murmur as her hand reaches slowly for my waist. 'What about here?' Her fingertips almost brush my skin, and I nod, shivering slightly when she touches me, featherlight. She kisses me again, her fingers trailing over the most sensitive part of my waist.

'What about . . .' She pulls away just long enough to murmur, and I swear I'm about to pass out. 'What about here?' She moves her other hand to the top of my stomach, her fingers tracing the skin below the wire of my bra. I nod again, enthusiastically, and she smiles into the next kiss. And, oh God, I was so right. This was exactly what we needed. This is everything I could ever need. 'And here?' she asks again, the hand on my waist moving to the small of my back.

I swear I'm about to drop dead when her fingers trail up the small of my back to my bra clasp. Like, I don't know how many documented cases there are of teenage girls dropping dead due to cardiac arrest secondary to severe horniness, but I'm pretty sure I'm about to spearhead that particular demographic.

And if there's anything standing between me and total and complete happiness in that moment, it's just a small thing. Nothing, really. It's fine. It's just that the words bubble to my lips, and I have to swallow them down. The desire to tell her how in love with her I am so easy and natural that the act of stopping myself jolts me out of the moment.

I'm not sure why I don't want to say them.

That's a lie.

It's just that the way things have been over Easter break, I'm not sure she'll say them back.

She seems to notice the shift, stepping away and dropping her hands fast as anything.

'You okay?'

I plaster on my biggest smile and dart back towards her for another quick kiss.

'Of course I'm okay,' I tell her. 'I apparently look hot, and my fit girlfriend can't keep her hands off me long enough to let the tan dry. What more could I want?'

She laughs, but it's stilted. Like she knows something's off.

'So, what's the dress you brought?' I ask, an attempt to break the tension, but it feels forced. 'Must be something special to take the detour to yours rather than borrow one of mine.'

It's the wrong thing to say. I knew that before I even said it. It brings up another moment of awkwardness, the moment we left school about to head to mine and I asked if she needed to borrow a dress. She scrunched her nose – involuntarily probably, I'm sure – and told me that my style *works for me, but isn't quite the look she's going for*.

'Oh, it's one of my favourites,' she says, looking away, pushing her hair behind her ear. I watch the movement of her fingers, the bronze of the tan now a startling orange against her pale fingertips, and I can't help but wonder if it looks natural on me at all, or if I just look trashy through her eyes. 'I'll put it on once I've finished my make-up.'

'Well, let's get cracking then, because I can't wait to see how you look in it.'

She blushes a little, and I wonder if it's enough that her

cheeks still turn pink at my compliment. I hope it is. It's got to be. Enough, at least, to give us a good day. A perfect day. The two of us glammed up, an afternoon together in this perfect meeting of our two worlds.

So I decide to start a little early. I finish my make-up faster than her, and, as soon as the tan allows, I slip on some pyjamas.

'I'm going to pick us up some Prosecco,' I announce proudly. 'There's a Bargain Booze on the corner that never checks IDs.'

'It's –' she checks her phone – 'half past ten, Eloise.'

'I'll get us some orange juice, too, then. Mimosas. It's a brunch drink. People drink all day at the National. The races are only running until like five anyway.'

She laughs at that, and my whole body reacts to the sound, relaxing as she does. But then she watches me slip on my shoes with such an unexpected intensity I have to steel myself before I look directly at her and ask what the problem is.

'Nothing, just . . . You're going out like that?'

The way her lips purse at my pyjamas, the rollers in my hair, I tell myself it's still enough. It's still enough to see the dried orange of the fake tan on the palms of her hands, enough to remember how her hands felt on me.

'Why?' I ask, smirking. 'Something wrong with my make-up?'

She laughs, at least. 'No, your make-up's perfect, really complements the rollers and the fuzzy pyjamas.'

'Oh yeah, the contour actually has nothing to do with cheekbones. It's a common misconception. It's actually designed to draw attention to the fuzziness of the pyjamas. It's very *in vogue* right now.'

She laughs again, but as she watches me grab my keys I see her shift back into discomfort. 'Are you actually, though? Going out like that?'

I shrug. 'It's just the corner shop. You never seen a Scouse bird in the wild? This is pretty standard – it's practically a rite of passage. Come with me. I promise we'll see at least three other women in pyjamas and rollers.'

She laughs again, but shakes her head firmly. 'I'm good,' and there's still laughter in her voice when she adds, 'I'd just die if I was seen out in public like that.' But something in my face puts an end to whatever amusement still lingers. 'Not that— I mean, you're fine. I just, it's me—'

'I get it,' I say, trying my best not to sound too bitter. I *so* don't want to start a fight right now. 'No worries,' I say when she looks like she might be about to apologise or defend herself. 'It's fine.' And I convince myself that's true, I really do.

I reach for her hand, smile at the fake tan dried into the skin – that's not going anywhere any time soon – and think about the matching streaks on all the parts of my body not visible under the dress I'll be wearing later. I really do a good job of convincing myself before I leave.

When I'm back, Prosecco in hand, and she's fully dressed – this gorgeous silk dress falling to her calves, the straps thin and soft against her shoulders, the silk clinging lightly to her waist – I forget all of it. For real this time. Nothing else matters

288

except that Isabel's here, smiling at me, pouring me a glass of Prosecco, looking like an absolute goddess, and seeming to think the same about me when I get dressed. When we leave the house finally, it really is like everything has fallen away to give us this perfect day.

'Who's winning?' Isabel giggles, peering over the crowd at one of the bars towards the racetrack.

'Fuck if I know.' I laugh, flushed and warm and a bit drunk, but content that Isabel – wavering slightly where she stands as she tries to see over everyone's heads – is right there with me.

'I just think, maybe if everyone slowed down a bit, it'd be easier to follow.'

I laugh, a loud, head-thrown-back cackle, and she looks so pleased with herself that I have to pull her in for a small kiss.

In front of us, the bartender clears her throat.

'Oh great, now she shows up,' I mutter, quiet enough so that only Isabel can hear, and she stifles a laugh while I order the drinks that we've been queueing about half an hour for. When they arrive, I pull Isabel away from the crowd, not stopping until we've found a quiet spot behind a marquee, nobody else around that we can see. We're both still giggling, trying to sip our drinks, but collapsing into laughter every time we catch each other's eyes.

It doesn't go very well, and the drinks end up mostly all over us by the time they're finished, but neither of us care much.

'Hey,' she says after a long while, in a quiet moment. She takes a step closer to me, my back pressed to the marquee.

'Hey,' I offer back with a smile.

'I'm glad we did this.' Her voice is sincere, her eyes searching for my reaction, and I nod.

'Yeah, me too.'

She kisses me. Swift and light and sweet, then pulls away for the briefest of moments before kissing me again and again, the tip of my nose, across each cheekbone, the space between my eyebrows. I'm laughing by the time she pulls away, and she's smiling, too.

'Just finally getting round to all the places I've wanted to kiss you since we met,' she says, and God, I love her I love her I love her. But I can't say that so I do the next best thing and wrap a hand round her neck, drawing her in for another slower kiss.

When she pulls away this time, her fingertips linger on my chin, and we lock eyes for a long moment. Something in hers, in the deep swirling brown, looks almost sad.

'We're okay, aren't we?' she asks, and my stomach drops as I realise it's the first time either of us has acknowledged that something has seemed off since Easter.

'Yeah,' I say, and it's knee-jerk instinct.

But something about this moment, this day, something about the way she holds my face up to hers, makes it feel safe. This moment feels less fragile than the ones before. Or at least like, maybe if it does shatter, whatever's underneath won't be quite so scary.

'I think so,' I say after a long moment, and this time she

nods, like she's accepting this as truth. 'I think we're almost entirely good,' I tell her. 'And there are parts that aren't, but they're manageable. We can work through them.'

She smiles then, all genuine warmth.

'Yeah. Yeah, I think we can, too. I think anything is worth working through for this.' And she kisses me again. Deeper this time. I stumble, wary of putting my whole weight on to the marquee, but she just laughs into my lips, and I grab her waist to steady myself, and she grabs back, and I feel myself sink into her, and we stay like that for a long time, just losing ourselves in each other.

Not long enough. It's a shrill, wordless cry that catches our attention first. We both falter, separating ourselves tentatively as we listen. Whoever made the sound is coming closer, two voices making use of the private space to argue.

'Please, Jay, please, please.'

Isabel's eyes widen, and I feel my heart wrenching in two. That's definitely Lily. And she's crying, desperate breathless sobs, like those of a toddler, powerless and helpless, who has no idea what else they can do but beg, keep begging, because they have control over nothing in their world. It's not something I ever expected to hear from Lily.

Isabel and I both freeze. Lily and Jay must be just round the corner, close enough to hear clearly now, but just out of our line of sight.

'Yeah, whatever, like crying's gonna do anything.' And I didn't think there was anything that could make me feel worse than the sound of that sobbing from Lily, but there is, and it's Jay Henderson sounding entirely unfazed. Cold and distant in the face of whatever she's pleading with him about. I'm suddenly glad I can't see Lily's face in response to that.

'Jay,' she almost whispers.

'Swear down if you say *please* one more time, Lil.'

'I don't—'

'You're being such a whiny bitch about this. It's not a big deal. But if you get on my nerves like this for much longer, it can be.'

My veins turn to ice. Because what starts off as a callous, unemotional dismissal turns into something else. Something calculating, something downright evil.

'No, Jay, please.'

'Nah, fuck this,' he says, and he takes a few steps away, close enough that we can see him now, even if his back's turned and he can't see us. 'Choice is yours, Lil. Keep being a bitch about it, and I can actually give you something to cry about. Or just get the fuck over it, and we'll be fine.'

He turns away from her so suddenly then, and if he's surprised to see me and Isabel just standing there, frozen, he definitely doesn't show it. He just winks at me. So quick I almost missed it. A small smirk and a wink as he strides off. I feel sick to my stomach.

A beat later, Lily turns the corner, too, taking a few helpless steps in the direction he's walked off in. She looks beautiful, or like maybe she did look beautiful before she cried through her make-up, and it hurts so much to see her like this. Whatever Henno's done to her, fuck him if he can't see what he had right under his nose. And it's so unlike Lily not to see that, too. Not to just say, 'Thank you, next!' to the fucker and storm off with her head held high. But she doesn't. She just stumbles after him, half-hearted, before coming to a stop, crying quietly as she gazes in the direction he left in.

'Lily,' I say, quiet as I can, but it doesn't matter. It scares the shit out of her anyway, and she jumps a mile.

When she recovers, clutching her chest, she narrows her eyes at us.

'God,' she says, and the word comes out hoarse and feral through her sobs. 'Of *course* youse are here right now. Of *fucking* course.'

'Lily, what's—'

'No, go fuck yourself, Lou. You don't get to suddenly give a shit right now.'

She makes a move to storm off, and Isabel steps after her, looking unsure, but the look of pure hatred Lily gives her stops her in her tracks.

'Oh, don't *you* even think about it. Coming in, swooping down out of nowhere, taking my place in the group. Don't you dare try to pretend you know enough about me to comfort me.'

And then she's gone.

CHAPTER FORTY-ONE

'I don't fucking know, do I?' I cry, exasperated. As if a post-Ladies Day hangover wasn't bad enough, now I'm spending my Saturday morning on FaceTime with poor Jas who's still ill, and Mel who's pissed about the lost morning of revision, trying to parse through what Isabel and I saw yesterday.

We all thought it better if we didn't involve Katie in this particular call.

'Well, what did he say exactly?' Mel asks slowly, as if speaking to a very dim child.

'We don't all have bloody photographic memories, Mel.'

'Actually, if it's sound, it'd be called an echoic memo—'

'Christ, Mel, it was something about her being a whiny bitch, about making a big deal out of nothing, and that if she didn't stop he'd *give her something to cry about.*'

That part I do remember word for word. Jas makes a face of such disgust at that part I worry she's about to puke.

'I've seen them arguing recently,' Jas adds quietly after a moment, her voice thin and raspy, and we both fall silent to let her speak. 'It's hard to tell what about because they always fight out by the bike sheds, but I've seen them. Whatever's going on it's been going on since before half-term.'

'Jesus, Jas, why didn't you say anything?'

'Didn't want to bring it up in front of Katie,' she says quietly. And that stops me in my tracks. Because isn't that what we've all been doing for ages? Tiptoeing round Katie to avoid hurting her feelings?

'I think we're past that now,' Mel says, and the bluntness of this shocks both me and Jas. 'I'm serious,' she insists. 'Whatever Jay's doing to Lily is clearly worse than Katie feeling a bit betrayed.'

She's right. It's not nice, but she's right.

'Maybe,' Jas says, 'but we can at least try to figure it out without getting Katie involved first, I think.'

'All right then, Jas,' Mel says, 'I think you should talk to her. You're all, you know, *you*. Maybe she'd—'

'Wait.'

They both stop when I speak, but my brain takes a second to catch up with its own train of thought, and there's a brief silence. Because I'm realising something.

'I think it should be me,' I say eventually.

'Didn't she already, like, shoot you down?' Jas asks as politely as she can.

'Yeah, because Isabel was there, I think.' I'm not explaining myself, but I've barely got this realisation fully formed yet.

'Lou, love you, but Jas is definitely the more tactful option here.'

'No, I think . . .' I hesitate as it all clicks into place. 'I think

295

it should be me because I'm the most like her. I think she's defensive. Ever since New Year, she's been defensive because she thinks everyone's judging her. But me and her, we're kinda the same. We're both messy. We're both kind of awful. I think, if it's just me . . .'

I'm right. I *know* I am. Because isn't this how I've been with Isabel recently? I think Isabel, her family and her friends are so much better than me, so everything they do or say puts me on the defensive. I *know* Lily's been the same way with us. So maybe if it's just me, not Isabel, not Katie or Jas or Mel, people she feels inferior to, judged by. Maybe if it really is just one piece-of-shit friend to another . . .

A text banner interrupts my train of thought:

Isabel: Eloise.

I pause, expecting there to be more, but there isn't.

'Speak of the devil,' I grumble, and both Jas and Mel widen their eyes.

'No, not Lily. Sorry, shit, I meant Isabel. My brain took a leap that I didn't make out loud. Look, I'm gonna hang up to text her back, but trust me, okay? If me talking to Lil one on one doesn't work, we can sic Jas on her.'

I wait for them both to grumble their agreement before I hang up, texting Isabel back.

E: ???

She responds almost instantly, like she was just waiting for me to acknowledge. It's a link to an article, one of those crappy tabloid monstrosities that they publish every year: *Scouse Birds Get Boozy at Grand National Ladies Day*. I fight an eye-roll. The preview shows a photo of a woman sitting on a kerb, high heels splayed out beside her, skirt riding up just a bit, clearly unaware of the photo being taken.

E: oh dw about that shit
E: they do it every year
E: spend all day lurking to find shots that aren't actually incriminating and try to frame them like they've captured the true seedy underbelly of Liverpool

I: look at the one of us though!

There's one of us? I'm normally so careful about spotting them. It's probably just taken from a bad angle, maybe mid-sip of our drinks or something to make it look like we're off our faces.

The next message she sends is just a screenshot from the article. A photo of the two of us behind the marquee. It had been such a tender moment, but here in the photo, blurry, mid-movement, it looks fumbling and messy. My hand is in her hair, her eyes half closed, our faces barely centimetres apart, but our mouths are parted. It's not a good look, for either of us. I call her right away.

'Fuck them,' I tell her, instead of a hello.

She takes just a beat too long to respond, and when she does her voice is tight.

'It's bad, Eloise.'

'Well, you've been out years, right? And I can deal with the backlash.' I mentally run through the people in my life I haven't come out to yet. My nan and granddad are the most important. I know they'll have questions. They'll be confused because I've had boyfriends before, and it just felt like too big a conversation to have. But, if they do find out from this, I'll deal with it. Pretty much everyone else is distant family, and I can cope with that.

'It's not that you're a girl, Lou,' she hisses, and if the way her voice breaks isn't enough of a clue, the fact that she calls me Lou is a dead giveaway that, no matter how hard she tries to keep it contained, this is bothering her more than I thought. 'It's the way they made us look. Like we're, like I'm . . . like I'm some kind of common . . .'

She trails off, and I can tell through the phone that she's hyperventilating, and I want to find a way to comfort her, but right now I'm struggling.

A fairly big part of me is fuming, to be honest. Because here I am thinking she'd been stressed for me. Thinking she'd be concerned that a photo of me kissing a girl has been published online before I've had a chance to come out to some of the people in my life. Before I've had a chance to figure out what kissing a girl even *means* for me. But she doesn't care about that.

298

She only cares about how she looks, about being seen with *me*. About her own pride.

'Like you're what, Isabel?' I hiss through gritted teeth.

'Nothing,' she says quietly.

'I don't think it's nothing, Iz. I don't think anything that's happened since Easter break has been nothing.'

There's silence from her end for a moment, and I scrunch my eyes shut, holding the phone tight. Because this is it, isn't it? This is the culmination of everything I've been feeling since we burst our bubble. I've been trying to bring her into my real life because I was using her as a life raft, and it wasn't fair. I thought she was doing the same thing, but she wasn't, was she? She was keeping me from the rest of her life because she *knew* how they'd react to me. Her bubble was never a bliss bubble. It was an embarrassment bubble.

'What do you mean?' she asks eventually. And her voice is so faux-casual, I lose my shit.

'You know *exactly* what I mean, Isabel. I don't think we're okay. And it's my fault because I'm obnoxious, and embarrassing, and maybe you'd just rather be in London with Caroline if you could.' I'm shouting by the end, throwing up a hand that she can't see, emboldened by the distance.

'So you *did* hear—'

But I'm on a roll, fury fuelling me.

'Then again, maybe it's kinda your fault, too. Maybe it's your fault because you were too busy being ashamed of me, being embarrassed by me, to realise that if you like me, your friends will, too, and maybe friends that won't are shitty fucking friends, Isabel. But you don't think about that. All you think about is whether or not I make you look like some kind of common . . . What, common chav? Real strong class-consciousness there, Isabel.'

'I didn't say that.'

'But you were going to, weren't you? If nothing else, I need you to be honest with me now.'

There's a long silence, and suddenly I regret it. Suddenly I regret asking her to be honest. I don't want to hear it.

'Yes,' she says eventually, her voice breaking slightly, but it doesn't make me feel any better. 'Yeah, I was going to say chav. But I *didn't*. I stopped myself because I didn't mean it.'

Yes, she did.

'We both know you did.'

'So how do we work past this?'

'I'm not sure we do.' My voice feels empty and alien. I can barely feel the words coming out of me because this aching hollow space in my chest is all there is. 'This isn't just you being about to call me a chav, Isabel. This is you being embarrassed of me.'

'I'm not. It's just—'

'There's no *just*, Isabel. Do I embarrass you or not?'

And the pause is enough. The tense silence after I finish speaking is enough to make it feel as if a hole has opened up under me and wrenched the world out from beneath me.

'Yes,' she murmurs eventually. 'Sometimes, yes. I don't think that makes me a bad person, Eloise. You're *loud*, and you're confident, but I'm not that way, and sometimes you can just be . . .'

'Too much?'

'It's not your fault. It's me that's—'

'Yeah, you're right. It's you that's the problem.'

The words come out barbed, and I hear her start to cry. And I hate myself for it, but that's been the problem the whole damn time, hasn't it? I used to know that it wasn't my fault. I used to love myself. And it's only Isabel who's ever made me feel like I wasn't worthy of that love.

'So, what?' she asks, and her voice breaks. I can picture how her face crumples, like it did back when we first kissed, and the memory stings. 'You're just . . . ending this? Giving up on us like your latest hyper-fixation?'

She's angry. She's hurt. I know that. It doesn't make it any less painful to hear her say that.

'Yeah, I think I am.'

I can feel myself getting angry again, getting loud, to compensate for my voice breaking, my eyes burning with tears. And maybe this isn't all about the phone call. Maybe some – maybe a lot – of it is about the realisation I've just had about Lily, about how we're one and the same, and about how fear of judgement from people like Isabel has been the root of pretty much every problem we've faced as a group this year. It's hard to parse through all that now, so I don't. I just keep ranting.

'Because actually you've done me a favour. Something's been

off about us for ages, and maybe I'd have felt really shitty about ending it if you'd been less insulting about it, but, as it stands, I feel just fine telling you that I couldn't possibly date such a pompous, stuck-up ... selfish ...' I'm starting to stammer, starting to run out of steam, and I stop before my words can turn into a sob.

'Well, sorry for wasting your time then.' Isabel's voice is tight but cold, and I can't think of anything to do but hang up.

I know it's not the best decision I've ever made, okay? But I grab my bike, fuelled by anger, trying my best to push it down and channel it into something, *anything*, more productive than this ache in my chest.

CHAPTER FORTY-TWO

I only get about halfway to Lily's. Turns out cycling's hard when your vision swims in waves, clearing briefly as the tears fall fast and hard, only to fill and blur again almost instantly. It's not until a close call with a little old lady crossing the road with her dog that I admit defeat, swerving off the road and stumbling into a side street to cry in peace.

It's hard to tell at first where the breathlessness from cycling ends and the crying begins, but after a while, despite all my efforts to pull myself together and keep going, the sobs don't subside, wrenching themselves from my chest in loud, mortifying gasps that are definitely going to attract someone's attention eventually.

I just can't seem to get my breath back. Because it's hitting me now just how final this all is. There are arguments, there are snipes and harsh words that can be said in anger and walked back with apologies. Those are fixable. Parts of that conversation were fixable.

But I can't stop thinking about her confession. That yes, I embarrass her. The way her voice got so small and sad when she said it. That wasn't her lashing out; it wasn't designed to hurt. That's the worst part, I think. It's clear she didn't *want* to hurt me. She just wanted to be honest with me. Exactly like I'd asked her to. Problem is, you can't fix the truth with apologies.

What if I changed my mind now? What if I turned my bike round, cycled to her house again, showed up on her doorstep just like I did after our first kiss, told her how sorry I am, told her how kissing her for the first time lit some kind of fire in me that would never be satisfied until I got to do it again. What if she let me? What then? Because I'd be happy, for a moment. My heart wouldn't be breaking any more, but then what about after? Because I'd know. After every tight-lipped smile, after every furtive glance round the room when I'm too loud, after every introduction to one of her friends, I'd know the shame she'd feel, and I'd feel it, too.

I don't think I can live like that.

I sit there for a while, letting that thought settle, and eventually the crying stops. I feel sick, but at least I can move. When I get my breath back, head still swimming a little and legs wobbly, I walk, dragging the bike beside me.

'Lily!' I call out, thumping on her front door. My voice is hoarse, but I call out a little louder anyway. This is one thing I *can* fix. 'I know you're hungover, too, there's no way you're not home. Stop being a little bitch and come talk to me, okay?'

Her face is, as I expected, furious when she opens the door, but it falls after a second.

'What's up with you?' she asks, and okay, fine, maybe I haven't done such a good job of pulling myself together.

'My girlfriend thinks I'm a chav,' I tell her, my voice flat and empty. 'What's up with you?'

She takes a long look at me. Like she's sizing me up.

'My boyfriend's trying to leak my nudes,' she says, a look of deep exhaustion in her eyes.

'Oh.'

'Yeah. Wanna come in?'

And I want to be happy that it was that easy. That we're suddenly back on speaking terms. But Christ, it's only going to get harder from here, isn't it?

We're both doing our best to be casual about it, but Lily's brought out mugs of the Good Hot Chocolate. The frothy kind. So I think that speaks to the seriousness of the situation as we both sit down at her kitchen table, the fight drained out of both of us. We both politely ignore the other's puffy eyes.

'Girlfriend?' she asks eventually. 'That's new.'

'Not any more,' I say, hiccupping a small, humourless laugh. 'So I guess it's old news now. You didn't know? Not sure whether or not to be offended that me dating Isabel wasn't hot gossip.'

She gives a dry laugh that echoes mine perfectly.

'I've not really had the energy for gossip recently.'

'That doesn't sound like the wonderfully problematic Lil I know.'

She doesn't say anything to that.

'I'm sorry we judged you.'

She just nods. 'You were right, though.'

'No. We were right to judge him. Not you.'

She gives me a weak smile.

'How long has it been bad?' I ask, and she looks up at me properly then, a hint of defensiveness in her eyes, but she seems to catch herself and shut it down.

'Dunno exactly. Bits and pieces since New Year. Before that, though, when it was a secret, it was . . .'

'A perfect bubble?' I ask. 'I know the feeling.'

'What's Isabel's damage?' She frowns, correctly interpreting the comment.

'She's been embarrassed by me this whole time. But it was fine until we kinda introduced each other to the rest of our lives.'

'Sounds like the opposite of what happened with Jay. Things got worse because we got too separate. I think he knew what he was doing, turning me against my mates.'

'That was him?'

She grimaces. 'Part of it. Most of it was me. Katie was getting too clingy. I knew she'd be on me about it as soon as she found out. And I was right. I knew you'd be pissed, too. I think I also knew you had good reason to be. Which made me even angrier, like the madder I got at you, the more I could pretend you had no right to hate me.'

'Lil, even if you were being the world's biggest bitch, I couldn't hate you. We're the same.'

306

She smiles, but tears spill from her eyes.

'I'm sorry I missed so much, Lou.'

'I'm sorry I forgot we're both the same flavour of messy. Of course we were going to have the same bad taste in lads.'

She laughs, and it's this snotty, ugly cry-laugh, and God, I've *missed* her. I've missed her so much. I'm crying, too, when I pull her in for a hug.

'What am I going to do, Lou?' She sobs into my chest as I cling to her, burying my face in her hair, the smell of beer and smoke still clinging to it from yesterday. 'He's going to ruin my life.'

'No, he's not. He'll have to go through the girls first.'

Chapter FORTY-THREE

The first day back at school after that weekend is awkward for a number of reasons.

First, there's Isabel, who's absolutely *everywhere*. It's like September all over again. In English, in the corridors, in the common room, everywhere I turn she's there, cheeks pink and staring furiously at the ground like she's trying to telepathically communicate all the things she hates about me to the floorboards.

But that's not even the worst part. Which is saying something because it's pretty damn bad. Every time I see her, my stomach twists; every time she brushes past me, head bowed so low her hair covers her face, I think I might be sick. So, you know, it's gotta be pretty awkward to outdo that. But somehow my reintroduction of Lily back to the gang manages it.

'What's she doing here?' Katie hisses when I walk into the sixth-form common room at lunch. I'd texted the group chat to meet up here. I think the others figured it out, but Katie hadn't known about anything that happened at the racecourse, and she jumps up in surprise when Lily and I walk in.

It's a shock on both sides, really. I've never seen Katie's face so twisted with venom. It's unsettling, but it might be more unsettling to see how cowed Lily is by it. I don't like any of this one bit.

'Katie,' I say, my voice small and slow like I'm afraid of spooking her, 'I know she's got a lot of explaining to do. But she *does* have an explanation.'

'You've got an explanation for the way you treated me last year? For making me keep your secret from all our friends? For just suddenly deciding you don't want to be my friend any more and ghosting me for months?'

I look at Lily, whose eyes dart between me and Katie in wide-eyed panic. Oh, I do not like this new Lily at all. It's weird, like watching a fierce lion taking a bubble bath or something.

'Er, well, not for those first few things, actually,' I say when Lily shows no sign of speaking up. 'But for the, y'know, the latter half of the ghosting, sure.'

Katie just scoffs. Which is definitely a noise I only ever expect to come out of Lily's mouth. Jas and Mel look freaked, too.

'Maybe we should—'Jas starts, reaching out a hand for Katie's, but Katie jumps back like she's been scalded, and Jas stops, looking hurt.

'No, maybe we should nothing. Maybe youse can, but I wrote Lily off months ago, so I'm out.'

She's gone before any of us can say anything, and Lily looks worse than ever. All I can do is put a hand on her shoulder and pretend I don't hear her sniffling.

309

'Er, so, I mean, I wish she'd at least heard us out,' I say after a brief silence, 'but we can deal with that later. For now, remember how we said we'd be here for Lily if Jay ever hurt her?'

Jas and Mel ask no further questions, just nod, pull Lily in for a hug, let her sit down at our table and explain in her own time.

'I mean. Yeah. I don't have a good explanation for the start of it. Just sorry. I mean, I felt judged, you know? Especially by Katie. I liked him, and I felt that you'd all give me shit for it, so I got defensive. And after a while it got too hard to just suck it up and apologise. Especially since you all hated me after the party.'

'We didn't—' Jas begins to say, but Mel shakes her head.

'We did a bit,' Mel concedes. And God, Mel's tactless, but honesty seems to be what Lil needs right now. She just nods while Mel continues. 'But only, like, a normal amount. And in a totally temporary way.'

Lily laughs a little at that. A watery, sniffling laugh, but it's definitely a laugh.

'Thanks,' she says, before looking down at the sleeves of her jumper, which she's stretching out over her hands while she finds her next words.

'He's . . . I mean, he's a shit. But you all knew that. Lou knew that. And I really thought I loved him. And he kept telling me that he didn't believe me. That if I really loved him I had to prove it.'

My throat goes tight. Lily's already told me all of this, back at her house over the weekend, the two of us sitting on her bedroom floor, puffy-eyed and hoarse, catching each other up on everything as if no time at all had passed. But it's still hard to hear. Especially since I remember Henno saying similar things to me, back when we went out.

'Nothing as bad as you're thinking!' Lily says quickly when she eventually looks up and sees the wide, horrified eyes of Mel and Jas staring back at her.

'Pretty much everything I did with him was stuff I wanted to do, honest. It's just Mum got a bit worried. Noticed Katie hadn't been round for a while. And she wasn't covering for me any more, either, so Mum worked out I was seeing someone and guessed he was kinda bad for me. So over Easter she wouldn't let me out to see him. And he asked for . . . pictures. I used Snapchat, but he screenshot them. Told me he wouldn't show anyone, that it was just for him to look at later. But at the races I heard one of his mates make some joke. It was like the smallest comment, something about my tits. And they all laughed like they were in on it. That's why we were fighting when Lou saw us. I asked him if he'd sent them to anyone, and he said no. He told me he'd just shown them, which he said was fine because they couldn't look at them again. But it wasn't fine. It was . . . I hated knowing that all these lads I didn't even like had seen me naked.'

Her voice breaks, and all three of us reach out to her. I put an arm round her shoulders, Jas wraps her arms about her waist, and Mel reaches out across the table to take her hand.

'I'm so sorry, Lil,' Jas says softly into her hair. But Lily just shakes her head.

''S not the worst part,' she sniffles after a moment, and we each lean back a bit to give her space to continue. 'He kept telling me I was overreacting, that if I couldn't get over it he'd give me something really worth being upset about. Now he's threatening to send them to everyone. Post them online with my full name. I can't even break up with him.'

And that's when she cracks, burying her head in the sleeves of her jumper, stretched thin and tight over her hands. 'He's gonna do it, I know he is,' she sobs.

We all move to comfort her again, but nobody says anything. Nobody knows what to say.

'No, he's not,' is what I come up with eventually. Fire rekindling in my chest, all the rage I've had burning in me for so long aimed at Lily now pointed directly at Jay the rat bastard Henderson. 'We're not gonna let him.'

I don't know how. None of us do. But we do know we'll tear him limb from limb before we let him.

We spend all of lunch brainstorming. Thinking of ways to steal his phone or otherwise blackmail him into deleting the photos, but none of them are foolproof, and we need them to be foolproof. Otherwise, what's to stop him from sending out the photos as soon as he takes offence at one of us trying to stop him? It fills up my brain for the rest of the day, leaving me completely unable to concentrate in lessons. Just me, the scabs on my neck, my bouncing knee, and a thousand vivid daydreams of various ways I can ruin Jay Henno's life.

It occupies so much of my mind that it almost takes me by

surprise when I see Isabel again at the end of the day. I'm on my way out of the school gates, wheeling my bike, and with the shock of it my resolve almost weakens. After a full day of dodging her, she's just standing there, leaning against the railings, turning her phone in her hands. I hesitate, and I hate myself for it, but I take a step towards her. I have to pass her to get home anyway. I'm not gonna, like, talk to her or anything.

But it doesn't matter because before I get to her she looks up. Not at me, but in the other direction, where this absolute supermodel of a girl is approaching her. They both squeal when they see each other. Actually squeal, at a horrifying frequency, and Isabel shoves her phone in her back pocket and flings herself at the supermodel. They hug, and when they separate they squeal some more, then hug again.

'Oh, Isabel, it's so good to see you,' the supermodel sighs after round two. And I can't tell if her accent is even *more* obnoxious than Isabel's, or if I just became immune to it coming from Isabel after a while.

'You too,' Isabel says, and I swear her accent has got extra obnoxious, too, but I'm focusing more on the fact that she sounds like she's about to cry. 'God, Caroline, thank you for coming on such short notice. Sorry I'm such a mess.'

Of course she's a mess. Because all of her tabloid-reading friends saw her looking like some *horrible chav* so now she's called Caroline the Supermodel to remind her that she's above all that. I guess it was easier for Caroline to come all this way to slag off Isabel's ex than it was to pretend to like her mess of a girlfriend.

'Don't be sorry, darling, you poor thing. Tell me all about it.'

Isabel shakes her head slightly, then gives a watery laugh as she dabs delicately at the corner of her eyes.

'Let's go back to my house. I don't want to cry in front of the whole sch—'

That's when she looks up and finds me. Just standing around, apparently.

'Oh, hi.' Her voice is pitchy, and she reaches up to tuck her hair behind her ears.

I just wave back. Because I'm not really sure what else to do with Caroline standing right there. Isabel seems to realise this at the same time.

'Oh yeah, uh, Eloise, this is Caroline, my friend from home— From my old school, I mean. Caroline, Eloise.'

Caroline's eyes widen as if she knows exactly who I am, and I hate it.

'Nice of you to visit,' I say to Caroline, smiling widely, but hoping she'll hear the insult in the words.

Yes, Caroline, we all know how reluctant you've been to come here until now.

I think she does because she gives me a smile in return where the mouth is all polite friendliness, but the eyes are practically screaming that she wants to kill me in my sleep.

'Of course, well, Isabel is having such an awful time right now, isn't she?'

'I'm sure she is. Well, you kids have fun.' I give my bike a little shove, make to move past them. What I really want is to hop on it right now and cycle away before either of them can see me cry, but there are too many kids around. It's just a sea of uniforms and book bags, and Isabel reaches out to stop me just as I start to move.

'Eloise,' she says, her voice low enough that I doubt even Caroline can hear her. 'Will you please talk to me?'

'Not now. You've got a friend visiting,' I say at a normal volume. Caroline, who had been intent on seeming as if she wasn't listening, looks over at that.

And I still can't cycle away, but I can damn well walk with purpose, and Isabel doesn't try to stop me this time.

'Oh my God,' Caroline whispers before I'm even remotely out of earshot. 'Her accent.'

I freeze, but either she doesn't notice or doesn't care.

'Have you asked her to say "chicken" yet?' she continues through a nasty giggle.

I turn on my heel. And I wish I could say I remain in the zone of calm-and-collected bitchy comments through tight smiles, but, well. *No.* I mostly just go absolutely batshit.

'Oh, fucking nice one, Isabel. Yeah, sure, I'll be your little chav girlfriend in secret until your posh mate comes back and then you can share anecdotes like I was some sociological experiment.'

Isabel looks like she might cry, but whatever she'd been about to say, Caroline steps in and interrupts.

'Christ, Eloise. She's already said she's sorry for that.' She flips her hair. If I'm a thousand miles away from the calm-and-collected

315

zone, she's the ruling monarch of it. 'You really want to keep picking that scab? Seriously, just move on.'

I take a deep breath. Try to get at least a little bit back to her level.

'I have unmedicated ADHD,' I tell her, attempting to match her air of indifference with a little shrug. 'Picking at scabs is kind of my speciality.'

Caroline looks more repulsed than I've ever seen a person look in my life, and I only chance the briefest of glimpses at Isabel – who now strangely seems like she might be suppressing a smirk – before I hop on my bike, tiny uniformed masses be damned.

CHAPTER FORTY-FOUR

'I'm still in favour of jumping the fucker in a back alley and just stealing the phone.'

'That'd definitely get us arrested,' Jas points out unhelpfully.

'Well, blackmailing's illegal, right?' I counter, 'so if he pressed charges so would we.'

'I don't think it'd stop us from getting arrested, though.' Oh, here's Mel, also being unhelpful. 'We can hardly go *sorry for the theft, officers, but he broke the law first.*'

I groan. None of this is useful. And Lily's running out of time. Every day she ignores Jay, the wilder and more real his threats become. It's last period, and at the end of the school day we all know Jay will be waiting for Lily at the gates. Just like he did yesterday and the day before and the day before that. We're not sure how much longer he's going to fall back on harassment before he bites the bullet and goes all in on revenge.

Lily's been getting twitchier all week. Which, you know, is bad. It's objectively bad. She's clearly very stressed. But in some ways it's easier to watch than the sad, beaten-down Lily we've been seeing recently. This Lily I'm familiar with. Angry Lily. Fiery Lily. This Lily makes sense to me.

'I'm with Lou,' she says then, crossing her arms, her knee bouncing up and down beneath the table. 'I say we just jump him. Wait until we're out of school, obviously, but then, you know, the five of us against him.' She falters. 'Four, I mean. But still. Four on one, that's good odds.'

Jas sighs, head in her hands. 'You *know* I don't like that idea.'

'What else do we have?' I ask.

'Maybe . . .' Mel begins. 'Maybe we compromise. Maybe we can confront him. *Not* jump him. But just square up a bit when he corners Lily at the gates. See what he wants. Maybe he'll delete the pictures if we give him something he asks for.'

'You're assuming he wants anything other than to fuck me over,' Lily says furiously.

'Well, right now, we're assuming everything. So maybe it's worth checking. And, if it doesn't work, then we've got the threat of four on one to fall back on.'

'That could work,' I say, considering it. 'I'm still not convinced he'd actually delete the nudes if we just asked, but yeah, maybe the threat of all four of us might mean we get the benefits of violence without having to actually, y'know, do the viole— *Jesus*, Isabel, how long have you been there?'

I'm not sure what makes me turn round to where she's standing – lurking might be a better word for it, actually – but Isabel lets out a little squeak of shock when I spot her. The others jump at the sudden shift from both of us, and I'm clutching my chest

318

while I wait for my heart rate to return to normal. It doesn't, even after the shock of seeing her there subsides.

'Sorry—' she says, approaching slowly, eyebrows tipped nervously. 'I just wanted to . . . but I overheard . . . Is everything okay?'

'No, Isabel, but it's none of your business,' I hiss, and I swear I see Jas shake her head in frustration. 'Don't you have to get back to Caroline?'

Isabel puffs out her chest. I watch her narrow her eyes, steel herself, but then she catches sight of Lily. I see Lily through her eyes then. And, even though she's vastly improved in spirit since the weekend, I note the dark circles beneath her eyes, the greasy hair, the jumper sleeves loose and thin from where they've been stretched tight time and again. Isabel's face softens, and she just shakes her head, spins on her heel and leaves.

There's a long silence.

'So . . . Lou, you wanna talk about that?' Jas asks quietly.

'Nope. Nope, not important. We're helping Lily.'

'I mean,' Mel points out, still unhelpful, 'we've still got, like, twenty minutes before the end of the school day.'

'Oh, would you look at that?' I say. 'Why don't we all get back to lessons for a bit? I'm pretty sure only Jas and Mel had a free this period, right? Maybe it was a bad idea to skip.'

I start to stand, but Lily pulls me back down.

'What's happening there?' she asks.

'Nothing, nothing's happening. We broke up, and it's not fun, but nothing's happening. So.'

'It looks like maybe something was about to happen,' Jas points out. 'Like maybe she came here to talk to you.'

'Why would she have come here to talk to me? I wasn't even supposed to be here. I was supposed to be in class.'

'English, right?' Mel asks. 'Which you share with her. So she probably noticed you were missing and came looking for you.'

I don't have an answer to that beyond a petulant grumble.

'All right,' Lily says decisively, standing up, and I just look at her in horror. 'I'm sick of all this shit. All this inaction,' she explains after a second. 'I just want everything to be okay again. And we can't fix things with Jay for another twenty minutes or so, but Isabel's come looking for you to fix things *right* now so I'm gonna find her and bring her back here, and you can thank me later.'

'Lily, *no!*' But she's already leaving.

I scramble out of the door after her, and I hear Mel and Jas's chairs dragging against the floor, too, because apparently we're all coming to watch whatever shitshow this is. But there's a pile-up a metre or so out from the common room as we all screech to a halt behind Lily's who's standing, dumbstruck.

'What's she doing?' Lily asks, her voice low and quiet and unreadable.

I don't know. I genuinely have no idea. But Isabel is at the school gates, locked in furious conversation with Jay Henderson.

I don't know what makes me march up to them, but whatever idiot spirit possesses me in that moment, it possesses Lily, too, and we both stride forward at the same time, Jas and Mel scurrying behind us.

'Lou!' Jas tries to warn me, but it's too late. Lily and I are right in front of Isabel and Jay, and while Isabel's face flushes a warm red, Jay just grins, this awful smirk, at the sight of us.

'All right, babes?' he asks, his voice thick with mockery. 'Didn't trust your mate to do the job?'

'What are you on about, Jay?' Lily asks and, oh God, I'm so proud of her. I cannot stress this enough. Her voice is tight with fury, her face warped and hands balled in fists, and I love her to bits. 'This has nothing to do with Isabel so leave her alone.'

Jay takes a step back, still smirking, and raises his hands in the air.

'Wasn't me, swear down. Lezza came to me. Trying to buy me out. Might have worked if youse hadn't come barging in. Maybe you didn't want it to work, though, hey, Lil? Always knew you secretly wanted the attention.'

'Shut your gob,' Lily hisses. 'And delete those photos. Or I'll do both for you.'

'What are you gonna do about it, daft little slag?' He laughs, actually laughs. Not a derisive chuckle or snicker, but like he genuinely finds the idea that a *daft little slag* like Lily might actually be a threat to him utterly hilarious.

'Oi!' I know. I *know*. It's stupid. I've got maybe five centimetres on Lily – he's a solid thirty taller than both of us. But the shout has left me before I can even consider this. 'What about two daft little slags? Think you can take us both?'

I'm getting in his face before Jas can even let out a groan of distress, but I swear Lily stands just a bit taller now she's got someone fighting on her side.

'Eloise—' I hear the soft whisper from somewhere behind me, and I know it's Isabel, but I'm ignoring it right now. I'm staring intently at Jay instead.

He looks like he's considering it for a second. Must hurt. To have that many thoughts in quick succession. I can see him weighing up whether or not he *could* take us, whether or not he *should*. Whether his reputation would better recuperate from hitting a girl, or from being beaten up by one. Two, going by the way Lily's eye is twitching.

He settles for spitting on the ground in front of us, then taking a step back and shaking his head, letting out a little scoff as he does.

I take two steps forward. 'Give me your phone.' I keep my voice low and steady.

'Not a chance.' He turns to Lily. 'You really think you can get your chavvy dyke friend over here to fight your battles fo— *Oof!*'

I hear the sound he makes before I fully register the hand that flew out from behind me. Half a second later, I see her barrelling after it, a flash of red hair out of the corner of my eye as Isabel falls through the space between me and Lily, where her fist has just connected square with Jay's jaw.

Honestly, it looks like it hurt her more than him. Even I could have told her never to aim for the jaw. But while Jay, Isabel, and I just stand there, all three of us gawping, Lily takes her moment.

A swift knee to the balls is all it takes before he's down, and I'm gaping not just at Isabel, who's cradling a swollen fist, but at Lily, who's suddenly looming over him, a leg either side of where he's curled up on the ground, prising the phone out of his hand.

She holds it to his face, which unlocks it, but then she's shaking too much to do anything, so that's where I come in, I guess. I go into his photos and delete them all, making sure there's nothing saved on his iCloud or anything like that. By the time I'm scrolling through his WhatsApp to make sure he's not sent anything to his mates already, he's scrambled upright, but he doesn't seem about to make any moves to stop me. He's just been absolutely bodied by a girl half his size. I don't think he particularly wants to risk it happening again.

I hold his phone out with a shit-eating grin, and, just as he reaches to take it, I drop it. It clatters, bouncing a few times on the gravel before he scrambles to pick it up. Lily even looks like she might be about to smile.

'Isabel, what the hell?'

As Jay pelts it in one direction, Lily watching him leave, Isabel and I both turn to the voice. Caroline has appeared behind her, a hand on each of Isabel's shoulders, pulling her away, but nothing in her face or voice suggests anything close to concern.

'So what, you're just scrapping in the street now? These girls hardly know you. They don't need you to defend their *honour*. Come on, before you embarrass yourself again.'

Isabel doesn't budge. 'They know me,' she says quietly.

Caroline just stares, eyes narrowed.

'They know me better than you do,' Isabel explains, and, before Caroline is even done rolling her eyes, Isabel flashes a look to me. 'And I—'

I only catch a brief glimpse of her face crumpling before she barrels off, too, Caroline chasing after her.

When I look back at Lily, she's watching Isabel running away. I only have time to see the faintest of creases appear between her brows before her gaze flickers back to me. Then Lily is flying at me, the soft thump of her throwing her arms round me the sweetest sound I've ever heard.

Chapter FORTY-FIVE

'I'm not in love with you any more,' Katie says simply.

I gape. Jas gapes. Mel gapes.

Lily, though, Lily just nods. Like she isn't shocked. Like she knew.

'I know. You deserve better.'

Jas gives me a look, and I shrug. None of us thought Lily had known. Maybe Lily hadn't officially known. Maybe she just guessed. I make a mental note to ask Katie about it later.

Katie sighs. 'Not better. Just someone who's in love with me, too.'

Lily nods again. It's the longest I've ever heard her go without making some snarky comment.

'I *do* love you, though,' Lily adds. 'Not in the way you deserve, but I love you. You're my best friend. I haven't acted like your best friend this year. But you're still mine.'

Katie looks up at the ceiling, as if she's trying not to cry. I feel like I shouldn't be here for this. Me, Jas and Mel are just standing a few metres away from Lily and Katie, where we'd basically forced them together. They both wanted to talk – we could all see that. Ever since the showdown with Jay, their friendship had been ready to be repaired. Neither would make the first move, though. Not even out of pride or stubbornness or anything, but just because each thought the other wouldn't want to hear them out. God, it was frustrating. So, here we are. Averting our eyes while Katie tries not to cry, and Lily makes no such effort.

'You're right, you haven't acted like it,' Katie says through gritted teeth. 'But neither have I. If I'd been acting like your friend, instead of someone who was in love with you, I could have, like, been there for you instead of getting all bitchy and jealous.'

'Yeah, that might have been helpful.'

Katie narrows her eyes at Lily, her nose scrunching up for a moment. I think we might all let out our held breaths at once when Katie finally rolls her eyes up to the ceiling again as she lets out a huff of laughter, but none of us more so than Lily, who seems to visibly unwind the second she hears it. Lily reaches out, taking Katie's hand, and Katie just pulls her the rest of the way in for a hug.

'You can be a real crank sometimes, you know?' Lily says through a watery laugh into the crook of Katie's neck.

'Yeah, well, you can be a real bitch, so.' But Katie's laughing, too.

Jas looks like she's about to cry, and I have to fight the urge to pull everyone into a big cheesy group hug. Mostly because Mel might actually claw my eyes out if I try.

*

What happens next might be better than a big cheesy group hug. Instead of more tears and grand gestures and apologies, we just sink back into normality. We spend that night, after school, in my living room, the five of us watching Netflix and eating every snack in the house. Like the last few months never happened at all.

That's the only downside, actually. Back to normal is good. It is, it really is. But it's . . . Well, not everything was better before New Year.

I'm picking at the scab when Jas catches me. She pulls my fingers away gently, hands me a tissue for the blood.

'It's worse than usual recently, isn't it?' She asks the question as quietly as she can, bless her, but Lily turns round anyway.

'What is?' she says, loud enough to draw everyone else's attention. Jas looks incredibly apologetic. Lily seems blissfully unaware that she's done anything wrong. I ignore her. Instead, I give Jas a small nod, and she pulls me in close.

'Wait, what?' Lily asks again.

'The picking,' Mel hisses, nodding at my bloody fingers, and I can't help but laugh at the obvious attempt to be subtle.

'It's not just that,' I say at a normal volume. Because, well, guess everyone's already involved in the conversation anyway. 'It's everything. Like, when stuff's perfect, I can put all my energy into functioning like a normal human person. But the second something's wrong, like with Isabel, or with Lily, it's as if it's one too many things for my stupid brain to handle.'

'Hey.' Jas pulls me even closer, plants a small kiss on the top of my head. 'I happen to love your stupid brain.'

327

'Someone should.'

'Oi.' Lily this time, clambering up on the couch next to me. 'Was that self-deprecation? Or was it to do with Isabel, because . . . Well, actually, I won't accept, either.'

'I mean, yeah, it was about Isabel. But no, you're right. I shouldn't be self-deprecating. That's the whole point. Ugh, God, I just— If I learned anything from this whole Isabel mess, it's that I'm never going to not be me. I'm never going to be able to be anyone else, and it's not doing anyone any favours to hope for it.'

'Nobody's asking you to be anyone else, Lou,' Katie says gently. 'Not even Isabel.'

I can only scoff at that.

'But see,' Mel starts, and she looks nervous. Pep talks are hardly her forte, but she soldiers on anyway. 'That's kind of it, isn't it? That immediate reaction, the instinct that Isabel wants you to change, that's part of the ADHD, isn't it? Rejection sensitivity?'

'Yeah, I mean Isabel said some shitty things, the way you tell it,' Katie adds. 'But it sounds like the only one being genuinely awful to you is your brain.'

I shake my head, wipe my nose with the bloody tissue.

'I didn't mean to make this about me,' I say, sitting upright, but nobody backs off.

'But you can. Whenever you want, you can make it about you,' Jas says.

'Within reason, obvs,' Katie points out. 'If one of us got horribly injured or something, it'd be pretty rude to show up

328

to our hospital bed, saying, like, *so Isabel said this thing to me the other day*, you know? So just, like, use common sense or whatever.'

I snort, throwing a cushion at her, and that seems to mark the end of the teary heart-to-heart. We sink back into normality again, and I try not to pick or fidget too much. But my mind is whirling from the conversation, running through the implications of it at a million miles an hour.

'You know a load about the medication, don't you?' I ask Mum later that night once everyone has left. I'm splayed across the couch, her at one end, me propped up against the other, feet under her bum, but now she's just looking at me like I've got three heads.

'I think maybe you didn't say the important context bit out loud again, Lou,' she prompts after a full second of staring.

'Oh, the ADHD meds. Like, what they'd do or whatever,' I say, only this time I drop her gaze because I do not want to see the look on her face when she realises she might have won this one.

I don't last long, though. When she hesitates, I can't resist glancing at her again, and she just seems surprised. Maybe even a bit concerned? She rearranges her face a moment too late, back into something more neutral.

I can see her work through the words slowly. She's had this conversation with me a thousand times except, no, not really. We've had this *argument* a thousand times. I'm not sure she knows what to say now that I seem to be actually listening.

'They're stimulants. Closest example that might make sense would be caffeine. You know how caffeine sometimes makes you calm, or even sleepy? That's because stimulants have a different effect on the brains of people with ADHD. It feels like it slows your brain down instead of speeding it up.'

'So it'd, like, change my personality?'

'God, no, you'll still be you. The meds just let you choose what to focus on. They let you channel your attention where you *want* to channel it. If you choose to channel that attention into being loud and obnoxious when I'm watching *Corrie*, then you'll be able to do that without distractions,' she says, grinning, 'and I'll still love you for it just the same.'

'But they won't, like . . .' And, oh God, it sounds so pathetic I can barely say it, but I have to. 'Fix me, right?'

When I glance back up, Mum's looking at me with the saddest eyes I've ever seen.

'Oh, hon, you don't need to be fixed.'

And it's stupid. It's so stupid. But I didn't realise how much I needed to hear that. And I think, in the same moment that hits me in full force, I think my mum realises for the first time that, in all our arguments, nobody's said that yet.

'Lou, love,' she says, shifting in her seat so she can wrap her arms round me, 'nobody's asking to change who you are. This world just isn't built for brains like yours. That was never your fault. And we can ask for as many accommodations as possible to try to help, but sometimes it's not enough. Meds just help make your life a bit easier. You're not weak or a failure. You have to work so much harder to exist in this world, and I've seen how hard you do. You're amazing. Meds just let you do that with a bit less effort. Because you shouldn't *have* to work so hard.'

And I know that if it was anyone else, I'd agree. Anything else. I know that when Jas thought she might need antidepressants I said exactly the same thing. And I know that if Mel ever considered antianxiety meds, I'd want nothing more for her than to finally feel at peace. I know all this, I know. And I also know that this difference, the feeling of failure on my part even when I'd be kinder to anyone else in my life, I know that's ADHD, too. But it doesn't solve everything.

'If the problem is that the world isn't built for my brain,' I ask after a long pause. 'If the problem is a world that won't accommodate me, why should I have to take meds to help my brain accommodate it?'

Mum seems stumped by that. 'You shouldn't,' she sighs eventually. 'You shouldn't have to. And you don't. Just do whichever makes your life easier.'

Problem is I'm still not sure I understand what counts as easier.

CHAPTER FORTY-SIX

I'm lucky that everything with Lily seems to be resolved because the last term of the school year is shaping up to be a circle of hell that Dante ended up cutting from the final draft because it felt like *a bit much*.

There's the pattern I've been following all year – one thing fixed, another falls apart. But I wish I could just count my relationship with Isabel as the thing that's fallen apart. Instead, everything seems to spiral with it. I have so much work to catch up on, and not enough headspace to deal with it. I keep thinking about Isabel, about her standing up for us, not just against Jay, but against Caroline, too.

The worst part is that she keeps almost speaking to me. I'll see her around, hovering in doorways, lingering after lessons, steps faltering in hallways. Sometimes she'll even get as far as looking at me, opening her mouth, but it always ends in a swift shake of the head, downcast eyes, marching away.

So I try to focus instead on catching up with work. Mock exams are coming up *soon* and I am too far behind. In every subject except English, apparently. I guess my early tutoring sessions with Isabel paid off somehow, but it isn't enough to stop me failing my other subjects. I feel like I have a different teacher calling home every other day.

But it's difficult. Made more so by the fact that every time I become aware of how difficult it is, my mind has a whole tangent to spin out on now about whether or not I should consider medication. I'll lose focus, my mind will slip away, and by the time I realise what's happened, instead of pulling myself back into work, all I can do is think about what Mum said. About making my life easier. About still being myself, but with more choice in where to direct my energy. And I think maybe she's right. Other people always seem to have so much *more* energy than I have. Which feels stupid to even think, mostly because I don't think anyone who's ever met me would describe me as lacking in energy. But that's how it feels sometimes. Because everything I've got, every last drop of whatever magic solution makes a person able to complete simple tasks like reading a book or finishing their bloody sociology essay, goes into scrabbling by, day-to-day, fighting against the current in my brain. It all gets used up on just *existing*. So, when something goes wrong, something unexpected, I can't cope because I've got nothing left. And maybe that *isn't* fair. Maybe, actually, it's deeply, horribly, seriously *unfair*.

When that kind of spiral hits, I run.

The running helps channel my thoughts, which is why I've been doing it so often recently. Problem is, I can't choose which direction my thoughts are being channelled in. They're definitely going in *a* direction, but mostly (and wildly unhelpfully) that direction is Isabel.

I spend so much of every run thinking about her. I don't know if it's the motion, or the quiet, but something about it just gives my brain free rein to go absolutely bonkers on the Isabel Williams Movie Marathon, reruns of all the good moments, flashes of touches and smiles and tender silences. Interspersed, of course, with word-for-word recaps of all the bad moments. Because what are brains even for if not to sporadically remind you of every mean thing you and anyone else has ever said?

And the worst part is, with all this procrastinating from exam revision, I'm getting faster and stronger and fitter. It's still a while off, but I'm getting closer to marathon-ready every day. Which I *know* doesn't sound like a bad thing, on the surface, but the problem with that is that now the Isabel Williams Movie Marathon becomes the Extended Edition. With all this extra run time to obsess over not just our past, but maybe some kind of future. A variety of different futures, ones where she starts talking to me again in school, ones where I show up on her doorstep in the rain, telling her *let's give it another shot*, ones where she throws stones at my window at night to tell me she couldn't possibly sleep until she lets me know how sorry she is, and then she kisses me like she might drop dead if she spends another second not kissing me, and I can totally pretend it's just the cardio that makes my heart rate skyrocket at the thought of it.

So, for a second there on one of my runs, sweaty and breathless and with my too-short hair escaping from the ponytail, I think I might have hallucinated her. But that's definitely her, sitting outside the Costa in Maghull square in one of those little two-person outdoor tables with . . . *No way.*

She's sitting there, awkwardly cradling a coffee, with Lily.

By the time I process the sight, I'm thankfully far enough past them that neither of them see me go flying, trainers hitting some crack in the pavement and just faceplanting straight into the path. A couple of passers-by hurry over to check that I'm okay, and I'm pretty sure I am. I'm achy, and I think my thigh might be a bit scratched up beneath my leggings, but I don't notice it at all. I just crane my neck over to check – yep, I saw right. They're chatting about something. And suddenly it's the most important thing in the world that I find out exactly what.

I do my best impression of *totally-and-completely-fine-thanks-for-checking-really-I'm-okay* girl, and hobble over to the Costa, lurking round the corner like a complete creep, just close enough to make out most of what they're saying.

'. . . still don't really get why you did it,' Lily's saying when I get there.

'Wanted to help,' Isabel says, and I can hear in her voice that she's being evasive. I didn't even understand the question, but I know it isn't the whole answer.

'Isabel, you offered him a fuckton of money. He's been sending me some nasty texts, told me exactly how *much* he was gonna get from you if it wasn't for Lou and me. You don't do that kind of thing out of nowhere.'

In the ensuing silence, I can almost hear her shrug, can perfectly picture the way her gaze falls to the floor, uncomfortable.

'I owed you. All of you.'

'Lou, you mean.'

There's another long pause. 'Yeah, but not just. Everyone's been so kind to me since I moved.'

'Not me, though. Literally everyone but me. I've basically been nothing but a dick to you for months.'

'No, not a dick. We didn't speak much. But you had no idea how much they all cared about you. Even when they wanted to hate you, they cared. And they didn't know how to help. And then I overheard the conversation in the common room, and realised that they knew what the problem was, but *still* didn't know how to help. But I did, so I thought I'd try and finally repay everyone's kindness. I *wanted* to do it in secret, but . . .'

I hear Lily chuckle. 'Yeah, my bad,' she says. 'I was trying to convince Lou to take you back, so I dragged her outside to find you.'

When Isabel speaks again, there's a new intensity in her voice, even as she tries to smother it.

'You did?' There's a brief moment of quiet where, I assume, Lily nods. 'Is that why you wanted to meet up?' Isabel adds.

'Yeah, kinda. To thank you for helping. And to try and repay you if I can, by helping with Lou. Oh, don't give me that sad, grateful look. It's mostly because Lou's insufferable when she's heartbroken.'

And I have to fight to stay hidden. Partly because I'd like to give Lil a stern telling-off, but partly – mostly, if I'm being honest – because I want more than anything to see what Isabel's face looks like at the word *heartbroken*.

'You *are* in love with her, aren't you?' Lily asks after a moment. 'Just gotta, y'know, make sure. Cos if you're not I've made a right tit of myself here, haven't I?'

Isabel laughs a little. 'Lily, not to sound nauseating, but I'm so in love with her I sometimes worry my body just isn't big enough to contain it. Have been since September.'

'Good enough for me.'

Well, fuck.

No, seriously, what the *hell* am I supposed to do with any of that information? Because here I am, finally just happy to have my friends back, just trying to get my goddamn brain to work right, and now it's all spinning out of control again.

Okay, so here's what we know, I guess.

1. Isabel tried to pay Jay Henno a *lot* of money to delete the nudes of Lily. That's what they were talking about when Lily and I ran out to find them that day.
2. Because of that, Lily now likes (?) trusts (?) okay, for sure doesn't *hate* Isabel.
3. Lily's helping her *win me back*? Because, well, here's the kicker.
4. Isabel loves me.

Still loves me. Finally loves me. I'm not sure which, but every time I think about it my whole mind just stutters. And then the panic comes back. Because I'm not allowed to feel this way. I'm not allowed to let myself get so light-headed and euphoric over finally hearing her say the words because nothing's changed, really, has it? She did a nice thing for Lily. Or tried to before we got to her. That's something, I guess. The fact that she can say out loud that she's in love with me is certainly a step in the right direction since Easter, but she's still not saying it to *me*, is she?

No, I'm wrong about nothing having changed. As much as I've hated it, I've had a few weeks now to really sit with my broken brain. And Mel was right, back during movie night. It was never *really* that Isabel was being a dick about the way my brain worked. Instead, it was more that my brain works in a way that was being a dick to me. And Isabel's embarrassment *should* have been her own problem, but I let it feed into that. Which isn't really her fault, is it?

But then does that really make anything better? Because all that tells me is that my brain is even more broken than I'd thought it was. And I don't think I can handle that, being around Perfect Isabel and feeling like I don't deserve her.

Things were much simpler when I thought we hated each other.

But God, being loved by her was beautiful. Even when I started hating myself, loving her, and having even just a portion of that love returned, it was, maybe, something close to worth it.

I'm not sure how much more of their conversation I can handle overhearing without bursting out and demanding an explanation, so the only rational thing to do when I feel the panic grip at my chest is to run all the way home.

In spite of my stupid fall earlier, the leg still smarting a little when I put my weight on it, I think I might break record times sprinting back, fuelled by an urgency that doesn't seem to have any action attached to it. Something feels pressing, and I need to *do* something about this feeling. But I can't think of anything. There are two options. I talk to Isabel or I don't. I try and figure this out or I let it die. I know, logically, that there's no deadline to either of these options. But the pounding of my heart and the itching under my skin tell me otherwise.

I should sleep on it. I shouldn't make any decisions like this.

And I try, I do. I take a scalding shower when I get back, washing the gravel and sweat away and hoping the heat soothes me somehow, but my blood is pounding just as fast, mind spinning just as anxiously, by the time I'm clean and dry.

I walk to the chippy to pick up some dinner for me and Mum when she gets home from work, just to give myself some way to burn off this anxious energy. I fidget through a few episodes of *Corrie* with her after we eat. I lie in bed, fingers tapping and limbs aching to move, scrolling through my phone, listening to half a song, watching half an episode. At some point during all of this, I've already made my decision. It doesn't help. It makes it worse, actually.

Before the sun even rises, I know I want to talk to Isabel,

but the decision just solidifies this feeling of urgency. I think I fall asleep eventually, my body exhausted, and when I wake up I definitely haven't had enough sleep, but the panic returns in full force, like somehow I've missed my chance, and I scramble on to my bike first thing, not even thinking to text her, just concerned with getting to her.

That was my biggest mistake, I think. After the third time I ring the doorbell and nobody answers, something in me deflates entirely, and I feel all the exhaustion of the past few weeks creep back over me. I think about calling her, but it's too late now – the momentum has gone. There's no urgency any more, only the cold trickle of doubt telling me this was a bad idea, after all.

By the time I've cycled home again, I'm mostly just annoyed. Bloody Isabel and her not bloody being there when I need her. It's fine. It's totally fine. It was a stupid idea anyway, and I'm glad she wasn't there. And if I jump off my bike with a bit too much force, tear my helmet off too roughly, then, well, it's for totally unrelated reasons, isn't it?

CHAPTER FORTY-SEVEN

I don't see her until I'm basically in front of her. She's sitting on my front wall, standing quickly to attention when I pass her, and I just about have a heart attack.

'Jesus, *fuck*!' I screech, dropping the bike, which clatters to the ground with my helmet perched on the handlebars. She looks about as startled as I do. 'Isabel? What the—'

'Sorry!' she squeaks, and she's already turning pink. 'I— Sorry, oh God, this is not how this was supposed to go. I didn't mean to scare you.'

I see her hand fly up instinctively to tuck her hair behind her ear, but it flutters near her face, awkward. Because, well, her hair's already pulled back. In rollers. She's got a head full of rollers. She's also wearing . . . well, the most hideous shirt I've ever seen, which is saying something coming from me. And pyjama bottoms, I think? Yeah, definitely pyjamas, but those are *not* Isabel pyjamas. Those are *fuzzy*. *Pink and fuzzy* with little pandas on them. They're eating bamboo. Two pandas repeated all over sharing little bamboo sticks, *Lady and the Tramp* style.

I've been staring at the pandas too long.

'. . . Eloise?' she asks after a moment, her voice small. I snap out of it.

'How *was* this supposed to go? And also what is this?'

She kind of holds her hands out, does a little jazz-hands kind of motion, and I hate it that, even after everything, something in me just softens at how cute she is. Something that was sharp and on guard just an hour or so ago simply melts into warmth and comfort.

'This is my grand gesture,' she says, and I watch as she catches her own insecurity and makes a conscious decision to puff out her chest, stand a bit taller. 'I was going to hold little signs like the guy on *Love Actually*, but that film is the pinnacle of straight culture, and it just seemed so off-brand.'

'So instead you're . . . No, sorry, walk me through this, please.'

'I'm proving myself.'

She's looking at me with wide, earnest eyes, but I am wildly distracted by everything that's going on with her right now, piecing things together, connecting the dots.

'Did you raid my wardrobe for that shirt?' I ask finally, because it seems the easiest point to address, and she lets out a dizzy, relieved little laugh at the question.

'Not quite. I got it from that vintage shop you love. I know I . . . I had some opinions about your clothes in the past. I never meant to be cruel. They're so *wonderfully you*, I wouldn't have it any other way. I've always been so scared of drawing attention to myself, and your clothes are attention-grabbing by *design*.

But I love that about you. You make me want to be bolder, Eloise.'

I try to ignore the way my heart jumps up a mile at the word *love*.

'The rollers and the pyjamas. They're because of the races?'

She nods, her cheeks darkening a little at the memory. Me, in my rollers and pyjamas, her looking up at me. *You're going out like that?*

'You told me that it's a Scouse bird rite of passage. I'm here as a *proud* honorary Scouse bird. If you'll have me.'

I'd just die if I was seen out in public like that.

But here she is. Out in public. Embarrassing herself for me. It's growth if nothing else.

And okay, I won't lie, my heart kind of does this thing when she says it. Like it might jump straight out of my chest. And I take her in again, the rollers, the pyjamas. She's carrying a plastic bag with Prosecco from the Bargain Booze. And I can't help but smile. It seems to reignite something in her.

'I'm sorry,' she says. 'I'm sorry for what I said over the phone, but more than that. I'm sorry for all the little comments and digs. For ever making you feel like you were something to be embarrassed about. Like you had *anything* to be embarrassed about. I'm easily embarrassed, and that's a problem for me to deal with, but the problem was never you.'

'It's . . .' I shift a little, uncomfortable with the sincerity in her words. I think I've already forgiven her. I think I forgave her weeks ago. I think a long time ago I decided it was all my

343

fault, not hers. But the damage had already been done. I already felt small, stupid. *Too much.* I think the thought of taking her back, of feeling that again, was too difficult. I try a different tack. 'Did Lily put you up to this?'

Her face turns just pink enough to answer my question before she does.

'Kind of. She suggested a grand gesture, said something about the five of you watching romcoms together recently?'

I laugh, but she continues. 'This, though –' she gestures again at her outfit – 'was my idea. I wanted to prove that I'm willing to learn and grow. That I admire you, in all of your beauty and your mess, Eloise. I'm not saying you aren't ever messy. But I need to do a better job of showing you I love the messy parts, too. And I need to learn to be okay with my own messiness, too.'

'Isabel,' I tell her, and I can hear in my voice that I'm letting myself fall for her all over again.

The word is barely a sigh, but she must hear it, too, because her expression just melts, her eyes wide and deep and warm, like she's on a cliff edge, and me breathing her name like that is the only sound in the world that can save her. Or, I don't know. Maybe I'm just projecting.

'It's okay, really.'

I take a step forward, close some of the distance between us on the pavement. Her eyes widen at my words, though, and she puts out a hand, and I freeze. We're closer now, but not touching. I'm just standing there, like a lemon, watching her shake her head and wondering if I've misunderstood something vital about what a grand gesture is supposed to mean.

'No,' she says then, and the firmness of it shocks me. 'Brushing it under the rug is what caused this whole thing in the first place.'

She locks eyes with me, and I see the seriousness in them, the way she looks at me. It's better than anything I've ever felt.

'I get self-conscious,' she says, and I can't help but notice that she doesn't blush or avert her eyes when she speaks. She keeps looking at me with that burning sincerity. 'I'm terrified constantly. Just petrified that someone might perceive me in a way I don't want to be perceived, or judge me, or think badly of me. But that's my own thing to work on. I'm sorry I ever projected it on to you. And I'm sorry I acted in a way that made you think I could ever be anything but madly in love with you, Eloise.'

I nod, and I must do a bad job of keeping it out of my face, the emotion that swells in my chest at the words *madly in love*. Because she smiles, just slightly. Still sad, still apologetic, but full of warmth at the way my eyes well with tears threatening to spill over.

'I projected, too,' I tell her. 'I took everything you said to heart. Sometimes it wasn't even what you said just . . . who you were as a person. I *expected* you to judge me, so I— Okay, this isn't going to be fun to hear, but is in the interest of not brushing anything under the rug. You know how I've always been so afraid of ADHD meds, right? Mostly because I was scared they'd make me, I don't know, *less*. Like they'd take away those parts of me that everyone always called flaws, but that I'd learned to love. But that's kind of what you did to me, I think.'

She looks horrified.

'Not on purpose!' I say hurriedly. 'It's more like I did it to myself. Like, when I was falling for you, when I thought we hated each other at first, you brought out the most insufferable parts of me, and it was so much fun. But then we became friends, and I used you as a distraction, hid away the parts of my life that stressed me out and made you my *everything*. And then, when we tried to burst the bubble and make you part of my life, my normal life, it was like everything fell apart. Like all the bits of me that made me *me* were the reason we weren't working out. As if we only worked when it was just you, and the person I was trying to be around you.'

'I didn't fall for you during our bubble, Eloise. I fell for you when you were being infuriating. I fell in love with those parts of you first.'

I nod. 'I think I get that now. But you see the problem, right?'

'I do. But I want to be with you. All the parts of you.'

'It sounds like we've both got our own shit to work through.' I laugh a little nervously, running a hand through my hair.

Her stare is still so intense, and I know this is so not the point right now, but I have to bite back a laugh at the situation. Her, looking at me with eyes full of love and hurt and reconciliation. The two of us having this conversation on the street in front of my house, the ugly shirt over fleecy pyjamas I'm sure she bought specifically for this grand gesture. The rollers in her hair, poorly applied, the silky straight hair escaping from them with every movement.

'We can work on them together, though, right? And maybe just, I don't know, promise to communicate.'

A small laugh escapes me. 'Yeah, communication sounds ideal. You'd think for two women . . .'

'You'd be surprised,' she says, and there's an implication of experience there.

'Okay, so, in the interest of communication, remind me to ask you at some point later about the girls you've dated in the past. Maybe I could actually, y'know, learn something instead of being jealous?'

'Wait, you were jealous? How did I not know you were jealous?'

'Haven't we just established that we've had communication issues?'

She laughs then, softly, averting her eyes, some of the intensity finally falling away from her features. I can't help it, she just looks so goddamn cute, so I wrap an arm round her waist, reaching up with another to gently brush away a strand of hair that's escaped from one of her rollers. She laughs lightly, but, when I'm done, I move my hand instead to her face. She doesn't laugh then. She only blushes furiously, and I can't even picture a world where I don't want to kiss the warmth on her cheeks and neck until it becomes that deep blotchy redness I saw that day we kissed for the first time.

But we're still technically in public, standing on my driveway, and I think that might be frowned upon. So instead I move to kiss her lips, just once, slowly and deliberately.

There's a whooping cheer from a car parked just down the street, and I spin on my heel, ready to go ballistic, but the head hanging out of the driver's side window belongs – I realise with a start – to Benji Williams.

'Woo, go, Isabel!' he's yelling, that huge puppy-dog grin stretching across his face as he flashes me a big cheesy thumbs up.

When I turn back to Isabel, she's hiding her face in her hands, groaning.

Laughing, I peel her hands away, and this time she's really red. Not just a cute, flustered pinkness in her cheeks, but her whole face is beetroot.

'Explain,' I say, and I laugh again, pressing the back of my hand to her forehead briefly to feel the warmth she's radiating.

'He drove me here,' she murmurs after a moment, eyes fixed on the kerb and her voice dripping with guilt. 'I wasn't going to get on the bus looking like this.' Then she seems to panic, eyes widening as she looks back up at me. 'But I still got some funny looks while I sat here waiting for you, so that's something, right?'

'Baby steps,' I tell her, unable to keep from laughing again.

'Uh, ladies?' Benji calls out again from the car, and we both turn to see him hovering awkwardly out of the window. 'Should I—?' He gestures vaguely with his thumb behind him. Isabel doesn't answer right away, just looks at me expectantly.

348

'Er, I mean, you can come in if you want? I can ask my mum to give you a lift back later.'

Her face breaks into this big, beaming smile of relief, and she dashes over to where Benji's parked to tell him at a normal volume that yes, he can leave. I'm full-on belly-laughing at the scene in front of me. Isabel, a fuzzy multicoloured mess, breakneck sprinting over to Benji, who whoops and cheers at whatever she's saying to him, reaches out to fondly mess up her rollers, then drives away, leaving Isabel to hurry back to me.

With Benji firmly out of the line of sight, she doesn't slow down until she's on me, cutting off my laughter, just scooping me up into her arms, and suddenly her skin is warm and flushed against mine, strands of hair escaping the rollers tickling my face, and I'm smiling into our kiss. We're still in the street, but neither of us care.

'Also, in the interest of communication,' I say softly when she pulls away, resting her forehead gently on mine, 'could you say that other thing again? The bit about being madly in love with me? I'd very much like you to communicate that just one more time.'

Her face splits into a dazzling smile. 'I love you, Eloise,' she says quietly. 'I love you, I love you, I love you.'

And then I watch in real-time as something truly devious happens in her mind. I watch her eyes narrow and sparkle, her mouth turn to a smirk that I thought belonged to another Isabel altogether, but maybe this Isabel, final-form Isabel, is a bit of all the versions of her I've known. She steps back from me, still eyeing me mischievously.

She takes a deep breath, throwing her arms out and her head back.

'I'M IN LOVE WITH ELOISE BYRNE!' she bellows, and Jesus, that girl's got lungs on her when she's not too embarrassed to use them.

It takes me too long to react, but I clap my hand over her mouth *after* she's finished yelling, and I feel her smirk widen beneath my palm.

'Maybe a healthy dose of embarrassment is good sometimes,' I say, biting down on my lip to keep from laughing. She prises my hand from her mouth, and locks her fingers into mine.

'See?' she says, letting me pull her back into the house. 'We're already learning from each other.'

I laugh. 'Mmhmm, if that's what you want to call it. I love you, too, by the way.'

EPILOGUE

One Year Later

The finish line comes with a medal, a bottle of Lucozade, a foil blanket, and a bunch of people asking me politely to please be respectful of the other runners and not lie down right there.

'Lou!' It's Mum, yelling from across a crowd of runners who all look ecstatic, and not nearly as dead as I feel. I push my way through, somehow, to where she's standing with the others. My legs probably got me there, but I can't be sure – they clocked out about three miles back.

'Am I dying?'

'You smell like you might be.' Lily wrinkles her nose.

'I smell like victory,' I protest weakly, and Mum laughs as she scoops me up in a hug.

'Oh, love,' she croons into the top of my head. 'You are . . . damp.'

Lily, Katie and Wil all seem to find this hilarious. Jas and Isabel, at least, press their lips together to politely stifle their laughter.

'Brought you something,' Isabel murmurs after Mum's let me go. She reaches into her bag, pulling out wet wipes and deodorant, and I bark out a tired laugh.

'Are you serious?' I tease, and there's that smirk. It comes out more often these days. The more comfortable we become, the less we feel the need to tiptoe round each other's feelings, the more we're able to have moments like these. Shining glimmers of rivalry nestled in among all this love.

'You need it more than me,' she laughs, nudging me.

I kiss her, but I make sure to undo my ponytail first, run my hand through my sweaty hair and place it on the back of her neck mid-kiss, laughing as she breaks away, shrieking.

'Okay, can I lie down in the grass now?' I ask.

'Nope!' Lily reaches out to grab my arm and physically stop me sitting down, then frowns, wiping her hand on her jeans. 'Photo for Mel first.'

I grimace long enough for her to snap a photo on her phone, Mum taking about a dozen in that time, too. When I collapse on to the nearest empty patch of grass, the others fold themselves down with me, but Mum cranes her neck to look at the crowd.

'I swear I saw a doughnut van nearby. Hang on, everyone, I'll be back in a bit.'

'I love you so much, Mum!' I call out after her.

'Mel's texted back a selfie,' Katie pipes up after a moment of quiet. 'She's giving you a thumbs up.'

'How's she holding up?' Jas asks.

Katie winces. 'She's holding. She just needs to not implode for another month or so.'

With A levels next month, Mel didn't even consider coming to London with us for this trip. I don't blame her. She's been on edge all year. The others were easy enough to wrangle, though. Isabel and Mum wanted to cheer me on – they'd have gone to the North Pole if that's where I needed them.

Jas is mostly here for me, though I suspect she's also a little bit here for Wil. I couldn't help but notice her decision to put a couple of London unis down on her UCAS application at the start of this year. I also can't help but notice the way she leans into them now. The heart-eyes they radiate when they look back at her. Good. Jas deserves nothing less than heart-eyes all the time. I make a mental note to ask Isabel about that later. Both her and Jas are staying at Wil's for the trip, so I reckon she's got some intel on what's happening there.

Katie and Lily are just excited to have some time away from revision, happy to cheer me on and have a little holiday in the meantime.

Lily leans over to see Mel's selfie on Katie's phone, and I watch Lily's eyes light up as the phone buzzes.

'That was a Hinge notification!' Lily squeals, trying to snatch the phone from Katie. 'Was it one of the girls I matched you with? Was it Glasses? Or, oh my God, did Mullet message you?'

'No,' Katie protests, holding it out of Lily's reach.

'You've been swiping without me?'

'You've been letting Lily swipe *for* you?' I ask in disbelief, sitting up to stretch my calves out.

'Don't sound so horrified,' Lily grumbles. 'She's worse at it than me – you should see some of the mings she set me up with.'

'What about Freddie? He looked nice.'

'He plays *Dungeons & Dragons*, Katie.'

'He also has a dog and seems to really love his mum.'

'Well, if he was fit, I could maybe forgive all of that, but . . .'

'You don't need a fit lad, Lil, you need a nice one!'

'I'm a firm believer,' Wil calls out then, 'that you can find both.'

'Lil doesn't go for both,' Katie reminds them. 'She only ever goes for fit dickheads. That's why we're doing this.'

'So, who's the notification from?' asks Jas after a moment.

Katie looks suddenly very guilty. 'I lied. It was one of the girls Lil matched me with.'

She holds up the phone. Definitely the one Lily called Mullet.

'She's pretty,' Jas croons.

'Yeah, she's also an anti-vaxxer.'

'Oo-er,' I say, but Katie turns on me then.

'No, you don't get to say shit, Lou. Ms *I found the perfect girlfriend before I even realised I was gay*.'

'I did, didn't I?' I say, unable to keep a shit-eating grin off my face as I lift Isabel's hand, already interlocked with mine, and kiss her knuckles. Everyone but Isabel and Jas fake barfs.

'Maybe I can set you up with someone from home?' Isabel suggests. 'How amenable are you to long distance?'

'Oooooh, what about Harriet?' Wil suggests excitedly. 'She's magnificent. People would cross continents to date her, so two and a half hours on the train isn't too bad.'

'As long as you don't poach *another* one of my friends off to London,' I groan as Wil produces a photo of the – fair enough, pretty magnificent, yeah – Harriet in question.

'This is part of my master plan, actually,' they grin, but their smile is aimed entirely at Jas. 'I convince you all to move to London one by one, start my own little commune, take over an entire borough. You telling me this trip hasn't convinced you?'

I've stretched out my calves as much as I possibly can, so at Wil's question I lie down flat on the grass, feeling the sweat on my skin beginning to cool and dry in the April breeze.

I can't see it from here, but I know Buckingham Palace is nearby. The long stretch of red gravel next to us leads to it, and even the trees and gates look regal around this neck of the woods. London is pretty. But it's no Liverpool.

'Wil, you try running twenty-six miles through this city, then look me in the eye and tell me you ever want to see another red bus again.'

'Point two!' Mum's voice makes me sit up again. She's struggling down on to the grass with us, massive box of doughnuts in her hands. 'Twenty-six *point two* miles,' she repeats when she's settled, handing out the doughnuts. 'That's very important. You get to brag about every step of that fifth of a mile.'

I laugh a little at her enthusiasm, reaching to grab a doughnut.

'Yeah,' I say, my mouth full. 'It's amazing how many fifths of a mile a person can run on *methylphenidate*.' Look at me go, I can pronounce it now.

'Hey!' Jas throws a piece of her doughnut at me. 'What did I tell you about the self-deprecating stuff?'

I roll my eyes.

'No, she's right.' Mum's frowning. 'The ADHD meds helped you focus on pacing or whatever, but *you* ran that marathon. *You* worked hard and trained for over a year. That's you. Giving the meds credit for a marathon you ran is like . . . giving last night's pizza credit for the marathon. The carbs give you energy, after all. Maybe we should hand over your medal to Papa John.'

'This is what I've been saying!' Isabel cuts in through Wil's laughter, leaning her head on my shoulder. Under the neon vest I'm wearing, there are scars visible near where her hair falls, around my neck and shoulders. Scars that used to be scabs that used to be spots. They've healed, mostly, since I started on the meds. Not completely because a lifetime habit is hard to kick, but it's become less of a compulsion over the last year.

'And when you ace your exams next month,' Isabel adds, 'that'll be all you, too.'

I don't know about that. Though maybe it's just the post-marathon endorphins, but I'm feeling good about next month. I don't know how my exams will go. I don't know what will happen with uni applications, what'll happen when Isabel moves back to London for uni, what'll happen if Jas moves. I honestly spent the longest time thinking uni wasn't even an option. Me

356

and all this shiny new dopamine hanging out in my brain have a lot of rethinking to do about the future.

It's looking good right now, though. With the people I love surrounding me, a medal round my neck, and my beautiful girlfriend resting her head on my shoulder. It's looking good.

ACKNOWLEDGEMENTS

As someone who has always read the acknowledgements just in case I ever got to write some of my own some day, I'm ridiculously prepared for this moment. Which is handy, because there are an awful lot of people to thank for this book.

First of all, *Lover Birds* wouldn't be anywhere close to what it is today without my brilliant agent Silvia Molteni. You poured a lot of time into helping me finish this book, and worked so hard to take it to heights I'd never even dreamed of. I cannot thank you enough for that. Thank you as well to Lucy Irvine for your support and kind words, and E. Latimer for taking time out to help edit and offer feedback, and to everyone else on the PFD Queer Fiction Prize panel for seeing potential in an unfinished manuscript and deciding it was worth the effort. In my cover letter, I wrote something about being so grateful that a prize like this exists. That only gets more true every day.

Enormous thanks to Tom Bonnick, my wonderful editor, for championing this silly little rom-com harder than I could ever have hoped for. For helping to create a story that feels perfect, and for encouraging me to keep the parts I thought I'd have to lose (especially the title). I am so grateful to you for patiently guiding me through this terrifying and exciting new experience. I'd also like to thank Jane Tait for doing a better job copyediting this book than I ever could, despite it being my day job.

I've also been incredibly lucky to have such fantastic people working on the book behind the scenes, so huge thanks to the rest of the HarperCollins team, Kate Clarke, Charlotte Winstone, Laura Hutchison, Jane Baldock, Jasmeet Fyfe, Caroline Fisher, Juliette Clarke, Kirsty Bradbury, Nick Lake, Nicole Linhardt – Rich and Deborah Wilton, for all your hard work. Thank you as well to Sina Shagrai for the gorgeous cover illustration.

I owe so much to all my friends for their constant support and for putting up with me when I was hyper-fixating on these characters. Especially to my NaNoWriMo buddies, Michaela Hook and Emily Ober, for the writing sprints and accountability. I'm not sure I'd have rediscovered the joys of writing for fun without you guys. To Ana Balaci, Cris Caserini, and Lauren Keller for reading this novel in its early stages and offering so much feedback and kindness, and everyone in *Isogaytion* for being constant pillars of support and listening to my plethora of Concerns. I'd also like to add an extra layer of gratefulness to Cris, who had to share a house with me through the panic attacks, the sleepless nights, the '*I'll never get shortlisted*'s and the '*maybe the book isn't even that good and they're all just humouring me*'s. Finally, Cai Hall, who sent me the link to the

PFD Queer Fiction Prize on the off-chance I might be interested in it. I owe you so much for that small thoughtful gesture. (Don't tell the others, but I promise never to kill off your D&D character.)

Mum and Dad, thank you. For reading endless bedtime stories. For letting me clear out the library every summer. For making me sign my old school photo because 'that's going to be worth something when you're a best-selling author'. For pretending *The Edninator* was going to be the next big thing. And Emma, for being an all-round wonderful sister, for letting me borrow all your books (when I was much too young for them), and for graciously granting me rights to your son's nickname. Let it be known that Izzy got there first.

I also want to thank my favourite writing community – the audio drama community. It's for a different medium, sure, but hear me out. Being around such a kind and supportive group of creators has changed my brain chemistry forever. So, thank you, especially to Waymon Alexander of The Liminal Lands for turning your Discord into a refuge for stray creators, to the professors at the Audio Drama Lab for doing the same, and to everyone in those servers for making the world of audio drama just a genuinely lovely place to be.

Finally, this book is partly an ode to English teachers — famously a safe haven for messy queer kids across the country. Thank you to every English teacher who ever encouraged me, all the way from high school up to master's level (a Publishing MA is close enough to count). Ms Price, in case you ever read this, you became the character's namesake because you saw a deeply uncool kid who liked to read and thought '*hey, you know what this kid would love? Pride & Prejudice.*' Thanks for the recommendation, you were right.